LIFE!
DEATH!
PRIZES!

Stephen May

B L O O M S B U R Y

LONDON · NEW DELHI · NEW YORK · SYDNEY

First published in Great Britain 2012
This paperback edition published in 2012

Copyright © 2012 by Stephen May

The moral right of the author has been asserted

Bloomsbury Publishing, London, New Delhi, New York and Sydney

50 Bedford Square, London WC1B 3DP

A CIP catalogue record for this book is available from the British Library

ISBN 978 1 4088 3119 9
10 9 8 7 6 5 4 3 2 1

Typeset by Hewer Text UK Ltd, Edinburgh

Printed and bound by CPI Group (UK) Ltd, Croydon CR0 4YY

MIX
Paper from
responsible sources
FSC® C020471

www.bloomsbury.com/stephenmay

'A real achievement . . . has a great deal to say about modern families and the world we live in . . . Full of surprises' Melvin ... ss

... ouching, truthful – sometimes shocking – and painfully ... portrayal of two brothers . . . a paean of praise for the ... side of contemporary youth, the side that, with all its ... s and failures, is still driven by love and connection' Mavis ...

... hen May manages to balance hilarity and sadness in nearly ... sentence of this deftly comic, completely engaging and at ... absolutely hair-raising novel. *Life! Death! Prizes!* deserves ... one of its exclamation marks' Suzanne Berne, author of the ... ige Prize-winning *A Crime in the Neighborhood*

... hen May has the sharp eye of David Nicholls and the verve ... ate Atkinson' Suzannah Dunn, author of *The Confession of* ... *arine Howard*

... turns bleak, funny, and tender . . . an intoxicating gulp of a ... el' Christopher Wakling, author of *What I Did*

... tty, witty, uplifting, sharp – it reminded me of Nick Hornby ... s portrayal of a modern family in all its glorious chaos' Kate ... ig

... hoes of J.D. Salinger and Dave Eggers . . . Stephen May is a ... jor new talent, sharply observant of the human condition' ... onique Roffey, author of *The White Woman on the Green* ... ycle*, shortlisted for The Orange Prize 2010

... he story is beautifully put together, with a strong cast and, not ... st, an extremely satisfying ending' *Reader's Digest*

STEPHEN MAY's first novel *Tag* was published by a small Welsh press and won the Reader's Choice award at the 2009 Wales Book of the Year. Originally from Bedford, he now lives and works in west Yorkshire.

BY THE SAME AUTHOR

Tag

For Caron, Hannah, Herbie and Joe

Chapter One

Mum's funeral takes place at the Millennium Cemetery, a pale brick square that stands cringing in the shadow of the Fun Junction on the edge of town. It looks like a Little Chef. Three council grunts in hi-vis jackets stand smoking in the soft cold rain, nothing to do but watch and wait before they can start filling in some hole. There's a tall, rail-thin man with a face so drooping he could only ever have become an undertaker. And there are great-aunts and neighbours and Office Angels and tight suits and hats and two kinds of faces. The melting ones and the blank ones.

There's Dean Hessenthaler, Oscar's dad, huge in his thick, expensive Kray-twin overcoat, meaty face grim as he pretends to look at the flowers piled around us. Christ, he's let himself go.

There's the Reverend Luke Newell, the vicar, twisting his hands like a nonce. Looks about my age though he must be older. This must be his biggest gig so far, and he's got the fear bad. Looks like he could piss himself any moment.

And there's Oscar, solemn and still, a six-year-old Kennedy in his suit and skinny black tie. He looks cool as, like he's in a band. And every time eyes fall on him they fill with tears. Damp tissues fly to noses. Oscar turns his gaze on someone and they dissolve. The blank faces become melting faces.

The only person who seems immune is Dean. When he first sees Oscar he murmurs, 'All right, kiddo.' And when

Oscar doesn't say anything back, he just nods like he's got the answer he's expected all along. Oscar doesn't even seem to see him.

Red eyes, red noses. Sniffles and murmurs. Even from the journalists, even from the police. Pale faces, black clothes. Red, white and black the colours of this funeral. Swastika colours. Death colours. None of that funeral-as-celebration-of-life bollocks today. No party dresses. No paper hats. No Hawaiian shirts. No football kits or teddy bears. None of the gimmicks you sometimes get at the contemporary burial.

Flick through the pages of the trauma porn mags, and you'll soon find a kid being buried in the QPR away kit, or a girl going into the underworld in a tutu. Or an old guy buried with his golf clubs, his car keys, or his Northern soul records: a kind of council estate pharaoh, proving that you can take it with you.

Not here.

'Come on, Billy, let's do this thing.' Oscar whispers it, but his voice is steady like he's a general leading troops over the top. Or rather, like an actor leading other actors over the top. Like someone whose learned his part. He squares his shoulders, stands up straight. One skinny metre of distilled heroism. He tugs at my hand, urgent and with surprising force for such a stickboy. I follow him and I can feel my own face beginning to melt like I was some stupid Office Angel. Well, fuck that. I'm not having that. I squat down, hold him by his shoulders, look him square in the eye and say, 'OK, bud, let's do it. Let's roll.' And I stand up and we're inside.

Every day I find stories sadder and more stupid than ours. Like this morning. This morning I read about a toddler from Inverness who died after falling and cutting himself on a

2

vase. Russell Poulter was enjoying himself with his favourite toys when he knocked over the ornament and fell on the shards which slashed his neck. All of this in front of his mother, a nurse, who must have known what was happening to her little boy but couldn't do anything about it. One minute she's washing up, listening to her first born playing, and next she's cradling his head while the life flows out of him. A sadder story than ours. And stupid because what could be more harmless than a vase?

Mrs Poulter didn't even like the vase. It was a cheap, gaudy thing, a present from her mother-in-law who was famous for her lack of taste. She'd been meaning to boot sale it.

Sad. Stupid.

I get all those mags now. *Chat*, *Bella*, *Best*, *Take a Break*, *Love It*, *Reveal*, *Pick Me Up* – most of the others. The sort that deal in real-life heartbreak. The sort that shout *Life! Death! Prizes!* in swirly circus writing underneath the title. The sort that tell me about the Russell Poulters of this world. It's good. It helps. It means that I can tell myself that I'm lucky.

I'm lucky because I'm still alive and Oscar is alive, and we have a house and enough money to go to Morrisons once a week and buy Cheerios.

Yeah, Oscar. Let's do it. Let's bury our stupid mum, the woman who thought it was worth fighting to the death with some random no one in a council car park.

From the outside the chapel looks like a motorway diner, and inside it's pretty much the same. Inside you could be in any modern parish church, any museum, any supermarket, any school, any jail.

The service itself is pretty retro. Poetry. Hymns. Psalms. Aunt Toni, Mum's sister, organised it all, and I can't say I'd have done it any differently but it doesn't mean that it's right. 'Cause it's not. It's all so, so wrong. The Reverend Luke talks about Mum's life and puts in all the stuff we – Toni and me – told him to put in, but he makes her sound small somehow. Like just another ordinary Office Angel. Someone you'd get in to fix your filing systems and organise the Christmas do. It's all just words. Not even words. Sounds. Noises bubbling away. And he doesn't mention the way she died. That pathetic playground tussle, that stupid push and pull. And I think that's a good call: it's such an embarrassing way to go, why would you talk about that? And Rev Luke doesn't talk about the one person who got us to gather here. He doesn't talk about Aidan Jebb.

The one more or less modern touch is a PowerPoint presentation of photos from Mum's life sound-tracked by Vaughan Williams's *Lark Ascending*. And in every picture Mum faces the camera with a wide-eyed, wide-mouthed, madly optimistic grin. From gurgling baby in 1969, to the glossed exec snapped at the Southwood Enterprise Awards 2009, Mum seems to be shouting 'Yay! ROFL!' Seeing all the photos like that, she looks mad. It makes me wonder if she wasn't sort of retarded in some way.

Is the funeral what Mum would have wanted? Probably not. She was an events organiser after all, she would have made it a huge occasion. An event organised by Mum stayed organised. She would have done Event Death. There would have been something spectacular, something to get it talked about, remembered – I can imagine her going into the chapel to the sound of 'Gimme! Gimme! Gimme! A Man After Midnight'. Or 'Going Underground' even. Something outrageous anyway.

And it wouldn't have been here, in this Little Chef chapel. The venue would have been exclusive, thought about. Hard to get to, but worth the effort when you were there. The hippest, happening boneyard. A cemetery with a view.

But funerals aren't for the dead. The dead don't give a fuck. No, funerals are totally for the living. And this funeral is a traditional, functional one, meant for those of us who are hoping just to keep functioning in the traditional English way. To keep putting one foot in front of the other until we're through and clear of it all.

Not all the living appreciate the effort. My dad's not here (a solitary text: *thinkin of U m8*. M8? He's not my m8. He's my father. He should remember that. And he should sort out predictive text) but mostly it's a success. And success here is measured by the volume of quiet sobbing in the church, the number of bone-crunching handshakes I get back at Oaks Avenue – and by the amount of bargain booze we shift at the wake.

You don't have to be dead to be a ghost. Look around and you'll see people who are ghosts in their own lives. Maybe most people are. Drifting through the streets and the shops and holidays, sighing and moaning. Or raging at the way they've ended up, wrapped in stuff. In ropes and chains. Jobs and houses. Tax credits. Rent and mortgages and parents' evenings and city breaks.

And there's worse things to be than a ghost. You could be a dangerous zombie, trapped in an endless tramp from dealer to police desk to social worker to hostel to street. That's us now. Our country: ghosts and zombies everywhere you look.

Aidan Jebb weighed less than two pounds when he was born. He was six weeks premature. The surviving half of twins. Aidan was the youngest by four minutes, but where Callum Jebb simply coughed once and died without crying

5

or even unfurling his hands, Aidan followed him already yelling, already fighting. Already elbowing the weaker kid aside. Grabbing for a life that didn't much need him, that was indifferent to him.

Aidan was the size of the palm of his dad's hand, a miracle baby, born into a house without carpets but with a widescreen TV and Sky Sports. When he finally left hospital, after six months, there were pictures in the *Gazette*. He was carried in triumph into that house, by now fully furnished with donations from local well-wishers. Aidan – named for his dad's dad, himself a legendary gambler – had brought good luck and the welcome home party went on for several days. Everyone remarked how quiet and good Aidan was. And Rosie, his mum – a kid herself – would laugh and say how weird it was: her being so loud and him being so quiet. Let's face it, she was a party girl, up for anything, and he just watched and dribbled a bit as he was passed around to be poked and prodded, as sweating faces loomed in and out at him. No, give Aidan a bottle and he was happy.

'Not so different from you then, Rosie.' That was some smart-arse.

Pretty soon, he was the sole permanent male in a house of girls. Men were around but strictly as visitors. They came but didn't stay and that was the way everyone liked it. Aidan gurgled and smiled as skinny lads tottered in with him and Rosie. He giggled as they fumbled and cursed trying to fold the pushchair. He clapped his little hands as they carried him upstairs to his cool room with its appley smells and the constant reassuring flicker of his dad's one legacy, the murmuring of Cartoon Network in the corner.

In the mornings there would be shouting and banging, but Aidan would be safe in his cot till they came to fetch him. It was never about him. Nothing to do with him. The morning storms were simply the weather of the house, brought in by the men and leaving when they did, with a final gust and a bang. Then it was just Rosie and him, and his nan, and Rosie's mates and the shops and the warm music of those pubs that didn't mind kids. Safe until the next smiling stormbringer with his rings and his easy laugh. Safe until the next guy with ready cash, careful hair and his way of knowing just when to get the drinks in.

After the funeral there seems to be a tacit agreement amongst the guests that it can all kick off now. Whether you're a glammy PTA type that got to know Mum at the school gates, one of the distant uncles with hair like a crash helmet, a marketing whizz in expensive shoes, the police family liaison, or my mate Alfie teaming his ever-present eyeliner with his job interview suit. Whether you're an Office Angel, or Mr and Mrs Khan from next door, it seems to have been decided: everyone can go mental now.

I hand out a few Pringles and that and then look for a place to hide. I'm not hosting this party. I can't. If anyone is the host it's Mum's sister Toni, and her partner, Frankie.

Aunt Antonia is sunshine. Everyone loves her: just like Mum but bigger in every way. Bigger hair, bigger laugh. She takes up a lot of room generally. It's odd isn't it? How the exact same mix of genes can produce such different results. I mean Antonia has the same face as her sister, but put together a bit wrong somehow. As if a keen-but-crap amateur artist was trying to paint Mum's face from memory.

The legend in the family is that they always used to think that Mum got the looks and Toni got the brains. Toni was the one who went to Oxford and all that. Then, after a while, that changed too as Mum started making a name for herself as the go-to gal when you wanted a business event organised properly. And then she started making real money at it, building a client list that took in most of the FTSE 100 *and* all those funky dot coms. Antonia meanwhile stayed settled teaching science at the girls' high school. Respectable, enjoyable, decently paid, but not the heights people had expected of her. Not that Toni minded. Big heart too as well as big everything else.

And now she's a few vinos in and, flushed and loud, looks bigger than ever.

Frankie, her partner – won't marry her, won't let her have children – he's loving it all. Frankie is an idiot but he's in his element here. He's some kind of sales guy and he's got a charm that comes from treating people in pubs. He has things to talk about. Football, the news, TV, money, gadgets, cars, diseases, the stuff people like to talk about. And he has jokes. Frankie tours all the little knots of people, filling glasses and pushing vol-au-vents and generally cranking up the bonhomie big style. At least Hessenthaler has made himself scarce.

I have only been to two funerals before, one for Granny Ann, Mum's mum, last year, where I skipped the wake and went off to smoke with Alfie – no trauma there that I remember – and one for my dad's mum, who I'd only met once. I was only nine for that, but I remember it as way too hormonal. The nervy atmosphere upset me. I couldn't wait to get home. All those adults coming apart. The sense that their grief might explode, wet and red and slimy from inside, like the alien in those movies.

It's not big news I guess, but death is a drug and not a smart one. A crude one. A dirty one. Premature death even more so. And then we add alcohol, light the blue touchpaper and retire. Only sometimes there's no standing well back.

They handle these things better in Arab cultures I think. Get the body underground inside twenty-four hours, make sure the weeping is done as theatrical as possible at the graveside and – obviously – there's no booze to act as an accelerant.

This funeral gets out of hand.

Pretty soon aged great-aunts are sweating, gesticulating, leaning too close to young guys in top-to-toe Armani. Office Angels look like cats on heat, arching their backs and purring. PTA mums are picking fights with their husbands about just who agreed to drive. Paunchy middle-aged policemen are getting all aggro about football. There's one fifty-year-old Liverpool fan starts yelling 'But what's your anthem! What's your bloody anthem!' at a baffled kid who has made the mistake of admitting he supports Man U. A dykey type with spiky hair and John Lennon specs is explaining the miners' strike to a voluptuous blonde in a LBD that is, frankly, just a little bit too L for her frame, and who I recognise as running Prontaprint in town. The words seem political, sociological, thoughtful and historically accurate and all that, but they are just so obviously a cover for her eyes that keep slipping towards the creamy flesh of Ms Prontaprint's tits. Ms Prontaprint smiles sleepily. We've done death in the afternoon, and now life – or at least sex – is making a play for the evening.

Toni is sitting on the sofa in the living room watching as Oscar, seemingly oblivious to the noise around him, sits and plays quietly with a couple of plastic knights on the floor. Frankie has switched on his thickest, richest Oirish voice – the accent that's so richly phoney they call it a brogue, the one the ladies are always so mad keen for – and he's telling funny stories about life on a Wexford farm to a little group of charmed Office Angels. Conscientious professional girls clearly not used to drinking in the afternoon.

It's all bollocks. I don't know that much about Frankie, I can't really be bothered with him – but I do know that he hated the Wexford farm, hated Ireland. Even now he won't touch potatoes. Not even chips. He couldn't wait to be out of there. Frankie rocked up in London in the mid 1980s with an accountancy degree and made shitloads of money selling prime bits of London to Arabs and music biz wankers.

On the fringes of the group, the partners of the girls glower, waiting for the old Paddy to shut up so they can start telling their anecdotes about great skiing holidays, or swapping top tips about the best route from somewhere to somewhere else.

I can feel my shoulders go tight. The whole thing is starting to sicken me. Toni's party smile turns her into something frightening and voracious. Jaws in lipgloss. I feel like I'm going to get bitten, chewed up and swallowed.

I know all this is natural. I know it's normal, but then so much of natural and normal is also disgusting and repulsive. Normal and natural doesn't make something good.

My mum's dead.

I want to shout it, like a little kid would. Like Oscar somehow isn't. I want to shut all these people up. Just for a second, make them face the truth they are busy hiding from. My mum's dead. My mum's dead.

A couple of curious faces turn my way, Frankie pauses in his blarney-talk and for a terrifying second I wonder if I actually did yell it out loud. But I think it's just the clenched fight-or-flight readiness of my body language pulling at my imagination, so I force myself to stretch and relax a little.

Toni appears. 'We need to talk about things, Billy.'

'Not now, Toni.'

'When though, Billy?'

I shrug. She sighs. All this sighing people do around me these days. Gets on my tits frankly.

She makes an effort. 'Well done on the clearing up though. Making the house look nice.' I shrug again. It wasn't hard. Yell.com and a phone. Even I can handle calling some cleaners.

'It'll make the house easier to sell if it's tidy.'

There's a commotion near my foot. Oscar has plonked himself down right beside us and those knights are jousting between our feet.

'Really, Toni. Not now.'

Me and Toni in the solicitor's days earlier. Mr Waddington looking tired and crumpled in his vintage worsted as he explains the mess of Mum's affairs.

'The will is ten years old,' he says. 'And obviously pre-dates the birth of Ms Smith's second child, er,' he shuffles his notes and looks up smiling, triumphant, 'Oscar.' A pause. 'And, er, it also pre-dates Ms Smith having property of her own. And of course, it er doesn't take any account of Billy reaching his majority. And it also fails to take account of the unfortunate demise of Ms Smith's mother.' A nod at me. 'Most unfortunate. And a real lesson in the importance of keeping your affairs in order.'

Mr Waddington runs his hand over his balding head. Smooths the long strands of his comb-over back in place. We don't say anything. What is there to say?

Basically this ancient will leaves me and Oscar in the care of Granny Ann, my mum's mum, who is also allowed to do what she likes with any of Mum's things. Of course, Mum didn't really have any things then, but now there's this house, the Subaru – Sooby-Doo as we christened it, Oscar and me – and Granny Ann is dead. All of which means that the estate is to be split three ways between Oscar, Toni and me, with Oscar's guardian – 'Whoever that may be,' says Mr Waddington carefully – keeping his share for him until he gets to eighteen.

And then he gets on to Mum's liabilities, which are a couple of maxed-out credit cards. Nothing major if you're pulling in £60K plus as a sought-after Events Manager, but problematic if you're not making any money because you've been reckless enough to get yourself killed defending your piece-of-crap Netbook from some junkie toerag after a ten quid fix.

In total Mum's estate owes Mr HSBC and Mr American Express about £30K and apparently telling them to go fuck themselves is not really an option. Or, rather, it is, as Mr Waddington puts it, 'Only an option in the short term.'

Things get blurry. I mingle. I probably smile and nod and laugh and murmur to all the faces that swim towards me and away from me, but I don't remember. A mashed Alfie comes over and gets all earnest at one point, but I don't think that I even bother doing the smile-nod-laugh-murmur thing to him. I certainly don't listen. Life is, as I've had occasion to notice recently, too frigging short.

The house is starting to feel too small. In their efforts to prove they are still alive, the ruined aunties are minutes away from groping the suits. Or at least so it seems to me. There's something going on anyway. I suppose it is just possible that I'm over-stating the scent of sex in the air, but I don't think so. As I stumble into the garden, Mr Khan – shy Mr Khan who says 'very good day to you, young sir', every time we meet – Mr Khan has his shirtsleeve rolled up and one of the PTA mums is feeling his biceps.

God knows what the funerals of toddlers are like. Must be a right clusterfuck.

I need a piss and head to the downstairs bog. And there's someone puking into it while some crone cluck-clucks and fusses. The Reverend Luke Newell. Of course it is. Has to be. I'll use the garden. Oscar appears. 'Hey bro,' I say. He nods.

I walk through the hallway with him. The dykey girl is still trying to do her number on the woman from Prontaprint. As we pass them, Ms Prontaprint swoops and holds him hard and fierce. Dykey Girl blinks rapidly behind her specs. Something me and Oscar are still getting used to is all this damp hugging. All the clutching and grabbing and squeezing. I wonder about the effect of all this middle-aged breast engagement on Oscar's future development. He's six now after all. A formative age. What happens when it stops? Will he pursue menopausal women with massive knockers all his adult life, hoping to get back to that brief time when he was guaranteed envelopment in perfumed and abundant female flesh?

Mum, we're going to be so fucked up.

Oscar breaks free at last and sprints the last few steps through the open French doors to the garden.

'Hold up, big man,' I say. When we're both in the garden, he stops and faces me. He has Things To Say.

'Aunt Tonia's going to make us live with her, isn't she?'

'She might try,' I say.

'I like her but . . .' he starts. He stops.

'You like her butt?' I say.

He giggles. 'Billy,' he says. And his face goes serious again. 'Can we stay here? Mum's here. Mum will always be here.'

''Course we can,' I say. And I mean it. But I'm uneasy. This might be a lie. I decide not to worry about it. After all, everyone around me is telling much bigger lies to each other. They are all finding new ways to tell each other that they are going to live for ever. If this party was a conversation in a foreign film the subtitles would read: *Other people die, sure, but us, those of us here now, we're immortal.*

That's what all this means: the laughter that breaks out now. The tears, the arguments, the desperate stories. It's all a huge lie. Other people die. We don't. We'll be here laughing at each other's stories until the end of time. LMFAO.

The fine rain keeps falling and we are getting soaked but I can't face the house with its sweat of grief and people.

'Hey Oscar,' I say. 'Shall we hide in the shed?'

'Yaay!' he says.

I don't think Mum ever went in the shed. She just chucked all the gardening stuff in there and every now and again, Mr Khan would go in to fetch the lawnmower. Was Mr Khan in love with Mum? Maybe. But maybe he just couldn't stand living next to all her uncontained wildness as symbolised by our garden. Perhaps cutting our grass every six weeks was an effort at controlling her. It could have been both of course.

Something, some instinct, makes me peer through the cobweb-smeared window.

What I see is shadowy but unmistakable. Dean Hessenthaler, trousers a murky blur around his ankles, surprisingly skinny legs bent awkwardly, is hauling himself in and out in that most ancient of dances. Dean Hessenthaler is doing someone from behind in our shed.

I'm thinking too slowly to do anything and just watch, numb, as Hessenthaler continues his animal rutting. I'm unable to turn away.

One of the tasks Dean Hessenthaler set himself when he became Mum's bloke – before Oscar was born – was to improve my command of what he saw as the necessary boyish skills. He was forever pointing out dead things to me, calling me over to examine the mashed-up raspberry splodge that was once a hedgehog or a hare. He once showed me the neat corpses of five baby blue tits whose nest had been blown down. They were all lined up in a row, like a conscientious blue-tit funeral attendant was ordering things.

'Like Goebbels's kids,' Dean said.

And then he told me the story of how, trapped in the bunker, Frau Goebbels had gently poisoned her six children to prevent them falling into the hands of the Russians. For a while it seemed that Dean Hessenthaler was on a mission to give me nightmares. Seems he might still be on that same mission even now.

Oscar guesses something is up.

'Let me see, Billy. Let me see.' And they must have heard because they spring apart and there's a blur of fumbling and tucking, buttoning and zipping. And I get a glimpse of her face. No one I know. Some random Office Angel.

'There's people in there Oscar,' I say. 'People kissing.'

'Yuk,' he says, making a face.

'Yuk,' I agree, making one back.

Oscar puts his hand out and I take it and we turn back towards the house. He stops.

'Was it my dad?' he says. Which just goes to prove that you can't ever fool the truly innocent.

I know what I've got to do when we get back inside. I find a quiet place and call PDQ. I say my name and the girl tells me they'll have all available cabs with me as soon as. They all know, you see. Everyone in Southwood knows. Mum's been on the front page of the *Gazette* for days and days and it has some weird effects. Old women force me to jump the queues in shops, assistants dash to serve me. Everyone talks

15

too fast and smiles too much. And now cabs turn up the second I call for one. A special kind of superpower.

Pretty soon there's gridlock in Oaks Avenue. A taxi jam. I go around the house telling people they've got to go. I'm polite but I'm firm. I don't take any shit. I amaze myself. And I get everyone out pretty quickly. Most of the crowd wobble towards the taxis, but there's a group going off for a curry. A fucking curry.

I knock on the shed but there's no one in there now. A few minutes later I see Dean shoving the Reverend Luke into the back of a taxi. I hear the cabbie whining, 'He better not mess up my car.' Dean hands him a note, the cabbie shuts up. Dean turns and raises his hand. I give him a tiny, tiny nod. He looks at me for a long moment. It means something, but I don't know what, and then he turns, hitches the collar of his coat up against the rain and shambles off, a big old grizzly, into the evening.

Aunt Toni and Frankie are the last to go. They spend a millennium or two trying to persuade us to go round to theirs. Or Toni does, Frankie carries on like some hosting robot. Loading the dishwasher, putting food away, wiping surfaces, clanking and clanging and all the time humming some stupid tune. I can't help myself, I strain to work out what it is. Oscar sits at my feet and starts with the knights again.

'Come on, Billy. You can't stay here. Not in all this mess.'

'It's not that bad.'

'But it's not right.' She sounds like a little kid. Like she's going to stamp her foot. 'We'll be fine.' This isn't me. This is Oscar and *he* sounds about sixty. He sounds like the most fucked off adult on the planet. Toni sucks in air noisily. *Don't start crying. Please. Don't start crying.* But you can see her taking a breath. Counting to ten in her head. Doing some breathing, yoga thing. Frankie appears. 'The

16

Dock of the Bay', I think. *Sitting on the dock of the bay.* The tune he's humming. I feel a flash of triumph. I smile at him over Toni's shoulder. I must look like a psycho. He frowns and picks up a stray Pringle off the top of the TV and disappears back into the kitchen.

Toni gives up.

They don't go straight away, there's still some faff about coats. And some hugging and kissing and crying to be done. She puts her wet cheek against mine and says, 'Billy, your mum was . . .' She stops and tries again. 'Your mum was . . . she was . . . she was . . .'

'I know,' I say, 'she was.' And we both try to smile.

'She was what?' says Oscar. But there aren't any more words just now, and she's off in a cloud of fruity soap and wine. Frankie shakes my hand. Winks. Actually winks. Tosser. The door closes. Oscar says, 'Thank Goodness that's over. Can we watch a movie? Can we watch *Kung Fu Panda*?'

'Yes, mate,' I say. 'We can. We can do anything.'

Chapter Two

School. Oscar is only six but he has to be kitted out like Sir Ranulph Fiennes on a polar trip. I mean, I know it's windy and wet and everything, but he looks less like he's spending a few hours with Mrs Bingley's Year One class, and more like he's doing Everest alone: without oxygen and without back up.

'Oscar, mate, do you really need two bags *and* a rucksack?'

His little face crinkles. He was a worrier before, and things aren't any better now. He closes those heartbreaking peepers and recites from memory.

'Packed lunch, reading book, colouring book, special pencil case, recorder, home-school diary, hat, blue asthma inhaler, spare clothes in case of accidents, scarf.'

'OK, Oscar, I get it.'

'PE kit, a favourite toy – but one we won't mind losing.'

'Yeah, I said. I get it.'

'Dinner money, wellies.'

Shit. Dinner money. Wellies.

Dinner money is easy. I unload a couple of quid from Oscar's special pig. He's always got tons of cash. Proper little miser. Hoards any money he gets at Christmas, birthdays, all that. Wellies is harder.

Spotting me cramming his yellow Fireman Sam boots into the top of his already bulging rucksack, Oscar pauses in his determined spooning of Ready Brek towards the vicinity of his mouth, and fixes me with a serious eye.

'Hippos,' he says. I'm baffled.

'I don't do Fireman Sam boots any more, Billy. I have hippo ones.'

I feel a pang. I realise that I love those Fireman Sam boots. Oscar has the whole outfit, and for a while he totally lived the life of the hero next door. He absolutely fused himself with the part. Did the whole De Niro thing, immersing himself in the role in his blue jacket and shiny yellow plastic hat. When did Sam go out of fashion? Why wasn't I told? And what hippo ones?

'The hippo wellies Mum bought when we went to Lakeside, you remember.'

'Yeah, of course.' To be honest I can't even remember the trip to Lakeside. They say torture victims are often capable of blanking out the horrors they faced. They couldn't survive otherwise, and I do the same. These irregular trips to the major retail cathedrals are deleted the moment that we're back home with the car unloaded and Five Live babbling out the footie results.

'Where are they then?' He looks at me blankly. It's plain that he really can't see how it's any business of his knowing where things are kept. And until a few weeks ago it wasn't mine either. It was someone else's job. Mum's job.

'Upstairs?' Oscar ventures hopefully. He tries to be helpful, bless him. I find them in the end under the living-room sofa and they are quite cute. Grey rubber boots, each foot given the face of a sulky hippopotamus. 'I know how you feel, mate,' I mutter to the hippo twins and return to the kitchen where Oscar is standing by the back door, biting his bottom lip like a reluctant parachutist. Like someone who is regretting rising to that late night, drunken dare to do a jump.

19

'Come on, my brave little soldier.' Brave little soldier, one of Mum's phrases.

'Billy, I'll be fine. I won't cry. You know that, don't you?'

And just then I think that I might. Weep, I mean. It's not so much the display of courage from the little man, but the use of the line 'You know that don't you?' This is another of Mum's phrases. As in 'I'm away next week, you know that don't you?' It became a_regular saying because, quite clearly, we never did know. Mum was super-organised, super-efficient. She always knew where all of us were going and what time we had to be there and who we were meeting and why. She had goals, targets. Not just for her, for all of us. She was the one who knew where things were kept. Those sodding hippos would never have hidden from her. They wouldn't have dared.

Oscar doesn't like to be taken right up to the school in the car. Like all little kids now he's a Nazi about pollution and that so I drop him at the corner of Kestrel Road. He likes to go in with the Walking Bus.

The Walking Bus is a council thing. It's an attempt to get all the PTA mums to leave the SUVs behind, and instead blahnick a little crocodile of shining Year One faces a few hundred metres between Kestrel Road Library and Sir Walter Scott Infants. It just means that for half an hour twice a day that library car park looks like the training ground of a League Two football club. All that shiny black. All those tinted windows. All those trying-too-hard motors.

I watch as today's PTA mum leads her troop towards the lollipop lady, a feature that, together with the red telephone boxes, tells you that this is a Good School in a Good Area. The sort of area you pay a premium for when it comes to buying a house. The lollipop lady has the jumpy look of a squaddie on duty in downtown Kabul. She looks all suspicious, as if suspecting this parade of fully reflective backpacks conceals explosives rather than the remains of Dairylea sandwiches. But I see her soldier-look melt as Oscar's little bobble hat moves past her.

As she shepherds the last kids on to the pavement she pulls Oscar back and hugs him. I see him standing resigned, tough as any guardsman himself, quietly enduring this bosomy, teary embrace. The lollipop waggles precarious and dangerous. It must be awkward to hug anyone, never mind a tiny person, while simultaneously holding a six-foot metal pole. I wonder for a moment about the ridiculous tragedy involved if it should slip from her arm and fatally clonk some passing tot. A top *Life! Death! Prizes!* story without a shadow.

I'm just beginning to think about physically prising Oscar from the lollipop lady's grip when she releases him and returns to duty wiping her eye on the back of her hi-vis sleeve. As she straightens up I notice that everyone is staring – all the kids and all the mums. We're going to overdose on sympathy, my little brother and me. We could get proper sick. Get emotional diabetes or something.

I sit in Sooby-Doo smoking, stroking my beard and half-listening to the new breakfast DJ guy flirting with the bird that does the traffic. The beard is new and it's not a fashion thing. It's not a topiary job. It's a tangled fortnight of forgetting razor blades and not being arsed. It's a beard born out of my own unique mix of laziness, absent-mindedness and defiance. I am my beard. My beard is me. I can't believe I haven't had one before this.

The fag and beard-stroking thing means that I'm late into the museum, and Jenny looks meaningfully at her watch, and then remembers about Mum. She looks stricken and immediately over-compensates.

'Coffee?' she yelps, and dives from the counter where we sell postcards, and into the old vestry that now houses our staff kitchen. The Social History Museum is in the old church of St Nicholas now converted and deconsecrated. I go and say hi to Mike. Mike is our team leader. A sixty-six-year-old ex-copper, a former superintendent no less, who in the course of a forty-year career in the force saw – and did – terrible things. It's a point of honour, already repeated many times in the weeks I've been here, that he can deal with anything. He even has a little saying: 'Nothing fazes the A-team.' He says this once an hour, a tiny mantra that's well annoying, but it's true that in the quietness of our own little place of worship there is very little that ever comes close to being in any way disturbing. The most disturbing thing here, is probably the door of the place. A thousand years ago the people of Southwood captured a Viking raider, tortured him and finally nailed his skin to the church door. You can, if you look hard, still see crusty, dandruffy flecks attached to the rusted nails that remain in the door.

He's dusting the exhibits when I come in – one of Mike's more remarkable characteristics is the joy he takes in the most menial of tasks. I can't do that. I can't fill my day with a round of little jobs. What I like about the museum is the time it gives for staring into space and daydreaming. It's the perfect gap-year job for me. Everyone else I know thinks the museum is boring. And I agree. But I find I like boring. Me and boring get on well. Especially now. Boring rocks. Other people can go trekking in Kashmir, I'll just stay here and get really, really good at Sudoku, thanks all the same.

Mike talks about football. He hopes someone else will break into the top five this year.

'We need your Spurs to do well. Your Aston Villas too. We need the Blackburns and the rest. We need it to be a proper competition.'

I barely know what he's talking about but I agree anyway and he's pleased. 'I remember when Burnley won the league. And Ipswich. And look what Brian Clough managed to do at Forest. European Cup Winners twice. On a team that cost buttons.'

'Amazing,' I agree, and Mike shoots me a look to check that I'm not taking the piss. So I carry on, 'Yeah, and Man United got relegated once didn't they? Hard to imagine it happening now.'

'Nineteen-seventy-four,' he says firmly. 'I remember it well.' Reassured, he goes off to damp-dust the collection of early modern lawnmowers. When he comes back he asks The Big Question.

'Everything all right?' he says. 'You doing OK?'

'Yeah. Yeah we're fine. As well as. You know.'

Mike nods. There's a respectful pause.

In the end he says, 'Busy day today, cock.'

'Really?'

'Yep. Party of sixth form urban geography students.' He says this with a straight face. I study him carefully. It can be hard to know when Mike is messing with me.

'Urban geography?'

'Apparently so. They say it's now a real live A level subject.'

The bait is there, dangling. We could now spend a happy hour arguing about the decline or otherwise of the education system, but my heart isn't really into another exploration of the shitness of modern times, and I'm pleased that Mike is prevented from getting into his stride by the arrival of Jenny, still flustered, with the coffee. Jenny hands me the drink and opens and closes her mouth a few times. I want to help her out but I find that I have no way to put her at her ease. I can't think of anything helpful to say. The pause drags on. Then inspiration comes. Hallelujah.

'Mike says we're going to be busy today. A party of sixth formers.'

Jenny smiles, radiates relief.

'Yes,' she says. And it's clear we've done it. All three of us have now negotiated the terrible awkwardness of my mother's death and can get on with making regular hot drinks, selling those sew-on badges for anoraks (I'm proud to think that we might be one of the last museums where you can still get these), chatting about seed-drills to middle-aged Mastermind fans, throwing the occasional drunk back out on to the streets – and dealing with school parties.

Aidan Jebb loved to sing. They noticed it early. The way he could harmonise with the radio, the way he could pick out tunes on this crappy little toy keyboard they had. Aled Jones was mentioned and, later, Charlotte Church. The primary school suggested extra lessons, though they never happened.

'He doesn't need lessons,' Rosie said. 'He's a natural.'

Nearly everyone who passed through the flat wanted to video him singing. Aidan quickly learned that songs meant prizes, attention, treats. It became quite a regular thing; Aidan woken up to sing and dance for the entertainment of Rosie and whichever bloke was round.

Not everyone liked it of course. Some of these men found it too freaky: the big alien voice coming from this scabby bag of bones. Some of these men weren't very nice. Because by this time Rosie was struggling. She'd always liked a drink and now she needed a bit of an eye-opener to get her up in the mornings. Something to kick-start her metabolism. And it was definitely true that the boys who came back to her flat were getting older, nastier. Sometimes they would leave money. Sometimes she would ask them to and they wouldn't. Sometimes they gave her a smack in the mouth instead, and called her a cheeky cow.

Rosie stopped seeing the girls she'd gone to school with and found new mates, and they'd spend the day watching daytime telly and drinking Vladivar and coke. Sometimes some blokes would come round and they'd take temazepam and have sex, and sometimes it was even a laugh.

Some guy filmed it once, and they played it back straight afterwards. All that red and flopping flesh, all that gasping and grunting. Those balding heads between fat, blurred thighs – it made Rosie hot inside and not in a good way. It made her cringe a bit. And she was embarrassed by the mess and grime of the flat. Not that anyone else seemed to care as they swigged and laughed and cheered every change of position and fast-forwarded to the good bits. The bits where the men made themselves come over the faces of the girls. It was sort of wild and the guy with the camera gave her forty quid 'for the use of the flat', but she still decided that it wouldn't happen again. And for a few weeks Aidan got to school on time and with his sweatshirt neatly ironed, and Rosie came to see him sing in Friday assembly. Everyone said he was going to be a star.

This school-group are weird. Keen, attentive, bright. It's a bit of a shock. We were never like that. We were just pleased to be out of school. Not as pleased as the teachers obviously, but pretty happy anyway.

This group is different, however. Half a dozen well-scrubbed young adults. The only one who looks dangerous

25

turns out to be the teacher. She looks like an S&M hentai cartoon made flesh. All shimmering purple lipstick and backcombed scarlet hair. A silver stud winks through ghostly, milky skin, just where a Georgian dandy might have painted on a beauty spot.

And I know her.

Her name is Lucy Avis and her younger sister, Katie, was in my class from Year Seven all the way till last year when we left. Until she went away to uni and got into Goth big-style, Lucy was famous in Southwood for being the star of the county table-tennis team. She was forever on the back page of the *Gazette* holding up some trophy. I'm surprised she came back. What's the point of going all the way to Nottingham Trent to reinvent yourself as the Queen of BDSM, only to return to the backwater you came from, where people don't recoil from your appearance on the High Street, but instead ask if you still like a game of ping-pong?

She's a decent teacher. Shockingly, her kids have not only read and absorbed our information pack, but they ask intelligent, thoughtful questions. They are a credit to urban geography departments everywhere.

Mike leads them around, gives them his old chat and they laugh in the right places (it's surprising how many amusing facts there are about the lives of lawnmower designers). At the end Lucy gives me a warm smile that gives a hint of the pink and silver of a studded tongue between two neat rows of expensively maintained teeth – teeth like one of those picket fences in a movie about small-town America – and I feel a faint, but definite, explosion go off inside my chest.

The kids – smart, intelligent, thoughtful – notice immediately.

A stage whisper hisses out from a trench-coated, bum-fluffed figure at the back.

'He fancies Miss. The perve.'

There's a sharp ssh from the girl next to him and, as I stare in his direction, Trench Coat drops his eyes but he's still smirking. And I'm of the opinion that all public buildings should be smirk-free zones. Lucy just grins and runs her armoured tongue around those A-star teeth. Then Jenny comes clicking-clacking over the old church flags. With her is a beefy chap with a shaved head. His appearance here is so out of place that I don't recognise him at first.

'Billy,' she mutters. 'It's Dean Hessenthaler.'

His hand shoots out towards me, like it absolutely didn't at the funeral. I don't take it.

'You've grown up kiddo,' he says. 'Getting to be a handsome young dude.' His voice is mild. I don't say anything. I can't think of anything, 'cept maybe 'Bloody hell, you've got fat.' And that wouldn't be polite now, would it? Not that he deserves politeness.

'Decent funeral I thought, Billy. As these things go I mean. I was really gutted about Suzanne. Gutted.'

'Yeah.'

He has Oscar's eyes I think. The same amazing blue. I never noticed that about him before.

'Do you want to come into the office?' I say, but he doesn't hear me.

Mum met Dean Hessenthaler on the day they started to paint a mural on the back of the old Co-op. Mum had been hired by the council to help revitalise the town centre. The idea was to show colourful local characters going about their business and Mum got in a couple of

27

League Two Banksies to help immortalise the people of Southwood in Dulux.

'I noticed him straight off,' she said. 'This great big boxer-type with an infuriating smile. Like he was saying "is that the best you can do."' In the end one of the professional artists cracked and challenged this cocky larrikin to paint a corner of the mural. And of course he turned out to be a bit of an artist himself. He may not have been a Banksy, but he could do a passable Rolf Harris. A few deft strokes and he'd painted a weirdly lifelike portrait of Mum, in greater than life-size. 'And I was annoyed,' said Mum. ''Cos it was a bit warts and all. A bloke that talented should have at least tried to flatter me a bit. Especially if he wanted to get his end away.'

But Dean Hessenthaler was too smart to flatter Mum. He knew what gave him his edge. It was the sense of not giving a flying fuck what she thought of him. And it turned out he wasn't just a dab hand with the matt and the gloss.

He wasn't good-looking. He was an easy twenty pounds overweight even then, with a drinker's face and a bit of a squint. But he had unbelievable confidence. It was so powerful that I'm guessing women felt he must be something special. I mean the guy seems so ordinary, but gives it the big one so massively, he *must* be special, right? That's the twisted logic that helps a certain kind of bloke get the A-star birds. You see it even in school where some runty scrote gets off with all the beautiful posh girls who do junior band and that. I should know, I have been that runty scrote. It's why I did drama instead of IT.

'It's ironic,' Dean says now, 'but I'd been meaning to get in touch before. About the boy and everything. I wish I had. Because it feels weird doing it after . . .' He leaves the sentence hanging. I can see now that he's nervous. He has rehearsed a little speech and is determined to deliver it and that's why he isn't going to be deflected into our little vestry. He pauses and his eyes, which have never quite settled on to my face but have instead roamed the shadows behind my shoulder, come into line with mine. He's thinking he's done enough small talk, it's time for business.

'I think I should get proper access now. I think I should get to know Oscar a bit.' This is so unexpected a suggestion that I laugh. Hessenthaler flushes. He never did like being laughed at. I remember that too. Which must have been a big problem with him and Mum, 'cause she laughed at everything.

A memory comes to me of Dean. From way back, before Oscar.

We're kicking a ball around in the garden. Dean taking little nips between passes from his silver hip flask, an object I thought then was almost impossibly sophisticated. I can sense Mum watching from the kitchen window so I turn on the skill, nutmeg Dean and he falls on his arse. I laugh. He laughs.

'She fell ov-er. She fell ov-er,' I chant, Millwall-style. Dean laughs again. What a sport.

'Let's play penalties,' he says.

I'm delighted and assume the attitude of a German goal-keeper, rubber-legging on the line, puffing himself up, waving his hands, bouncing up and down. Dean plants the ball on a little tee of mud.

'The crowd is hushed,' I say. 'It's a last-minute penalty. Last kick of the game. Can Southwood Town equalise and take the FA Cup Final into extra time?' I'm taken aback to see the venomous look that Dean lazers out at me. He takes a short, five-step run up and blasts the ball hard as he can towards the centre of the goal-line. The shot is perfectly flighted and smacks me with a gunshot crack, straight on the nose, and I'm flat on my back and crying. It feels like I've been punched. Mum comes flying out of the kitchen. Dean makes a bit of an effort.

'Soz Suzanne,' he says. 'Don't know how that happened. Foot slipped. Bit out of practice.'

Mum is curt but civilised as she puts a Kleenex to my bleeding nose. 'Never mind,' she says. 'These things happen.'

'Yeah,' says Dean. 'He'll get over it.'

Here in our little church now, Dean takes a deep and noisy breath.

'Actually, there's a case for saying that Oscar probably should live with me. I mean it. Maybe he should be with his dad when he's got no mum. Maybe he shouldn't be looked after by a teenager. Not when his father's around. It's not right. No offence.'

'Bollocks,' I say, far too loudly. I can feel all the heads in the gift shop area swivelling towards us. The kids giggle. Hessenthaler runs a hand over his death-row scalp.

'Look, we should be able to sort this out sensibly like adults.' And of course he's right, that's exactly what we should be able to do.

'Fuck off,' I say. 'Fuck you.'

He takes a step back. He looks genuinely hurt. Meanwhile the air around me starts to resonate. I fight a temptation to look up. This is a church after all, deconsecrated or not, and even though I'm pretty militantly atheist, I'm still half-expecting some kind of trouble for swearing in the house of the Lord. Hessenthaler takes another heavy breath. He needs to get that sorted.

'At least let's give the little lad the choice.'

'Oscar,' I say. 'And no, you can't see him.'

'I don't think you can stop me, bud.'

'I'm not discussing it,' I say and turn away. He cracks. I feel a hand on my shoulder.

'Don't you turn your back on me.'

And I spin round, and suddenly we are rolling over and over together on the floor. I am able to see the shame of all this grunting and heaving at each other, playground-style, but then the red mist really comes down and I'm just trying to hit him as hard and as often as I can. I'm aware of a couple of digs in my face, and can taste blood in my mouth, when there's a kind of animal noise, a strangled moo like a cow in labour, and Hessenthaler is rising off me. Mike has him in a head-lock with his arm up behind his back, wrist bent at an almost impossible angle.

I lie back on the floor, I'm finding it hard to breathe and I wipe my nose with the back of my hand and it comes back streaked with blood and snot. Mike marches Hessenthaler back to the doors flanked by the astonished faces of the urban geographers.

Before he lets him go Mike says, 'Official channels please next time chum.' And, as he releases him, Hessenthaler straightens up and looks like he might take a pop at Mike who gazes back, level, calm, every inch the seasoned copper. Hessenthaler turns and leaves, and our Saxon door – the door with its memories of torture still attached – bangs behind him.

I feel the church flagstones cool through my museum sweatshirt, and listen to my own breathing coming ragged and rasping.

Someone claps. It sounds sort of sarcastic.

By the time I open my eyes again the school group have gone, and Mike and Jenny are both standing over me like concerned corner men at a title fight.

31

'Cup of tea?' says Jen and goes off to make it before I can answer. Mike helps me up.

'You'll have to work on the old jab son. Still, you gave as good as you got considering you were pretty out-gunned, weight-wise I mean.'

'I think,' I say carefully, once I've got my tea and I'm sure that I can talk normally, 'I think I maybe need some time off.' Jenny and Mike both nod.

'We can handle things here mate,' Mike says, and Jen nods again. 'Take as long as you like. Nothing fazes the A-team.'

Chapter Three

Oscar and I are choosing our Chinese when I see him. Thing is, we don't even need to be getting a takeaway. We have a monster chest freezer in the cellar stuffed full of nourishing heartiness of every description. Casseroles. Lasagnes. Irish stews. Toad-in-the-hole. Spag bol, curries from Mrs Khan. You name a carb-packed national dish and we've got it. Over the last couple of weeks, when they haven't been cleaning, Mum's mates have been baking. We won't starve.

And even my own crew have been at it. Alfie for instance: normally as tight as a gnat's chuff with his gear, he has been dropping off humungous lumps of hash. And I hardly smoke dope. It gives you throat cancer and, worse than this, can turn you into the most boring person in the whole world. And far worse than this even, is the fact that I haven't really learned to smoke it. I'm always coughing and choking, my spliffs fall to bits and it all makes me feel incompetent. But still he's been pressing it into my hand every couple of days. Like Mum's friends, he wants to do his bit. And, yes, I know it's because they all care and are trying to help and fiddly-dee-fiddly-fucking-dee, but sometimes I just want to shout: I get it. You're on our side. Stop now. Let me have fish fingers and oven chips, *please*. Let me unwind by watching crap TV or playing Empire on the PC. Just like I've always done.

And today, when I picked up Oscar from the Walking

Bus, and looked at the way his shoulders drooped under that rucksack – he looked like a tired but determined snail – I thought, fuck it: a Chinky. The nutritionally balanced homemade stuff can stay in the freezer for another night.

It's a proper wild evening. The weatherman in his wacky red blazer has smiled his way through the announcement of driving rain and freak twisters, and the old windows rattle and the sky is getting more low-budget British horror by the minute. The wind blows mournful hymns down the chimneys and Oscar is spooked by the rumble of distant thunder and the prospect of lightning. I go to draw the heavy curtains and that's when I see him, standing still in the rain, staring across the street into our house. Aidan Jebb. The reflection from the room makes it hard to see, but that skinny outline is distinctive. Aidan Jebb. I press my nose up against the glass and shield my eyes with my hand. It bloody looks like him. Even though he's not officially a suspect, even though he's disguised as youth-who-cannot-be-named-for-legal reasons in the *Gazette*, everyone round here knows that Aidan Jebb murdered my mum. Everyone in this town could tell you what he looks like. This kind of info doesn't leak, it spurts. Stains everyone.

In an odd way I've been expecting it – Southwood is a small town – eventually you get to meet everyone, even someone who is meant to be in hiding. But not like this. Not outside my own window. It's full-on shocking and I must make some kind of sound because Oscar says, 'What is it Billy? Is it lightning? Has it hit someone?' And yes, I suppose it is. I suppose it has. But I don't say anything. I glance down as Oscar scrambles over, and by the time I look up, less than half a second later, he's gone, leaving me doubting myself. Have I conjured him up out of bad weather and fear? Stuck his features on to some random passer-by?

'I can't see anything.'

'That's 'cause there's nothing there, Oscar. Have you chosen what you want to eat yet? If you hurry up there'll be time for a bit of Empire before Ricky and Alfie come round.'

Western civilisation is finished. How do I know this? I know this because of Wings of Empire. I started playing this a lifetime ago when I was ten. The deal is you join a tribe and gather tools and skills and build villages and then towns and then cities and conquer countries until you are Lord of Everything. Until you are fucking God.

When I started out I didn't know squat and kept getting eaten by any passing animal. Not just lions and things with sharp teeth either. Once I got mashed by a zebra. Once by a giraffe. And I was murdered by any marauding warrior. Before I was eleven I had already been enslaved, raped, tortured and killed hundreds of times. I built pyramids for emperors with my bare hands, toiled day and night in the gem mines for archbishops. I begged and starved and wept and cursed the world, while Mum laughed at me and suggested I might be better off with a book.

So I stopped her coming into my room and, gradually over months and years, I got pretty good. I got a bit A-star at it. By the time I was onto my twenty-first life I was enslaving others and making the people of weaker tribes wash my feet with unguents. It felt easy, I can tell you. It felt like sunshine.

But there's a limit.

With Empire – and with the surname Smith – you don't ever get to be too good. You don't get to be God.

There are two million players of the game all over the world. Two million players, 59,000 tribes in 259 worlds.

But no British leaders. Not many Americans either. In Empire, the big stars are all Korean, or Chinese, or Uzbek or some such.

Every time my people rise up and begin to carve out some prosperity, a Chen or a Chung or a Kwok will unleash a plague he's been developing in his factories, and I'll find my workers coughing up blood in the fields or in the marketplace. Or my armies will be distracted by dancing girls, or by strange lights in the sky. Or my fish quotas will rot in the seas, or my mountains turn overnight into volcanos, which bury my cities with molten hate.

The jealousy, brutality and skill of these Asian kids is pure total beyond. And they never do anything else. They don't work. They don't go to school. They don't have girlfriends. It's 24/7 nation-building with these guys. They never even sleep. They never fucking sleep.

It's 7.30ish, there's still all sound and fury outside but we're OK. There is beer and weed and we're not playing Empire. We're going total old school and we're playing Scalextric. Me, Oscar, Alfie and Ricky. Since Mum got killed I'm never short of visitors. I like to think that it's because they are helping me through my time of trouble, but it might just be because I have this whole house to myself and everyone else my age is being nagged to empty the dishwasher and all that.

It's brilliant playing Scalextric with Oscar. His favourite thing is to chase after the cars when they fly off the track – which they do all the time – and put them back on, so that Ricky and I can just concentrate on going as fast as, without worrying about slowing down on the bends. Fun for all the family I think you'll agree. It's like being a little kid again, in a good way. Alfie and me

– we've been mates since primary. When we were about ten we used to go shoplifting sweets from newsagents together. Alfie said once, ' Hey, Billy, you nick stuff. I nick stuff. We're a pair of nickers.' We pissed ourselves. The tragic thing is, it's still the funniest thing he's ever said. His comedy peak. People even say we look alike, like brothers. But we don't really. People just can't be arsed to look properly.

Ricky I've known for years too. He joined Southwood High in Year Eight after he got kicked out of his private school for wearing the wrong colour socks or something.

Alfie is on his Dreampad uploading crap, looking at other people's uploaded crap, and generally wasting precious time. We're going to watch a shit-but-somehow-good movie, play some music, talk bollocks, get pissed, and then Ricky and Alfie are going to student night at the Library. The Library used to be an actual library, now it's where the bands play, and where you go if you want to meet those posh girls who like to self-harm. Beautiful, rich girls who hate themselves. Rick and Alfie have decided that's their new target market.

This is the evening we're into when the doorbell goes. Oscar, who until now has been making us piss ourselves at the way he's like a crazy puppy chasing the cars flying across the carpet, stops dead and looks towards me with a comical expression of surprise and alarm. I would laugh but just at that second I'm struggling to contain my own surprise and alarm. It's never good news when the doorbell goes without any prior warning, is it?

People who call unannounced are trying to sell you things you don't want. Or tell you things you don't want to hear.

* * *

It was a couple of coppers who broke the news about Mum to me. A man-cop and a girl-cop and I felt proper sorry for them. They both looked like they were shitting themselves. They had a script to follow of course. They get training and counselling in all of this, but there's always one person improvising in the scene – me in this case – and they had to take their cue from whichever way I might go. Would I go for disbelief? Denial? Would I kick off? Start ranting, screaming, bawling? Or would I go into quiet shock? And of course it's not quite true that I was totally unprepared. A hundred thousand TV police procedurals have taught the nation how to behave when the worst happens. None of us need fumble our lines any more.

I think – hope – that I made things as easy as possible for my coppers, Lee and Sally. They interrupted me on a Tuesday morning. It was my day off and I was half-watch-ing an ancient *Top Gear* on Dave.

I took the news quietly, and I let them make me sugary tea and call some people on my behalf. I let them take me to the hospital with lights flashing and siren on. And I let them call friends of Mum who could pick up Oscar, and I let them withdraw quietly once they'd delivered me safe to the nurses, gliding through the whoosh and bleep and murmur of the new hospital, the statement building they built to replace the old one that always smelled faintly of old men's wee-wee. Even from the outside.

I reckon I was part of a textbook breaking-bad-news operation. We all played our parts magnificently, with real A-star dignity.

But the sense of panic at the unexpected ring at the door is going to take years to drop back to the level of normal every-day anxiety. It goes again, insistent now. And it's followed by loud banging. Suddenly, I think I know who it is and I'm up and off my chair in one moment. If Aidan Jebb wants a piece of me, well then he can have a piece of me. I fling open the door and, so certain am I about who I'm going to see, that I'm momentarily unbalanced, disorientated, unable to place the face in front of me.

'Aunt Tonia!' squeals Oscar behind me and wriggles past to leap into the arms of Mum's big sister.

Toni, of course. Had to be. She stands uncertain on the doorstep, probably wondering what she's done wrong. I can imagine how it looked, me yanking the door open like that, red in the face, chin out, fist already half-raised, words forming like bullets in the back of my throat.

I laugh. 'Don't just stand there, Toni, come in.'

Toni has brought wine and another bloody homemade lasagne and enters the house carefully, unsure what to say about her initial reception, and then visibly deciding to say nothing. Oscar pulls her along by the hand. He's always delighted to see her. Then again, one of the proper sunshiny things about Oscar is that he's always delighted to see anyone. The world really is his friend. It was hard for Mum to teach him the usual modern guidelines about the stranger danger and all that, because Oscar doesn't really believe in strangers.

'You're just in time to put Oscar to bed. Would you like that Oscar? If Aunt Antonia does bath, bed and a story tonight?'

'Yaay!'

This is shameless, I know. But the whole bath, story, bed thing has been wearing me out. Doing my head in. A while back I invented a game called The Drying Machine, which was basically me making machine noises while towelling Oscar down. That progressed until now the machine has to explode noisily, with Oscar whirled around in the air before being chucked – towel and everything – on to Mum's bed. The drying machine explosions are getting massive. He wants the machine to be set to 'triple maximum explode'. And this means more noises, fiercer scrubbing, more whirling, bigger throws with a bumpier landing. It's proper hard work at the end of the day.

Somehow Oscar has now negotiated a situation where his minimum expected nighttime requirements is all this followed by three stories from books, plus one that I've made up.

And lately he's moved from books that are cheerful and short – *Hairy Maclary*, say – to the grim and long, like the ones from the *Treasury of Classic Fairy Tales* that some fuckwit cousin bought him at Christmas. Don't get me wrong, it's all lovely and that, and yes I know that childhood goes by all too fast and so on, but a break from the routine is always good too.

And the stories I have to make up? Right now I'm doing a series of adventures by creatures no one has much time for. Action thrillers starring slugs and rats and cockroaches. They're going down all right, though Oscar is pretty well out of it by the time we get on to them.

But everyone needs the odd night off.

Toni huffs a bit but she's snookered. She can hardly say no, can she? Not when Oscar has gone 'Yaay!' like that.

Oscar's birth. It starts out cosy enough, everyone sitting around in candlelight in the living room. Mum on the sofa, reggae on the stereo, everyone with a glass of wine. Even me. Especially me. Actually, I don't think Granny Ann had wine. I think she had a cranberry juice or something. 'Someone has to stay sober,' she said. And this was a bit of a pointed remark because the midwife, Caroline, was well up for wine. And there was cake. Everyone definitely had cake.

So. Hours of chat and contractions, until even Mum and Caroline are running out of talk, and I notice that the midwife is frowning more and smiling less, and I know that Gran sees it too but she doesn't say anything. I can't tell if Mum suspects something is up. She's bright, glittery. Fidgety. Her face slicked by a thin sheen of sweat. But what do I know? Far as I'm concerned this might all be normal.

After a while – a long, long while it seems to me – the contractions start to lose power and Granny Ann suggests going up to the hospital. She's been a very good girl. She's waited hours to say this. I could tell that she wanted to call for an ambulance more or less from the moment Mum cracked open that first bottle. Caroline declares that it is Mum's call, but it's obvious she doesn't think it's necessary, and Mum won't hear of it. She puts Black Uhuru on and we wait some more. I remember thinking that the whole situation was a bit like one of Dean's war stories.

'War is all about waiting,' he said once. 'You wait and you wait and you wait, and then just when you think nothing is going to happen, Hell kicks off around your arse and it's all noise and shouting and blood and guts for a few minutes – though they feel like years at the time – and then you wait some more. My time in the army was ninety-eight per cent waiting and two per cent shitting myself.' And nearly all the waiting was spent with a drink in his hand. And I think that's how Mum saw having children – warfare for girls. And she was Special Forces. SAS. Not subject to the usual rules.

An hour or two later – by this time I'm completely losing track, I'm only twelve remember – Mum still isn't fully dilated and Caroline produces a little machine and a drip and persuades Mum to allow some twenty-first-century magic into the room. This is a chemical that forces the body to produce contractions when it can't be bothered to. Mum's cheeriness is turning to a tetchy kind of growling, and Granny Ann wants me to go to bed. Mum doesn't care whether I'm there or not any more, but I've lasted this long and pride forces me to stay.

Nevertheless, I do doze off – for how long? A minute? An hour? Three hours? – and am woken by Mum screaming, proper screaming. At first it's wordless, a terrifying, primeval howl but she catches her breath, 'Just knock me out. Please. Please, just knock me out!' And Caroline is flushed and her voice stays calm, but everything else about her is jerky and sweaty and this panics me. I want to run upstairs but my legs won't work. I'm stuck here.

'Shoulder dystocia,' Caroline mutters.

'What?' says Gran, and Caroline has to repeat it as Mum starts screaming again.

'A fucking shoulder dystocia,' says Caroline, biting out her words as if Gran is a retarded student nurse who doesn't know the basics. And she snaps that it's too late for drugs now, and Mum screams again and Caroline presses a button on a pager thing that is clipped to her belt. Long minutes of wailing follow and I cover my ears but still can't leave the room. Then there's a fierce banging at the door, of the kind I dimly remember and associate with people wanting Dean and wanting money.

A huge man enters in a dinner jacket. He looks like a retired heavyweight boxer down on his luck, corpulent and squeezed into a stained tux in order to be paraded at some awards dinner. Which is close to the truth in a way. This turns out to be Dr Simons, a consultant called away from a colleague's retirement party to heave Oscar into the world using brute strength and Iron Age weaponry.

I don't know what you think of when you imagine forceps, but before Oscar I imagined a kind of delicate tongs affair, the sort of thing someone might use in a deli for picking up slices of cooked ham. But they're not like this at all. I was in a fog of sleep and wine but I remember twin flashes of curved steel. Swords. Forceps are like proper fuckoff swords. It's like a medieval execution in reverse as Dr Simons braces himself with one gleaming handmade shoe up on the sofa and heaves away. It's ugly, ungainly and as far away from the idea of modern medicine as you can imagine. No whooshes and bleeps here. Mum's screaming, Gran's whimpering and Dr Simons is grunting and growling like a wounded bull.

I remember the surprisingly vivid crimson of the blood all over the white sheets that we had placed over the sofa. The sticky gleam of it in a perfect circle, like the Japanese flag.

The screaming has become background by now. Or, more than this, it's like I've absorbed it. Like it's part of me. It's almost industrial. A soundtrack that I could imagine lasting the rest of my life.

And this is how Oscar is hauled into the world. Nine bruised and bloody pounds, purply-black like a half-sucked sweet. And silent. I was sure he was dead. I'm sure everyone else in that room thought so too, except for Mum who was gasping in an ecstasy of folding and unfolding her body on those slippery, rising sun sheets. Grave, Dr Simons took a long serious look into Oscar's face and pinched him hard on the arm. Nothing.

And again.

Still nothing.

At last he just whacked him, sudden and furious on the thigh, exactly as a frustrated parent slaps a naughty child – the way you see it every Friday evening in Morrisons – and Oscar came through. A thin, high cry of surprise. The noise of a sudden betrayal that cut through both Mum's sobbing, and Black Uhuru's bass-heavy ch-chunk. This is how it starts, Oscar: a lifetime of sharp pains delivered by the ones you trust.

With Toni and Oscar upstairs, we stick on *Flight of the Arachnids* and it is as gorily hilarious as we had all hoped. It's about these killer African spiders that run amok on a plane. Sixteen deaths in (not that long, believe me) Toni reappears with glasses and the wine. We're on the Red Stripe and decline. Toni takes a deep slug of Shiraz and parks herself on the sofa next to Alfie. I can see him stiffen slightly. I'm also a bit tense. I keep my eyes on the orgy of blood and venom on the screen but still I see – feel – Toni's gaze wandering around the living room. And I know what she's seeing. She's seeing a happy, ordinary Friday night. She's seeing lads and joints and beer and the takeaway cartons and the fluorescent yellow Southwood Sound and Vision DVD cases, and she's thinking that this is so wrong. There should be misery and keening and, I don't know, choral music on the stereo. There certainly shouldn't be lads giggling as giant spiders cause mayhem on a New York-bound 747. I can feel my shoulders start to tense up. Why shouldn't we be able to relax a little? Unwind a little? Live a little? Be a bit bloody normal.

Her brooding presence on the sofa affects everyone's enjoyment of the killing. After another fifteen minutes or so Alfie stands and stretches melodramatically.

'We should get to the Library, Ricky.' It isn't nine yet.

The Library isn't even open. And the weather's still shit. They'll get soaked. But I'm not pointing that out. I think Ricky might, but they're already on their feet.

'Yeah, best get off,' Ricky says. 'We'll see you soon, yeah?'

I see them to the door in silence.

'See you, bruv,' Alfie says and pats my arm. Pats my arm. Tosser. He's not my bruv any more than my dad's my 'm8'. They're all tossers. And I have the sudden thought that Mum and her mates wouldn't do that to each other. If any of Mum's mates had promised to come round to eat curry, watch crap films and hang out, they'd stay till the film was over and the beer was gone. As I close the door, I find my eyes are full of tears. I take a few seconds just to lean against the wall, then I take a deep breath and I'm into the living room and turning the TV off.

'Don't do that just for me,' says Toni.

'I'm not,' I say. 'It was giving me a headache. It was Oscar's choice.' And I realise that I'm furious with her. How dare she come in here and start judging me and scaring my mates away, and sit there implying that I'm not suffering enough, that I'm not in enough pain? She hasn't said anything but I know that's what she's thinking. I just know it and I'm not having it. The red mist is coming down. It's a physical sensation and I almost enjoy it, revel in it. I'm going to have a full-on row with my aunt, and I'm going to grind her drooping fat face into the carpet.

'I don't need another lasagne.'

'What?' She looks confused and God knows I was clear enough.

'I don't need another bleeding lasagne. Freezer is full of them. I don't even like it. Neither does Oscar.'

There's a pause while her face dissolves and I feel like shit.

Through wet, hiccoughy sobs she says, 'My sister's dead, Billy. Your mum. And it's like you don't even care.'

'That's crap.'

'I know. I'm sorry. I'm fucking sorry.' And then she picks up one of the kitchen chairs and throws it at the wall. Of course she doesn't do it right. The chair hardly even reaches the wall. It doesn't splinter like I guess it was meant to. Just sort of rests there. I almost laugh, have to turn it into a cough. Toni never does stuff like that. Mum, yeah, all the time, but Toni no. There's a sort of silence. Just Toni panting like she's been in a race.

'Toni. It's OK. It's going to be OK.' And it helps, even though we know that I'm probably wrong. That it's probably a lie. And we hug for ages and then laugh for no reason, and then we finish the wine and the beer and we don't talk about Mum. And we don't talk about wills and shit. Toni even smokes a joint. Expertly, without coughing, which is more than I ever manage. We watch *Life is Sweet*, Mum's favourite movie – Mike Leigh did it for Mum big time – and we laugh at that too, and then we find that it's suddenly easy to talk. And we stay up late talking about how sunshine Mum was and I laugh at the stories of what Toni and Mum were like as kids – even though I've heard them all before. And then Antonia says that she'll kip on the sofa, and I say no, she should have my bed. We've got Mum's bed spare too, but neither of us are ready for that yet. It's still got all her stuff on it. I wouldn't let the cleaners go in there before the funeral. And they were relieved, I could tell. Didn't make a fuss. So, her make-up's in there. Her GHDs. All her clothes and shoes and shit. It's still more or less the same as it was the day she was attacked.

And so I doss down amid the glasses and the dirty plates

46

and the Chinese congealing in its silver foil cartons, while Antonia lurches heavily and unsteadily up the stairs.

Aidan Jebb believed in Jesus. Every night Jesus came to him and sometimes during the day too. They would play games together, sing together.

For a long time Jesus was Aidan's best friend. Aidan would ask Jesus to help his mum stop drinking and stop being so moody and to stop having people over all the time. He asked Jesus to bring his dad back from wherever he was, and Jesus said that he would try.

Sometimes people would ask what Jesus looked like and Aidan would tell them that he didn't know. Jesus was invisible, didn't they know that? He had to be careful though. Some grown-ups thought it was funny when he talked about Jesus and other grown-ups would get cross. People never seemed to get cross about other children's secret friends. Jerome Finlay had a friend called Rowley and no one seemed to mind that. And Aidan never knew if his mum was going to be cross about Jesus or OK about it, so it was safer not to talk to her about him. And some grown-ups got more than cross. Once, one of his mum's friends hit him really hard when he was playing with Jesus. And hit him again when he started to cry.

And then Jesus stopped coming, and after a bit Aidan stopped asking for him to come back. For a while he wondered what he'd done, why Jesus wasn't his friend any more. It made him sad at school because they said that Jesus helped everyone, but they didn't say that he got bored and went off just like everyone else.

I don't sleep. But I'm ready for this. Completely prepared for the whole insomnia trip 'cos it's not something that started with the dead mum thing. It's not grief or any of that bollocks. I started not sleeping ages ago, before GCSEs, so it's not worry about exams and all that either. I started the not sleeping habit in about Year Eight, so I'm a no-sleeping expert. It's like a specialist subject. I did go to a doctor about it once. On my own, without Mum or anything. I wanted her to give me some pills or something, but she wasn't having it.

'So you can't sleep? So what? Think of it as a gift.' And when I asked her what she meant she sighed like it was obvious and said, 'If you want, you can see the sun rise, watch old movies, write letters, read books. Your days are longer than anyone else's, your life twice as long. This isn't an illness, this is an opportunity you've got here.' She was from Liverpool. Proper hard-nut, even though she was a doctor. You wouldn't go to her if you wanted a sick note or anything. No wonder she had to get out of Merseyside. Anyway, now I have a system. I don't see the sun rise and I don't write letters, but I read a bit, watch crazy internet stuff, listen to some sounds, jerk off, play some Empire, and then repeat as necessary. Sorts me out. Mostly sorts me out.

Fact is, however, that this time things go awry. Empire doesn't work out so well for a start. There's a recession looming in my world and I take some advice from my governing council and act on it. No bunker mentality for me and my tribe. I run a listening government.

I stimulate the economy with heavy investment in roads and schools and hospitals. On the social side I head off some ugly rumours of political dissent by experimenting with directly elected mayors in a few key cities.

I come back to my nation after listening to a few tunes only to find my outer provinces burning, my best soldiers crucified by the side of my new motorways, while chirpy messages of victory ping in from Tashkent and Hanoi.

'Hey man,' they say in cruelly flawless English. 'Bow down, mofo. Bow down.' I guess I've got to try harder.

After that debacle I catch up on some *Life! Death! Prizes!* and I read about a kid with cancer who was set on fire by two other kids. She's five and the kids that did it are eight and ten, and this isn't in America or anywhere, this is in Northampton. And then I read about someone selling film of Dick and Dom having a real live scrap in the BBC car park. So I find it on YouTube, but to be honest it's hard to tell if it's the real Dick and Dom. Could be any two blokes having a ruck. Yeah, she was right that granite-faced Scouser doc. You've got to work with this insomnia thing. Use your extra hours wisely.

And then somehow it's morning: Oscar is in, hurling himself at me and catching me right on the tip of my chin with a bony knee. It hurts. Proper hurts.

'For fuck's sake Oscar!' I yell, and stand up, which means he face-plants himself on the floor. 'Can't you just be normal for once you little—' and I stop myself just in time. Or more or less just in time because he's already started whimpering. 'Don't be such a cry-baby,' I snap. 'You could have broken my jaw.'

Oscar stops crying. He does his shocked face. Like a man doing a double-take in a silent film. Stan Laurel. He looks like Stan Laurel. And he's pissed himself in the night again. I can smell it on him. Jesus.

'And you're going back on the pull-ups tonight.'

Antonia sails in and scoops him up and, with Oscar half-hidden by her own mane of wild early morning hair, they look like some two-headed creature with both faces shooting me reproachful looks. I drop my arms and step back.

49

'What are your plans Toni? Because, no offence, but we're a bit busy today.'

'Can't Aunt Tonia take me to school?' says Oscar.

'No,' I say. 'We're going together me and you. Together as a little threesome. Me, you and Sooby-Doo.' He frowns. 'It's my favourite part of the day, taking you to school. And you're going to enjoy it too. It's an order.' This is meant to lighten the mood but it just comes out as stupid.

Chapter Four

Then it's Sunday and Oscar wants to go show-homing. This is a game we used to play with Mum. Her favourite game. She had all the apps to help her. She had RulerPhone, the app that turns your phone into a laser measuring thing so you can check room sizes. She had Mouseprice, the app that tells you how much any house is worth. You tap in the postcode and the info from the land registry comes up. She even had Walk Score, the app that tells you how easy it would be to live an eco-friendly lifestyle in any particular address: how far it was from supermarkets, doctors, pharmacies, hospitals and cinemas, all that. But it wasn't really the value of a house that Mum was into, it was more the overall look. She was always looking to see what was contemporary in architecture and soft furnishings. Always keen to see what the modern house was wearing. She was looking at fabrics and trends, seeing in the textures of the new-build house the way design was going – the way culture itself was going. She said this was important if you wanted to stay top dog in the event management world. And this is why she had ShopSavvy, the app that scans barcodes and finds the lowest price for home products.

It's funny because Oscar never really got into show-homing before. He was irritated at the way he was always being reminded not to touch, not to climb, not to be a small boy basically. But now – this Sunday – he's begging for us to do it. And, faced with the long stretch of tranquillised time that is a wet Sunday, I agree.

Southwood is a pretty good place to go show-homing. In common with every other small town in the south-east, our town has been asked to do its bit in the battle to provide affordable homes. A call that the developers have chosen to answer by providing hundreds of 'Luxury Mews Apartments'. Most of them empty. What this means in reality are ghost villages of low-rise flats on the flood plains next to the river. Today we're going out to a development called The Limes.

Seen from a distance these urban fuck-pads designed for the aspirational young professional are indistinguishable from the warehouses and DIY centres of the new retail park that they are also building out that way. They all have that Wal-Mart look. All that magnolia brickwork, enlivened here and there with primary colour trim, as though these new homes are nurseries for depressed children. Which they kind of are.

Somehow I don't think that the transformation of St Luke's – the old nuthouse – into The Limes, an estate of 'Executive Town Houses' complete with triple garages and gyms, is quite what the Minister for Urban Renewal had in mind. I can't remember the minister's name but I do know he's a lord and owns half of Kent. Which figures.

We head for the show home, past the middle-sized saloons that trumpet middle-sized success outside those few middle-sized executive boxes that have already been occupied.

What's total sunshine about show-homing is the way that it enables you to try on other people's lives. And not even their real lives with all their mess and clutter and shouting, but fantasy lives where the cushions and the rugs are nicely coordinated.

The best fun Mum and me had from show-homing was when we were pretending to be in the market for some stately pile out along the Essex/Suffolk border. My imagination was fired up by who the estate agents might be thinking we were. Once Mum and I pretended to speak Russian the whole time, so the agent would think we were the trophy wife and offspring of an oligarch. Another time, Mum spent a scarily realistic hour pretending to be a footballer's wife, making the estate agent piss his pants with her ideas for adult playrooms and en-suite apartments for her poodles. She was good at all that. She was pure A-star at acting, was Mum.

But if it was a right laugh at the top end, lower down the housing ladder could be entertaining too. The attempts by a developer, to cheat and skimp and fool the eye – that stuff delighted Mum. And we were happy 'cause she was happy. And she used to love the pure codshit bollocks of the estate agents who, at this level, were generally much younger and more eager than the ones who sold the mansions, and would bang on about 'feechas' in the hope that they were going to palm off a Legoland box on to a single mum with a good credit score but no sense.

The show home at The Limes is a classic of contemporary good taste. All the rooms are small except for two. Downstairs there is the enormous kitchen designed as the hub of the house in the same way that Houston was the hub of the Apollo moon missions. It's all a pleasing collision of light wood and chrome. It's like a hospice.

Meanwhile the one big room upstairs is the master bedroom with an en-suite that is less a bathroom and more a spa retreat. This is Oscar's favourite room 'cause it contains around a dozen little stained-glass bottles. He thinks they are toys, and in a way he's right. They are meant to put potential purchasers in mind of sensual love-making sessions. This whole room is meant to make the middle-aged couples think they can recapture the passion of their honeymoon if they fork over £250K for a hutch with underfloor heating and a wet room. There are also other clear bottles filled with smooth stones and strange fronds and twigs all hinting at Swedish-style decadence.

The other rooms are disappointing. Claustrophobic. Cell-like. From the point of view of a social historian, which I suppose I might be one day, then what's most interesting about the place is the fact that there are more bathrooms than bedrooms. Four bedrooms, four en-suites plus a 'family bathroom' that is considerably lower in spec than the one reserved for the master and mistress of the house.

If you had to guess at who might make this their home then you might suppose it's aimed at obsessive–compulsive foodie swingers with high levels of self-importance who don't like their children much. Does this sum up aspirations of the modern family? Maybe it does.

I put my hand in my pocket and touch the sharp fold of Dean's note. The one I found waiting for me this morning. The one I haven't read yet, but I know it's from him. I recognised the writing on the outside. The huge and hurried scrawl: 'To Billy.'

It was OK at first, having Dean around. He brought with him a new kind of sweary, sweaty, blokey stardust. I hadn't had much to do with blokes before. All Mum's friends were women, most of them single for long stretches, and here was the most complete burger-eating, football-loving, beer-guzzling, farting, belching, groin-scratching hairy specimen of manhood. I was impressed, and Dean was a good role model for a while. A bouncer by trade and an ex-soldier, he was popular with Mum's mates. There's nothing like knowing someone who has actually killed people to make an eco-warrior feel turned on. Especially when he can also get you into singles night at the Andromeda for nowt.

He was noisy of course – big, booming voice – but he only got proper mad during *Question Time* and *Match of the Day*. When they were on he would shout and swear and storm out of the room like these programmes set out to personally do his head in.

Hessenthaler supported West Ham, so I did too. Took to calling them The Irons, like a true fan, and we even went to a couple of games. We seemed like a proper family there for a while. And he could talk about exciting boys' stuff. He'd tell me of bayonet charges in Afghanistan, of the look in a man's eyes when he was dying a few centimetres away from you. Stories of stunts that even then I thought sounded less like warfare and more like the sort of showing off you get in the playground. He'd tell me about blokes who would run under fire through a minefield with a mate on their back and then put that same mate back in hospital during a scrap over a pool game. Mum liked these stories herself, but hated him telling them to me. And they did frighten me. But I was a boy who had been banned from watching horror films, or anything rated higher than a PG, so this was new and thrilling territory for me.

I even sort of got used to the sex.

They did it everywhere at first. And all the time. I'd come home from school, push open the door and have to run out immediately. Sometimes I could hear the shouts and groans from outside, and I'd go on past the house and to the shops without bothering to go home. Mum's mates would give me sly looks if they met me in the street. 'How's your Mum?' they would twinkle. 'How's Dean?'

'Oh, they're still shagging like rabbits,' I would say, all brisk and grown-up. But I wasn't that cool with it really.

I wasn't an innocent. We'd done it all at primary school. We'd copied the diagrams and labelled the parts. Our textbooks were ultra modern. They included the clitoris and everything.

We'd seen smiling cartoon people go at it in a variety of positions just before playtime. We had watched Miss Morgan unfurl the pink skin of a condom over a cucumber.

'Some men make the excuse that condoms are too small,' she smirked. 'I'd love to meet the man who is bigger than this.' There was just a hint of smiling emphasis on the word love, and we all tittered dutifully.

And I'd had a personal education too. At eleven years old Mum was driving me north for one of my increasingly rare weekends on Dad's boat, and I was rummaging amid the detritus of the glove compartment for a barley sugar, when a small golden missile had tumbled out and landed between my feet. I picked it up. I turned it over in my hands, puzzling over its smooth metallic sheen. Mum laughed.

'That's just my weekend kit, Billy. To stop me feeling lonely. Put it back, mate.' And she laughed again as I blushed furiously and shoved it back amid the tissues, the sweet wrappers and the change. And we never spoke about it again.

I think it's hard for women on their own not to treat their sons like their boyfriends, and their daughters like their mates. Those relationship muscles are ones that they can't help flexing. It means that the children of single mums get too much information, too much of the time.

The thing is, no matter what people tell you – no matter what you know – at eleven your mother having sex sounds like she's being attacked. It sounds like pain. It sounds like a sacrifice to an angry God. And the fact that your mum is cuddling and kissing, purring and rubbing up against the perpetrator doesn't make it easier – it makes it harder. More confusing.

They did settle down though, after a while. They still did it loads, but generally it took place at night and almost always in the bedroom. Dean gave up working the doors, and got a day job fitting fancy fireplaces. Good money, regular hours. With his army pension and Mum's job, we felt rich for a while. More importantly for me, the night-mare scenario of coming home and seeing a flash of erection as Mum and Dean ran naked and giggling for the stairs, well that diminished as more or less normal rules of behaviour reasserted themselves.

And maybe we would all have made the long haul. Maybe we would still be a family, still gathered around *Final Score* on a Saturday night, still pissing ourselves at the *X Factor* auditions, still going to see The Irons. All things we did with Dean that we hadn't done before. Maybe Dean would have started going to parents' evenings and enrolling me in boxing classes. Maybe I would have joined the army cadets and wouldn't be having a gap year work-ing in the Social History Museum. Maybe I'd be all signed up for the paras and contemplating my first stint in Iraq, or the Sudan or wherever. Maybe Dean would have handed on his trusty bayonet with the dirty stain of Taliban blood still just about visible on the blade.

All of that might have been possible if Mum had remem-bered some of her own sex education lessons. If she hadn't let Dean get her up the duff.

Being with Mum softened Dean – he brought her tea every morning, all that – but the prospect of a baby freaked him out. It freaked me out. And it freaked Mum out too.

57

But our shared fear somehow didn't unite us. I think now, looking back, that we each needed one of the others to embrace the new kid with enthusiasm. We needed someone to cheerlead and it didn't happen. Mum could have been the most gutted actually. She was enjoying her work, enjoying her life and now it was all complicated again. It was as if she'd got to the top of the hill and just seen more hills appear. The horizon appeared further off than ever. We were each miserable in our own way and, if we ever realised that the others were suffering, we were irritated rather than comforted. Of course I had the best excuse. The only excuse. I was just a kid.

The atmosphere went sour. Mum wouldn't let Dean tell his war stories in the house, and anyway he'd started to repeat himself. And he took to watching football in the pub rather than at home, and I punished him by affecting to have grown out of it, started talking about twenty-two poofs kicking a goat's bladder around. And then he started working nights at the Andromeda club again, coming home in the early hours a little bit pissed, just in time to wake Mum who was then noisily sick.

She was sick for most of the pregnancy, way past the time the nausea is meant to pass. And not just in the mornings. Dean was soon associated with sickness and tiredness and I last saw him about a month before Oscar was born. He was trying to pick his pants up from the front garden in the rain. Not just his pants. All his stuff. Mum had tipped it there three days earlier and it had sat on our lawn like an installation. Like a piece of modern art titled *My Boyfriend Is A Wanker*. When he came round to get his stuff, she took the piss out of him for a bit from an upstairs window, he booted in the front door and that was that. I never saw him again. I think there might have been threats of injunctions and court stuff afterwards but Mum didn't talk about it and I wasn't interested. And then the full-on hurricane that was the birth was on us, and I was suddenly a birth partner, filling the gap where Dean should have been.

The arrow hits Oscar in the show home's garden. He's out there beyond the French windows playing some strange game of his own. I'm looking again at the gleam and glare of the black marble of the kitchen when there's a flicker of something in the corner of my eye. And I'm already turning and striding towards him before his unmistakable wail goes up. I'm not sure what has caused the movement at the edge of my vision but something was very, very wrong about it.

'What's the matter, Oscar? Come on. Tell me. Stop crying for God's sake.' Fear has made me sharper than I mean to be. I ease up when I see how quickly he does try and stem his tears, swallowing his sobs and trying to turn them into coughs. He's lying on the ground rubbing at his leg. He looks fearfully over my shoulder and I turn to follow his eyes. Peering over the uncreosoted back fence of the garden is an ugly tyke. Crop-haired, ginger, and snot-nosed he looks about twelve and his eyes shine with a ferrety intelligence.

'Can I have my arrow back?' No please, no apology for wounding a little kid. I glance at the ground and see a stick sharpened at one end and notched at the other. A home-made arrow. A Blue Peter kind of arrow. I pick it up and I snap it in half. And that should have been that.

I pick Oscar up and, without looking at the snot-nosed wannabe, walk back into the statement kitchen and through the thoughtfully planned, thoroughly contemporary super-luxe living room, and out into the real world where seconds later we are confronted by snot-nose and several others who look the same but older and, if anything, even uglier. It looks like the underclass are show-homing too. Casing joints for future breaks and entries. Eyeing up the driveways looking for executive saloons that might be available for a little light twocking at some future date.

I'm not too bothered at first. I count them. There are six kids in total. The oldest about fifteen. Snot-nose is by far the youngest. He's snivelling now.

'He broke my arrow,' he whines, and I can see that I might have been wrong about his age. He doesn't look like twelve now, more like ten, puffed up on chicken nuggets and all-day breakfasts.

'You broke my kid brother's arrow.' This is another tiny kid dressed like all the others in shiny blue trackie bottoms with a ball cap pulled down low over his eyes. Even though he's small you can tell that he's the leader. There's some kind of fire in his eyes. A sort of ambition. The other kids stand in a ragged anonymous group just behind him, hoods up, caps jammed tight on to their heads, hands thrust deep into pockets, as though auditioning for some generic movie about teen gangs. But in truth they are not very frightening. Then it comes to me who these would-be Bad Motherfuckers remind me of: they're like the kids in *South Park*.

'Fanta pubes is your brother is he?' I say now. 'I wouldn't be admitting to that, my friend.'

The boss kid flushes and someone snorts behind him.

'Think you're clever don't you?' says Cartman or whatever his name is, and he reaches behind him and pulls out a knife. A bread knife. It's laughable. Pathetic.

And it's terrifying.

We're all aware of the stories: the bloke shot for his cufflinks, the dad kicked to death because he slaps the kid

60

caught scratching his car, the grandad who has a heart attack chasing some yobs who spat at his grandkids on the swings, the teacher stabbed while breaking up a fight in the playground, the dead mother who wouldn't let some lowlife take her Netbook. Those stories.

Oscar's getting heavy in my arms but I don't want to put him down, not now. Cartman comes close to my face. He has deep, purplish bags under his eyes and his skin is way too thin for a kid his age. He looks like he needs a decent kip. The only thing that is recognisably teenage about him is his deodorant. Lynx obviously. He sticks that ordinary bread knife under my neck.

'Not so clever now, eh, knobhead?' And now I can smell something else, something apart from Lynx. He smells of the need to prove himself. And you know what that smells like? It smells like cider.

And now I am proper worried.

Knives, cider and a need to impress his mates – it's sort of a lethal cocktail. I can't run because I've got Oscar – I wouldn't get two metres – and I can't fight for the same reason. I feel Oscar quiver and whimper into my neck.

I look around The Limes. There's no sound or movement anywhere. I could holler for help, but there are only a few occupied houses and, anyway, this is England – who's going to come rushing to our aid? They've read all the same stories. Those stories. The *Life! Death! Prizes!* stories.

'OK, lads, look. I'm sorry about the arrow. I wasn't thinking. Let me make it up to you.'

I really need Oscar to get down now and I try and shake him a little bit, but he just whimpers again and clings tighter. I put my hand into my pocket. There's some crumpled paper and some loose coins. I pull it all out. Some coppers spill and roll on the floor. Snot-nose hurls himself after them, chuckling. I glance at my fist. There's a twenty and a ten there. Thirty quid.

'Maybe take yourself off to Maccy D, buy yourselves a slap-up meal. Make up for it.'

The knife doesn't move and his eyes don't leave mine. 'I don't eat that shit. It's full of hormones and crap.'

'Get yourself a salad from Simply Food then. You might just have enough there.'

I swear that he almost smiles. He lowers the knife anyway.

'No, I tell you what you should do. You should go round the corner to the Paki shop and get us some booze and some crisps. Cunt won't serve us no more.' The P-word and the C-word both sound very loud here in The Limes. The crew shuffle uneasily behind their leader, who puffs himself up a little more as he senses the fading enthusiasm of his troops. It probably makes him more dangerous.

'OK,' I say. I'm thinking that I'll stroll the couple of hundred metres out of the gate and round to the Indian newsagent. The old gent in there will, upon my request, phone the old Bill and then, after a suitable interval, I'll stroll back, get in Sooby-Doo and drive home.

I'm not expecting that the police will be able to catch anyone but the appearance of a cop car in The Limes should have all these little trolls running for cover. But Cartman is ahead of me.

'OK then, it's a deal.' He puts the knife back in the waistband of his trousers. 'Thirty quids' worth of White Lightning. You'll have to leave the kid here though, to make sure you come back. And don't call the filth or anything like that.' He's grinning, exulting in his own criminal genius.

I really do have to put Oscar down now. My back and arms are proper aching. It's a struggle because he's squeezing my neck so tightly, but eventually I manage to wrestle him to the floor. He grabs me round the legs, burying his face in my stomach.

'I'm not leaving Oscar with you lot. Sorry lads.'

'He'll be safe. We wouldn't hurt a little kid.' This is mumbled by one of the anonymous hoodies.

'Not 'less we have to,' Cartman seems put out. This is his big scene, and he doesn't want minor characters screwing it up.

'It's not negotiable. Sorry.'

Cartman's frustrated at this, and shows it by hawking up phlegm and spitting it down at my feet.

'Come on Curtis, let's just go.' This is another kid, but their leader is reluctant and has, in case, formulated a plan B. He's a quick thinker. You've got to give him that.

'OK, we'll all go to the shop. You buy the drink, and we'll just stand close and make sure you don't try anything funny.'

And so this is how I find myself in AJ's 24/7 Supastore buying ten huge plastic bottles of White Lightning with a mob of Year Nines at my back. I'm hoping he'll ID me, but he doesn't. Ludicrously, the bottles I pick out are labelled 'Family Size' as though they were a necessity like bog roll or cornflakes. What kind of family can they have in mind?

The Indian guy, AJ himself perhaps, doesn't make conversation as he rings up the bill. He has me down as one of those losers who buy booze for underage kids just because they're asked. He's learned enough street diplomacy not to make an issue of it however. Oscar doesn't seem frightened any more. He stares around the shop curiously, taking in the profusion of stuff on the shelves, the wild party of smells in the air. Then Lucy Avis, the urban geography teacher, Katie's sister, walks in.

She's not looking much like a goth goddess right now in her tracksuit, all red in the face. She's obviously been jogging or at the gym. She looks like the old Lucy Avis, the County Ping-Pong Champ, her only concession to gothic eccentricity is that her scarlet hair is held up off her boiled, sweaty face by a biro. She twitches as she sees me, then takes in my little tribe of blackmailing hoods. She includes us all in a shy grin.

'Hello boys,' she says. 'What are you up to?'

There's a ragged chorus of mumbles all of which add up to a generalised 'Nuttin' Miss.'

Suddenly it all seems like bollocks. Like a stupid dream. *What the fuck am I doing?*

I put my hand on AJ's arm as he's loading the cider into a cardboard box he fetched especially for the purpose.

'You know what, mate. I've changed my mind. I don't want the cider. I'll just have a *Sunday Mirror* and a packet of plain crisps please. Sorry to be a pain.' I wouldn't normally get the *Sunday Mirror* but I notice they're giving away a download of *Battle of Britain* and Oscar and me, we're partial to a classic war film.

AJ rolls his eyes, and starts doing whatever thing on the till is necessary when some tool of a customer messes up your transaction.

I turn around. 'Sorry kiddies,' I say. 'The bar's closed. Oh and I'll have a packet of those Pampers pull-up things please.'

I keep my voice cheery, but I'm watching Cartman's hands. If he goes for his knife then I've got to go for him. And I'll have about three seconds to proper hurt him. He doesn't of course. In the shop, in the presence of Miss, he looks even smaller. He looks like what he is. He looks like a kid.

'Wanker,' he hisses, and he starts to swagger to the door past Lucy.

'Curtis Hughes, you stop right there.' Lucy has a teacher voice that is pure old school when she wants. It works too. Despite himself, the kid shuffles to a halt and turns around. His homeboys take the chance to scarper. The shop-bell jangles manically as they leave. 'Do you want me to call your mum?' she says, her mobile is ready in her hand.

'No.'

'No, what?'

'No, Miss.'

'Because she's not going to be too impressed, is she?'

Cartman/Curtis shakes his head unhappily. 'And I *should* call her because that's what we agreed at parents' evening, didn't we? She said, "Whenever Curtis steps out of line, call me and I'll deal with it." And she will too, won't she Curtis? Deal with it, I mean.'

'Yes Miss.' His cheeks are glowing a fireball-red now.

'So don't you think that you should apologise to this gentleman?' His eyes flicker up to mine. He's searching for a dignified way out. And I'm not giving him one.

'Sorry, mate.'

'That's OK,' I say. I pause and just as he turns to follow his friends out of the shop I add, 'Best give me the knife though, eh?'

'What?'

'The bread knife. Best give it to me.' I hold my hand out. Lucy's eyes are wide as he pulls the weapon out of his waistband and hands it over. He does it the sensible boy scout way too, handle first. 'Thanks,' I say, trying to keep my voice neutral, as though he was giving me a light or something.

'We were just messing,' he murmurs.

'You are in such shit,' breathes Lucy, as he starts to move away.

'Don't tell Mum, please Miss.'

'Curtis, I've got to. You know that.'

'Fuck,' he says. 'Fuck.'

And suddenly Oscar is over at him snarling, sinking his teeth into his wrist. Curtis yelps. 'Fuck!' he says again.

I prise Oscar's jaws away from the pale flesh. There's a perfect dental impression of Oscar's mouth left on the skin, here and there blood is breaking through to the surface.

'Don't. Say. Bad. Words.' My little bro is purple with rage.

I pull Oscar away and wrap myself around him, pinning his arms to his sides. I look up as the shop-bell jangles again and I see poor ole Curtis rushing past his mates who are gathered outside. He has his hands over his eyes and his head down. He's trying and failing to hide his tears. Just a kid. Just a fuckwit kid.

'Absolutely sure you don't want this cider?' says AJ.

By the time he got to high school Aidan Jebb wasn't really singing any more. His voice hadn't broken but lots of other lines had been crossed. He'd been done for nicking sweets, for vandalising motors and for throwing stones at smaller kids. He was still going to school more or less every day though and he didn't really play up all that much. Except in music. For some reason he hated music now, always did his best to stop Miss Morgan teaching. He called out, he pushed other kids off their chairs, he picked fights. And at lunchtimes he could often be found trying to break into the performing arts block to bang around on the drums. Or he was running across the roof. In music he was a menace.

And Rosie had a boyfriend now. She loved him. She'd do anything for him. She wanted babies with him. He was her partner. Titus Cooke. A businessman. Wore a suit. Drove a big black Lexus that cost about £45K new. It wasn't not new but that wasn't the point, it almost looked like it could be. Titus Cooke didn't really have a house as such. There were rumours of a luxury apartment on the edge of London, like there was word of an exclusive beachside villa in Northern Cyprus. What he had for sure were a number of places around Southwood where he was guaranteed a bed. Titus Cooke had seven children already and he made sure that they were all looked after. If the mothers played ball with him, he'd see them right. Titus Cooke had plans and schemes and quite often they came off. He was a well-known face around town. There were bars where he had unlimited credit. And he could always get you stuff. Stuff was what Titus dealt in. Hard to get stuff. Tricky stuff. Titus always had a friend, someone who knew someone who knew someone who would find the stuff you needed. Or something very like it. And if you couldn't afford stuff – exotic stuff or basic stuff – then Titus would give you a loan. Titus was the Daddy.

When Rosie had sex for money now it was a bit more organised. Titus, or one of his mates, looked after her. Titus called her his favourite rock star. Someone who put in a lot of effort to get what they needed. He saw she was all right. He sorted it. Rosie did massages, Swedish therapies, executive stress relief in the comfort of the client's own home, hotel sessions, stag parties. And she did amateur for the internet.

She had her face blanked out obviously. Or she had a mask on. She wasn't thick. Didn't want someone recognising her in the Spar.

To be honest she'd never thought she'd say this but she liked the girl on girl stuff best. The girls were clean and gentle and you could have more of a laugh. Sometimes they'd send the camera guy out of the room and tell him to come back in a couple of hours and they'd make sure there was plenty of usable material on the tape.

She made some money. She wasn't some slag on the street, down at Castle Road. And it wasn't every day either. She didn't need to do it every day. Which was just as well because some days she didn't get out of bed at all. Some days she just needed to take some time out, get a few cans in, or some Vladivar, watch TV with Titus, listen to music. Just chill. It's not a crime. She wasn't an addict either, most of her drugs were prescription. Plus a bit of weed, bit of coke. Bit of this. Bit of that. And there was food in the house.

And Aidan was loved.

She liked to see his face. He made her smile. Even if he was an irritating little shit at times. It would be nice if he wasn't so bloody rude to Titus. And it'd be nice if he would sing once in a while instead of going round with a face like a slapped arse.

Little sod always had his dinner money now. Nearly always.

I tell Lucy the whole pathetic tale of the show-homing trip as we leave the shop. She only popped in for a Nutri-Grain bar and a pint of milk. Now that she's scattered the opposition with such ease, I feel like a real turd. I feel cowardly and embarrassed. Furious with myself. Even Oscar put up more of a fight than I did.

She says, 'I better give you a lift home then.' I tell her that no it's OK, my car is parked in The Limes. 'Oh, they'll have trashed your car,' she says with weary certainty.

And she's right. Sooby-Doo has been comprehensively, systematically kicked to death. In the three minutes it has taken us to walk back from the shop to The Limes, they have turned our old but tough family saloon into something you might see on the news as part of a barricade. Sooby is without wheels, without headlights, without windscreen, without more or less every sodding thing and, as we approach, the car goes up in flames with a Hollywood whoomph.

'Sooby!' wails Oscar. I don't know what to do. If this was a leadership exam, I'd be failing. I'd be getting an Ungraded. I'd be in the Special Needs group, after-school catch-up lessons, support teacher and everything. Lucy, though, she seems pretty A-star at it.

'Hey there dude – don't cry. A car's just a car. It's a thing, like a ... a ... brick. It's not important. An earwig, an *ant* is more important than a car.'

Oscar stops crying. He's not convinced, but he's giving this idea some serious thought. Lucy presses home her advantage, uses the time this dubious philosophy has bought. 'So why don't we go to my flat, have a drink. I'll get cleaned up and then we can all do something together. Play a game. Is that a good idea?'

I think there's no way Oscar will go for that.

'Have you got Coke Zero?' he says.

'Yes, I think I do.'

'OK then,' he says. 'Let's go.' And that's how easy it is for Oscar to move on. RIP Sooby-Doo the Subaru – the car he named – and hello to skilfully marketed caffeine-free fizzy pop. I'm a bit shocked to be honest.

Chapter Five

Lucy Avis's flat is cool. An estate agent would call it 'charming', 'deceptively spacious', 'well maintained', 'full of character', 'with considerable potential', meaning it's small, old, and in need of a complete revamp, but I could really get to like it. The carpets are beige, the walls magnolia and the kitchen looks like it's come straight from a B&Q clearance sale, which it probably has. But there are radical paintings. Huge, dramatic abstracts. And even better than the paintings, there are also two huge board games on the wall. One is Risk, which I love. It's a kind of analogue Empire. There's a map, exactly like the one in the normal board game version, but massive. And the other oversized game is snakes and ladders. This board has pictures of places in Southwood on it. There are snakes leading from the Fun Junction, and from the Ship and the Library and the kebab shop, and ladders coming up from other places, like Lucy's house. And, glory be, the Social History Museum. Inspired.

'Who did these?' I say.

'My boyfriend. Milan. He's an artist.'

The corners of all the rooms are filled with an eclectic collection of ethnic musical instruments. There's a balalaika here, a bouzouki there, a djembe, a gourd, a sitar, a tabla, a set of bagpipes, a bodhrán . . .

'Wow,' says Oscar, 'can you play all these?'

Lucy laughs and shows those amazing teeth.

'No, sweetheart. But Milan can. He's a terrific musician as well as an artist.'

'Oh,' says Oscar, flatly. And his audible lack of enthusiasm for this boyfriend character would be comical if it didn't so clearly echo my own.

'Where is he now?' I say, careful to sound genuinely interested.

'Milan? He's on tour. He's Musical Director and Set Designer with a physical theatre group.' Of course he bloody is. He would be.

'Where's he from?'

'Coventry. But his parents are Czech, hence the name. He did the paintings as well.'

'Talented guy,' I say. I hate him.

'Yeah. And it's weird that he's so artistic because he's really a scientist. Got a PhD in something to do with artificial intelligence.'

'Bit of an all-rounder then.' I can't help it. I'm trying to be nice, but it comes out as flat as Oscar's 'oh'. Lucy laughs again. She's probably used to this.

'I'll grab a shower.'

Oscar and I distract ourselves while Lucy showers (she's *naked*. All soaped up. Just centimetres away behind a flimsy B&Q door) by setting up the table-tennis table that is folded in half against the living-room wall. The bats are there too. Everything to hand if she gets the ping-pong urge. We quickly get into a rhythm, Oscar and I. I serve, he takes a wild swing, misses and then chases the ball, as it bounces around the room. He's doing his puppy thing again. He's happy. Lucy comes out wrapped in a towel. (She's *naked*. Wet. Under a few millimetres of cheap towel.)

'I hope you don't mind,' I say. 'Oscar wanted to play.'

71

She smiles and shakes her head. 'Maybe I could give you a game one day?' I say. She laughs now and all those beautiful, architectural teeth come out again.

'I could give you a lesson,' she says.

'Does Milan play?' I say, sure that he'll turn out to be a former West Midlands area champ, or a Czech international or something.

Lucy is thoughtful. 'No, it's funny. He's rubbish at table tennis. Doesn't get it at all.'

'Yaay!' says Oscar. Lucy scoops him up, presses him against her towelled breasts. 'Meanie,' she says. Oscar blushes.

We spend the afternoon playing snakes and ladders. Snakes and ladders – who knew it could last so long? And it would have taken even longer if we hadn't fixed it so that Oscar's counter takes a final ladder from the Town Hall to the winning post. He's proper thrilled by his victory and then he falls asleep on Lucy's chaise longue thing. It's a copy of the famous one by Dali, the daybed in the shape of a pair of scarlet lips, no doubt knocked up by Milan in a spare five minutes between painting a masterpiece and composing a symphony for bouzouki and harp.

Lucy makes tea and hot buttered toast and we talk of this and that. People we know. Her job. My job. Bands and stuff. And we make each other laugh a bit. And then there's a quiet time and Lucy smiles.

'You're very good-looking you know,' she says suddenly. 'I could quite fancy you.'

What can I say to this? I mutter something – even I don't know what. She carries on. 'Yeah. I could quite easily fancy you. If you weren't too young. If you didn't know my sister. If I didn't have a brilliant boyfriend already. And if you didn't have that beard.'

72

Which I suppose is her way of saying that it's never going to happen. A case of being kind to be cruel I guess.

So I call a cab, and when I leave we sort of half-hug awkwardly on the doorstep. Lucy takes both my hands, looks into my eyes and I notice that hers are so dark they are almost black. She takes a moment and then says, 'Billy, I think you should always remember that you are a lover not a fighter. From what I've seen anyway.'

I see him as we get out of the cab back from Lucy's. It's dark and it's raining again and he's only there for a second but I know it's him. He's standing over the street, a little black hole of misery. A darker space amid the winter murk. He's not wearing a coat and the hood's up on his top. He looks so ordinary he's almost invisible. He could be an evening jogger I suppose, one of those lightweight types that have to pause every few steps. Only I know it's not. It's him. Aidan Jebb. My heart bangs against my ribs but I stay cool. I pay the cabbie and wave away the proffered change and we stand facing each other, silent across Oaks Avenue. It's a long second. I'm holding the sleeping Oscar and have time to wonder if I can get into the house, get a weapon and get back out in time to smash his pathetic little face in when a car passes and he's gone.

Inside I wake Oscar up. I want to get him into those pull-ups. He'll thank me for it in the morning. But he's not having any, and I'm just too exhausted for a fight at this time of night, and so I let it go, knowing that we'll both pay for it later. Oscar proves himself tougher than me and so he goes to bed triumphantly commando. Un-nappied and promising a whole dry future. Like a victorious president he is all euphoric, promising a change is gonna come. Yeah, yeah, I think, we all know what happens to those kind of promises don't we?

When I'm sure that Oscar's asleep I creep back into his room and stand on the third step of the ladder that leads up to his bed and just watch his face for a few minutes. He breathes like a little mouse, fast and shallow. His face wrinkles and twitches in sleep and a tear edges out of the eye that I can see.

'Hush up, kiddo,' I say. And then I remember that kiddo isn't my word. It's Dean's word. A word from the forgotten dream when he lived with us.

I look out into the night and there's nothing there. I open a window to feel the wet wind on my face. I listen and I can hear the usual. I can hear the usual scuffling that means that a bin is being raided by a cat or a fox, the distant screeches that mean something is being killed out by the park. A dog barks. Somewhere, in Southwood or somewhere nearby, somebody is being raped, beaten, killed. Someone always is aren't they? In every small town someone is doing a world of viciousness to someone else. Usually it's to someone they really love.

I need two things now. Music and alcohol. I have thousands of tracks on my phone and tonight is one of those nights when I hate them all. We use up music too fast these days, I think. At least I do. From Click-Click to the Ha-Ha Germs. From Rosalita to Razorblade Picnic. From Fay Barclay to The Infected: everything is stale, old, done in. And if I leave it on shuffle then the goddam machine seems to choose the crappest selection. My iThing makes a terrible DJ. And I know it's all random but it doesn't feel like it. It feels like my own phone is deliberately trying to bring me down. But when I try and take control I find that I'm just as bad. Nothing suits.

As for drink, there's nothing in. I make a vow: that will never happen again. While I'm in charge, there will always

74

be booze. Actually, a second look reveals that there is something. It's bound to be rank but desperate times call for desperate measures.

When they first got together Mum and Dean went for long romantic cycle rides. I'd be left with Gran or Aunt Toni or one of Mum's mates, while they packed butties and ginger beer, and went off exploring the byways of the National Cycle Network. It was a chance for Mum to do the proper courting she'd missed out on because of becoming a young mother. Of course, it ended up with her becoming a slightly older mother, so maybe proper courting – whatever that is – wasn't such a top idea either. To become a single mum once is an accident: to do it twice, well, that just makes you look like a retard.

On one of their expeditions they found some sloes and, with the help of a recipe downloaded from some celeb chef website, they made sloe gin. It's the easiest thing to do, it takes no skill at all but still it felt like an adventure, something real couples did together. Playing and working together all at the same time. And the beauty of it was that you had to wait. You can hurry love, but you can't hurry gin. As their relationship matured, so did the drink.

Dean moved in on the day that the sloe gin was finally ready, the day the website gave permission to crack open the bottles. It tasted sweet, like undiluted Ribena. Slipped down nice and easy. Dean said, 'Christ, this'll rot your teeth before it gets you pissed.'

They only realised how potent it was when they tried to stand up. And they just laughed and drank more and danced. Danced. Hessenthaler danced. That must be some powerful magic in those sloes. Hessenthaler dancing. I wonder where I was? Not at home that's for sure.

So they drank and they laughed, attempted a rough and ready tango and they gave each other easy, powerful Hollywood orgasms. Made love like they were in a film. Yes, Mum told me all this. Single mums see. They just don't have the same boundaries as other parents.

It was thrilling and romantic and beautiful and dirty. Properly, wonderfully dirty. And they fell asleep in the early hours twisted around each other like an ancient knot.

And woke up sick as dogs.

Two bottles of the sloe gin got drunk, but the hangover cost was so extreme the next morning that even Dean never tried it again. And that last bottle has been sat at the back of the kitchen cupboard for eight years. It'll be rank, but it'll do the business. In any case, it was time it was gone.

So. I end my evening smoking Alfie's weed in the bath, sipping Mum and Dean's own special love potion and listening to Mum's 'Abba Gold'. Mum's two last musical passions were Abba and Nick Cave, and you might think that there is a long stretch of highway between those two points, but now, for the first time, I pay proper attention to Abba's lyrics. There are some pretty melancholy stories. Some well-thought-out personal politics. Even 'Super Trouper', which has the cheesiest oompah-loompah bounce to it, is actually the story of a woman who, despite being gutted at being stuck in a lonely hotel room in Glasgow of all places, goes on to the stage every night to perform, smiling, for the uncaring masses. And 'Knowing Me, Knowing You' is about divorce and so is 'Winner Takes It All' – Abba are obsessed with divorce in fact. Every second track seems to be heading for the family courts. You get more jokes from the Bad Seeds that's for sure.

Even Abba's happiest tune, 'Dancing Queen', is about how quickly youth vanishes, how fast all that power goes.

It's pretty clear that Bjorn and Benny's view on dancing is that it's OK to be lost in the moment at seventeen, but pretty soon those easy days will be gone, and you'll be dividing up the welcome mat with your ex-partner. As for making your soon-to-be-ex wife open a hit song – a song that she will have to sing for the rest of her career – with the lines 'I'm nothing special . . . in fact I'm a bit of a bore', well, it takes a special kind of cruelty to do that. And a special kind of masochism to agree to it. No wonder Agnetha became a recluse and married her stalker.

As I lie in the bath letting the ash drop sizzling into the water, I flick through the pages of *Life! Death! Prizes!* This is what I read about: James Pownall, aged 37, a bloke who, in the midst of a divorce, came around to the family home and hung his wife, Julie, aged 29. There was a messed-up attempt to make it look like suicide. Two texts sent, one to Julie's mother and one to her sister, both saying that she had had enough, that this was the only way out.

What transpired later was that his two young sons had watched him do it. Two little boys, aged five and seven, saw him haul their mother's unconscious body from her bed to the landing, watched while he improvised a noose and dangled her over the balustrade. This is the point where, according to the coroner, Julie probably came around. There were marks around her neck consistent with clawing at the ligature. And, after the choking and flailing and gasping was all over, Pownall sent his crying children back to their room with the instructions to come down at seven and call Julie's mother to say that they had just found their mummy hanging. Which is what these kids – good kids obviously – did.

The oldest one, Tobias, phoned his granny on the dot of seven saying that something was badly wrong. He didn't say – couldn't say – exactly what it was. His granny phoned the police. And those brave, good kids didn't mention their father for three days, until the youngest one, Henry, finally murmured what he had seen to his granny who was giving him a bath.

Seeing the police arrive outside his house James Pownall tried to top himself, taking a Gillette Mach 3 to his wrists. These cuts were later said to be 'superficial', thus proving himself to be an incompetent and a coward. But he was also a man who had never given any sign of a murderous impulse. The article was full of quotes from neighbours and friends attesting to his quiet, polite, hard-working personality. And you can tell from the kids' names that this was not a scummy family.

This is a story from the leafy suburbs of Godalming, Surrey. Pownall was a solicitor, which might account for the delusion that he could out-wit the peelers. I suppose that we should be grateful for the fact that he didn't kill the kids too. Apparently the angry, repressed, middle-class control freak is the classic profile of the family annihilator.

That's what I read about as I lie in the bath, getting ripped, drinking eight-year-old sloe gin and listening to 'Thank You For The Music'. And in the morning, I wake with a fire behind my eyeballs and with a pissy kid brother whimpering next to me.

'I'm sorry, Billy. Sorry, sorry, sorry, sorry.'

Chapter Six

Aidan Jebb was making decent money getting stuff for Titus and his clients. He'd race all over town on his BMX with packages and envelopes and rucksacks and bring cash back to his handlers. A big lad for his age, he was often around when interest on loans needed collecting. It was easy. He just needed to put his hood up, maybe wear some shades. And Titus gave him a sword. Titus Cooke was a collector of militaria. That sword cost £350. It was a genuine Scottish claymore used at Culloden to put to death God knows how many wounded Highlanders. Titus Cooke liked to be on the right side of history. Titus Cooke liked to be on the side of the winners. Titus had a lot of swords. Knew his stuff.

'You gotta have a collection,' Titus said. 'Police told me that. You have one sword, you're a psycho. If you have loads, you're a collector of antiquities and they can't touch you.'

And Titus let Aidan walk his dogs. Aidan was scared of dogs but he wasn't going to tell Titus that.

Titus's dogs. They looked mean but they were gentle enough. Obviously you wouldn't let them near any babies – only a fool would do that – but they were meek as anything if you treated them right. They just wanted to please really, just wanted to make their daddy proud of them. If they scared people then it was only the people Titus – and Aidan – wanted them to scare. Walking those dogs, Aidan was a superhero. And he had a sword at home.

A fucking sword. Titus told Aidan about Culloden, about the army that backed the wrong guy. About the prince who thought he was an ace fucking general and screwed up the battle plan and sneaked off while his tired and hungry army – the men who had followed him all over from Inverness to Derby and back, in bare feet some of them – were butchered on a wet, misty morning. And Aidan's sword was used there. Some of the Highlanders were scalped. Some of them ended up as slaves in the West Indies.

'White slaves man,' said Titus. 'Imagine that.'

I'm back in the museum, our secret oasis in the heart of the town centre. Outside our cloisters the crowds bounce from major high street brand to major high street brand, only getting a rest by paying the hefty cappuccino tax in one of the many coffee shops. Southwood has a population of 22,000 and 31 places where you can drink Fair Trade, free-range skinny lattes. If Mr and Mrs Joe Public ever came in here, they could sit for free or, for £1.50, they'd get a perfectly decent instant Nescafé. All you get for your £3.95 in one of the corporate chains is a nicer cup. Here you might very well get served with Mike's old 'Justice for the Dinner Ladies' mug, itself an industrial relic from a forgotten local government strike of the early 1980s. But here you'd also get to look at some interesting artefacts. For example we have the earliest working model of a motorised lawnmower (1912, Germany, rescued from a Lowestoft scrapyard in 1973), not to mention a complete horse-drawn fire engine from the 1800s. Though I admit the horse is stuffed. But you don't get any of that in Coffee Republic or wherever.

I've been sat down for about a minute when Jenny pads over.

'Everything all right, Billy?'

What can I say? The obvious. I can say the obvious.

'Yeah everything's cushty, Jen. Tip-top.'

Jenny nods and then hands me a note. Oh God, not another one.

'It's from that fella, the one you were fighting with. He collared me outside this morning.'

This is the third note I've had from Dean. They all say the same thing, which is sorry and can we talk properly. And they're all written on headed notepaper. Total Security Solutions. Which I guess is the name of who he's working for now. He's either still hired muscle or he's a bailiff, and he thinks he should be in charge of Oscar. *Oh, behave Dean*, I think, as I very deliberately drop the note straight into the paper recycling box. Jenny sighs. 'You're going to have to deal with him eventually, you know.'

I'm not sure about that. In my experience if you ignore a problem long enough it goes away. It's been a policy that has served me well for my first nineteen years and I see no reason to stop now.

Toni calls late one night. We do the usual: Oscar. Mum. The rain. I'm wondering what's up. I've known Aunt Toni all my life, I can tell when she's nervous. She has something to say. I wait. And I wait. And I wait. Eventually it wobbles out, her voice going quavery and high as she says, 'Billy . . . I've seen him.'

'Yes, me too!' I cut in all excited.

'You've seen Dean? When? He told me you haven't even answered his messages . . .' Her voice tails away.

'Dean? I thought you meant . . .' I stop. There was something extra in the way Toni presented this. A bit of edge. 'Toni,' I begin, and I don't have to say anything else. Don't even get the chance to.

'No!' she sounds outraged. 'No. It's not like that. Nothing like that. I've got a partner, remember?' Her reaction tells me more than I'd ever have guessed. And yes I do remember that you have a partner, Toni. I remember that he's an idiot. A bloke who laughs at his own jokes. A bloke who *only* laughs at his own jokes. One of those blokes.

'But you like Dean. You think he's OK. You're on his side. You think he should see Oscar.' I say all this as facts not as questions.

'Oh Billy. We need to stick together. Life's too short . . .'

I hang up.

Oscar wants me to help him learn some spellings. He has twenty words to do look-cover-write-check with. I'm just going to finish a bit of Empire business first.

After my previous setbacks my world is embarking on a period of unusual peace and plenty. This is probably a result of all the time I've been spending managing affairs of state lately. If you want to compete with the Chens and the Chungs, you got to put the hours in. And all this enforced babysitting has given me the opportunity to get things moving.

I know it's a dumb level of micro-management but I've recently been overseeing the re-organisation of the national football league. In Empire, as in life, if you want something doing you have to do it yourself. I certainly can't trust my Minister for Sport. His avatar shows him to be sort of reptilian and I suspect he's well up for plotting against me. I'm keeping an eye on him. Meanwhile I've been releasing state reserve funds to build new stadiums, appoint administrators and set up Centres of Excellence. I'm considering a bid to host the continental championships.

Thing is, I've done all the nation-building essentials

– there are reservoirs, mines, new cities, roads, train stations, airports, power stations, air defence systems and inter-continental ballistic missile silos. The people have jobs, now they need bread and circuses otherwise they get a bit mutinous. That's world leadership 101. Every dictator knows that, even the special needs ones.

Eventually Oscar starts getting proper agitated that we're going to run out of spelling time and pulls the plug out of the wall. Just after he's done it, he looks at me all wide-eyed like I'm going to batter him or something. But for some strange reason, I find I don't care all that much. A few months ago I'd have gone pure batshit.

Lucy Avis comes into the museum. She's not on her own. With her is a weasel-faced kid of about fifteen. I know weasel face. His whole skulking demeanour speaks of smashed streetlights, kitten-baiting and the extorting of cider from his elders and betters. This is one of The Limes lot. Curtis's gang. I can't be sure, but he might have been the muttering hoodie who interrupted his leader's minipop gangsta spiel to say that they wouldn't hurt Oscar. I take Lucy aside.

'Lucy,' I say, 'three words: W.T.F.'

She looks blank. Then laughs. 'Oh, I get it, what the fuck? Do you mean why have I brought Lyndon Bowers here?'

I look over at this lanky hoon who is examining our prize lawnmower, a baffled frown contorting his nasty little features. Lucy follows my gaze. 'Work experience. Lyndon likes history. I rang your boss. He was quite keen, said that you were short-staffed. Said that you were all over-worked and could use an extra pair of hands. Said that someone else taking on some of the more routine tasks would free up the professionals to do some of the more analytical, strategic work they don't normally get time for.'

And yes, that does sound like Mike in one of his more satirical moods.

'He tried to kidnap my brother.'

Lucy sighs. 'No, Billy, his mates tried to get hold of some cider and some idiot said he'd buy it for them.'

'That's a generous view of the incident.' Lucy shrugs and calls the weasel over. He keeps his eyes firmly on the ground.

A minute later we're all in Mike's office trying to have a conversation with an averagely monged-out set-three type kid. He's tall but he hangs his head, won't make eye contact and grunts into his chest. So far, so normal.

Mike attempts to loosen him up with chit-chat. Enjoy school? What team do you support? Films you like? That sort of thing. Just as Mike seems to have run out of reliable conversation starters, Weasel Bowers does a surprising thing. He seems to droop even lower and says, 'Msosferthrtninyoutime.' I look at Lucy. She rolls her eyes.

'I'm sorry, I didn't quite catch that,' I say.

'I'm sorry for threatening you that time.'

'And you want to do work experience? Here?' He nods mournfully.

'Miss said I'd like it.' He looks like a man beginning to lose his faith in human nature. I feel almost sorry for him.

Lucy cuts in. 'Lyndon had work experience all sorted out. At Debenhams. But there was an unfortunate incident there the other week. And they withdrew the offer.'

'So coming here is a sort of punishment? Like doing lines or detention?'

'No, Billy. Lyndon working here is a chance for him to redeem his sorry ass.'

Mike laughs and looks Lucy up and down. Randy old

goat. She smiles blandly back. Being mentally undressed by dirty old men is part of the hazards of A-star womanhood I guess. Affirmation of a sort. Smart girls learn to take it in their stride, work with it where they can.

He says, 'What was the unfortunate incident? Talking too much?' He laughs at his own joke.

'A teeny-weeny bit of shoplifting, nothing major.'

Lyndon cringes at this witty banter between his teacher and the crumbly museum guy. I don't think I've ever seen anyone look so uncomfortable. And, despite myself, I soften towards him. He wasn't the male lead in whatever movie those kids were running in their heads. He was a supporting actor at best, standing shuffling behind the star turn. His big line was saying that they wouldn't hurt the kid. The improvised line that upset the star. He looked bloody uncomfortable then too – a boy with no future in hard man roles – and it's that memory that decides it for me.

'Come on Mike, we might as well give him a chance. Remember, nothing fazes the A-team.' This is shameless and I'm a bit embarrassed. Mike takes his time. Rubs his chin, makes gargling sounds in his throat and generally acts like a right old *X Factor* judge, cranking up the tension before giving the final verdict.

'Yeah OK. For a week is it?'

'Three, I'm afraid. He's on extended work placement as part of his pap.'

'His what?'

'Pap. Personal Action Plan.'

'Right. Pap. 'Course.'

I escort Lucy to the door. Her eyes flicker to the tiny slivers of Viking skin clinging around those warped Saxon nails. She shudders.

'Does he really like history?' I say.

She smiles. 'As much as he likes anything else. I have to visit him while he does work experience and I like it here. I owe you one.' She pauses. Looks at me coolly. 'Billy. You really need to lose the beard. It's getting out of control.' She grabs it in her fist and tugs sharply. It bloody hurts. I'm too shocked to do anything as she pulls my face forward by the beard and kisses my cheek. Her touch is light, like a daddy-long-legs brushing over you in your sleep. But nicer obviously. I feel her hot breath rustle through the unruly growth of the beautiful mutton chops.

'The beard is sacred,' I say when she lets me go.

One of our more regular customers is Steve Mantel. He's not a lawnmower nut, though he does know a lot of random stuff. He's homeless so he spends way too much time in libraries and museums. He sells the *Big Issue* across the way outside the Early Learning Centre. It's an A-star pitch. Lots of middle-class guilt going to and fro there. He takes a break round about eleven and often pops into our place for a coffee and a Hobnob. Sometimes he's completely wazzed and then him and Mike do this dance, a kind of slow waltz, as Mike ushers him out. Him and Mike go way back. Mike arrested him about a hundred times when he was just a uniformed plod in Southwood and Steve was just another small-town boot-boy into cider and Mott The Hoople. And then Mike went off to fit up big league crims in the Met, and Steve settled for the dreary workaday life of the nine-to-five alcoholic.

Today Steve is very excited. They were having a jumble sale in the church hall opposite the hostel where he lives, and he's bought a painting.

'The museum should have this,' he says.

'Yeah, like we need more junk,' says Mike, but not unkindly.

Steve is outraged. 'You don't even know what this is, do you. Look at it. Really look at it. Impressed by his vehemence, we all lean in closer, Jen, Mike and me. We take in the street scene. At first I assume it's just another piece of Victorian romantic bollocks. A cheery crowd out for the day in the mid nineteenth century. Burly costermongers in colourful neckerchiefs. Flowersellers. Urchins. You know the kind of thing. Portly beadles with red faces.

'This is the hanging of Joe and Mary Goddard,' says Steve. 'They were convicted of thieving and were taken to the edge of the town and hung. You must know about them.'

Mike says that yes, he does know, but that he's not sure that the museum is the best place to commemorate such unpleasant goings on. Steve gives him a contemptuous look. He coughs wetly into a rank tissue.

'A tenner,' he says. 'Got to be worth a tenner.' Mike just sniffs but when he moves off, Jen and me, we fish out a fiver each. And later Mike lets us put the painting on the wall, with a little laminated card next to it giving the bare facts of the case.

I decide that I had better neutralise the threat from Dean. I need to get him to cease and desist. I've thought about this carefully. Donating the spunk does not make you a dad. You can't just waltz in and say 'Hi babes I'm home' if you haven't done the groundwork. He hasn't changed any wet sheets. He hasn't got up in the night. He hasn't fished turds out of the bath, or organised a play-date. He hasn't set up the MMR jabs or done CBeebies at five in the morning. He can't come in now and expect to go for pizzas and ice cream. There's an old Smiths song on my phone, one of Mum's faves – 'You Just Haven't Earned It Yet, Baby'. I should ping it over to him. I could do it too. That Total Security Solutions notepaper has his number and his email address on it.

I try to think about what Mum would do. She would call him and, with a mixture of charm and firm authority, would put the whole issue to bed. Mum was a phone genius. Everyone she was talking to became her best friend for the time that she was talking to them. Mates, work contacts, even cold callers from credit card companies, all of them were made to feel uniquely special. And it wasn't fake. Mum genuinely loved people. All people. She loved to hear their stories and to tell hers. She was an A-star performer, but an even better audience. It could be frustrating for us of course, her kids. We always had to share her with all these no-account others.

Once I said, 'Mum, why don't you just email these people? Quick message and boom it's done.'

'Billy,' she said back, 'you're such a boy. Who wants "boom it's done"?'

Mum had this theory that email and the phone had been invented in the wrong order. She said that email should have come first and then, after a while, along would come another inventor who would promote his super new product – the phone – by saying 'It's just like email only now you can *actually talk to each other*.' And everyone would go 'Yeah, wow, that is *amazing*.'

I should say that she was pretty A-star at email too. Funny, personal, entertaining, all that – but she was queen of the phone.

'Business isn't about jobs. It isn't about money or products – it's all about personal relationships. It's about people.' That was her line.

So, even though I know that phoning Hessenthaler

will put me in the driving seat of our difficult relationship, I decide on an email. And an impersonal, legal-type one at that.

I'm sitting at the desktop in Mum's office. No one has been in here for ages. No one has had the chance to nudge her presence out of the way with their chatter and noise. I can practically feel her behind me. Smiling, but shaking her head.

The sense of her is so strong that I turn around and of course I just see the wall with its poster, a blow up of the cover of an old girls' adventure annual. It's from the late 1950s I guess. Against a bright yellow background, two girls on Vespas head off waving and smiling into the future. Underneath it says *Popular Stories For Girls*. There they go, the luckiest generation of women in history, sprinting all excited towards Beatlemania. The Stones. The Pill. Moon Landings. Feminism. Thatcher. *Sex in the City*. Before parking up at *Mamma Mia!* How old would they be now, those girls? Sixty-six? Sixty-eight?

I shiver as I turn back to my fuck-off-and-leave-us-alone letter. 'Just bloody write it, Billy,' I say out loud to myself. And I listen, holding my breath, as the air recoils from the first words spoken in here for nearly a month. I feel I've prodded the whole room into waking and now I'm waiting to see how it will take it.

My message to Hessenthaler is a masterpiece. If poetry is about putting all the right words in the right order without a single one of them wasted, then my email to Hessenthaler is a proper poem. It reads, in its entirety, 'Fuck off and die.' In your face Simon cunting Armitage.

I am called in for a special meeting at the school. Mrs Bingley wants a little chat about Oscar's progress. I know enough about schools to know that the words 'a little chat' can't mean anything good.

At Sir Walter Scott Infants I park my shiny courtesy car next to a row of three girls' cars. A Clio, a Punto and a Mini; cars that say 'successful young women coming through, stand back'. They are the hip chicks on the block. Sooby-Doo would have looked so out of place here. I can imagine a collective shudder through their shiny aluminium parts if that grotesquely dinted and scratched piece of steel had taken its place next to them. The courtesy car is a Ford Ka. Another girl's car. Courtesy is a feminine trait I guess.

The whole world of schools is also a girls' world now. A world of emotional intelligence, constant praise and encouragement. A world where kids are more likely to be told 'I like your top' by their form teacher, than they are to be bollocked for running in the corridors. And the car park reflects that.

Mrs Bingley. The head of reception at Sir Walter Scott Infants is a big, big woman who likes flowing linens in vivid hues, especially favouring golds and scarlets. She's all blinged up like an old-school rapper too, clinking and jangling as she bears down upon us outside the Head's office. Mrs Bingley moves like the luxury super yacht of some Russian billionaire, exuding confidence and power. She's one of those women built for middle age. Middle age is clearly her time. If I had to guess, I'd say there was a divorce not too far back. Or maybe a young lover picked up on the Turkish coastline. Or both.

She's worried about Oscar. More than worried, she's *concerned*. And that is, as we all know, much much worse. Concerned is worried with A levels. And what is the cause of this concern? The nub of her complaint is that Oscar

– poor, motherless Oscar – has not been behaving as he should. It's not, she stresses, that he's been difficult exactly. It's not that he's been biting, or scratching or breaking toys and pencils. It's worse than that. Far worse. It's that he insists on playing quietly on his own. He's polite but distant with his peers, ignoring them as far as possible. Worst of all, he won't open up to the support assistant, the key worker, assigned to help him work through his grief. Just sits staring at her in silence.

'In fact, when Loretta – his key worker – tried to get him to talk about his feelings he became quite rude.'

'What did he do?'

There's a little jingle-jangle as Mrs Bingley straightens her back. A triumphant ripple runs up and down her impressive bulk. 'He told Loretta that he was going to disembowel her. She was quite upset.'

I guess she would be. I resist the temptation to comment favourably on Oscar's vocabulary – there's surely not many six year olds who could use a word like disembowel correctly – and instead make soothing noises, and when these have minimal impact I ask the hard questions like: 'What exactly is your problem?'

Mrs Bingley sighs. Another one. Jesus. She says, 'The main thing that concerns me is that Oscar is simply afraid to be in close relationships with others. And I'm concerned that his present reserve might develop into a real and lasting fear of intimacy.' There's a pause and then she says, 'We thought initially, it might just be a phase because of what happened to his mum. But really I have to say . . .' She pauses again.

'Have to say what?'

'I have to say that maybe there's more going on.'

'Like what?' I'm going to make her say it.

'Look, Billy, any child is a lot to take on but when you've got someone like Oscar who has been through such a major trauma then you need a particular skill-set. Particular expertise. I've been doing a lot of reading and discussed Oscar with professionals more used to handling this sort of thing.'

'What sort of thing?'

Mrs Bingley sighs. More sighing. There's always more sighing. 'Come on, Billy. Can you honestly tell me that you don't think Oscar – and you – would benefit from some family therapy?'

I don't say anything. And the silence makes Mrs Bingley nervous. She can't help herself. She goes rushing on. 'I discussed the symptoms in some depth and my colleagues agreed with my assessment.'

'Which was?'

She takes a breath. Decides to go for it.

'That Oscar is a child at risk.'

'At risk of what?'

She sighs again. Her jewellery rattles. Her gold and scarlet silks rustle. I do the Blinking Game on her. I keep my eyes on hers without blinking and she looks away. She can't play the Blinking Game at all, which must be a problem for her when dealing with Oscar because he's a Blinking Game master. A Blinking Game prodigy.

She's proper hacked off now. Good.

'Billy, it is my honest belief that Oscar is at risk of emotional neglect or abuse, and is consequently in danger of perhaps developing a significant personality disorder.'

And, having dropped the bomb, she sits back to view the impact. Clearly this is a knock-out punch as far as she's concerned. I work hard at giving her no satisfaction, concentrating instead on the pain from sitting on these ludicrous chairs.

92

In the end I say, 'Which one?'

She looks confused. 'What do you mean?'

'I mean which personality disorder do you think Oscar is developing?'

She looks flustered now. Maybe the conversation wasn't meant to get to this point. Maybe I was meant to give in, fall sobbing into her bosom. Fuck that. She ers and ums a bit, gathers her forces. Rustles, clanks and sighs. 'Oh, er, the diagnosis usually takes some time and some proper observation but my provisional assessment points to Avoidant Personality Disorder.'

Oh, come on. 'Oh, come on,' I say. 'There's no such thing. You've made that up.'

She is very offended and huffs about genetic and environmental factors combining to mean that some individuals move from a normal childhood shyness to developing an extreme dislike of being in contact with others. Their fear of ridicule and criticism is so strong that they avoid any new situations. This can, she says, become so ingrained that it can seriously hamper an individual's ability to take his or her place in the world.

'It is most commonly seen in children who have not been supported in social interactions and made to feel confident. Sometimes it happens when a child's adult role models function well socially and expect children to follow suit automatically. Sometimes it is the result of the memories of disastrously painful social occasions. Sometimes, in the most extreme cases, it can develop from a fear of the danger and uncertainty of the adult world. A terror caused by unpredictability or even' – she takes a breath – 'violence in the home.'

It is so obviously something she has got from an evening class or a mass-market paperback. Teach Yourself Child Protection maybe.

I think about Oscar mauled and smothered by teary strangers at Mum's funeral. I think about Mum herself with her laughing and her parties. She was a bit of a life and soul was Mum. Her phone was always singing and pinging as the calls came in and the texts rained down. And she was often entertaining. Long boozy Sunday lunches, themed dinner parties with Mum dressed up as Ann Boleyn or Che Guevara. Nights playing poker. SingStar with the women doing 'Big Spender' and the blokes doing 'My Way', and music and cackling coming up through the floorboards.

Once I came downstairs for a drink of water to find half a dozen drunk and half-dressed grown-ups playing Twister. Didn't do me any harm. I liked all that when I was really small. Later on it got on my tits I guess.

And I think about Dean's possessions on our lawn. And I suddenly remember him booting his way in to our house. It's like a TV drama in my head. The crash of glass. The glitter of it in the hallway, as he lurches in, head and shoulders down. Mum, the whole huge nine-month-pregnant ball of her, screaming and barricading herself in the bathroom. Dean's hand in my face as I try and stop him getting to her. Yeah, but Oscar wasn't even born then.

I think about Toni throwing a chair against the wall. I think about me knocking Oscar to the floor the other day when he smacked me in the jaw with his pointy stickboy knee. I think about Mum throwing her slippers at *Question Time*. I think about Curtis Hughes pulling a knife in The Limes. I think about homemade arrows. Difficult new social situations? Yeah, there have been a few. But then again, too few to mention.

If Mrs Bingley had read the mags I had, she'd know how totally everyday this sort of thing is. How mickey mouse in the scheme of things.

'Has Oscar witnessed violent scenes at all?' She says this casually, like she is some kind of TV detective trapping a suspect with an apparently harmless, but actually killer, final question.

'No,' I say.

It has taken Mrs Bingley over half an hour to get to this point and by now I have the back pains of a ninety-year-old ex-coal miner. Bingley seems all right with it. Her body, stately though it is, has adapted to her working conditions. Maybe she can no longer sit in grown-up furniture. Maybe if you were to go to her house everything would be infant-sized. Maybe Mrs Bingley's Turkish lovers all have to pass the test of coping with a munchkin-sized bed. She's talking again but I'm not listening.

I tune back in when she starts on about his personal action plan.

'His pap,' I say.

She seems disconcerted. I'm not meant to speaka da language, that much is clear.

'Yes, his pap.'

Oscar's pap is a scheme designed to help him develop both his self-esteem and appropriate behaviour, and basically involves a cardboard cut-out of a plane.

When Oscar does something good – plays a game with some friends for example, or speaks up at show and tell – then the plane will move up off the runway, and on to a little fluffy cloud on a special board. When he does something else good then he'll move on to a higher cloud. And this process is repeated until he reaches the sun, where he can get a suitable reward. Should he threaten to disembowel anyone again – or do anything else 'inappropriate' – then the plane will nose-dive towards the ground. It seems vaguely Buddhist to me, though whoever thought up the sun-landing business clearly knows less about Greek mythology than a teacher should. And a plane that deliberately moves into cloud formations is a crash waiting to happen IMHO.

'What about Icarus?' I find myself saying, inappropriately. 'And what about the dangers of sunstroke and melanoma?'

Mrs Bingley purses her lips, sighs, clanks, rustles. 'Billy, this is serious you know.'

'I know. Sorry. Sorry.'

And I put on a serious face and decide to treat this whole thing like it was an A level oral. A piece of empty theatre. I explain that my experience of Oscar is quite different. In my experience people warm to him instinctively. They like the fact that he's quiet. That he doesn't tug at sleeves and attempt to tell them the story of his life so far. That he doesn't tap dance for sweeties. Mrs Bingley listens with the patience and indifference of a rock. She's not to be moved.

'As I say, our assessment of Oscar's personal and social education suggests that he's struggling to achieve a level two.'

'You assess friendship? You assess likeability?'

Mrs Bingley is puzzled by my ignorance, annoyed by my incredulity and completely fucked off by my tone.

'Well, yes we do. The extent of social interaction in the early years is one of the key indicators of future academic and social success.'

'Bollocks.' And too late I find I've said that out loud. Mrs Bingley jingles indignantly, her impressive rack heaves and wobbles. Those imperial clothes shimmer and radiate.

'And the Social Services Department will want to be in contact obviously.'

Obviously.

*   *   *

What does emotional abuse actually mean? As far as I can see, every child is an emotionally abused child. Ask anyone to describe what it was like when they were a little kid and they will give you a list of random cruelties inflicted on them by brothers, sisters, teachers and parents. Even in the nicest homes. Even in the poshest houses. Maybe especially there.

And what about the properly emotionally abused? What about Derek Hecht of Loughborough, whose dad killed his mum and then tried to fit him up for the murder? What about the kids kept in cellars and sheds who only see their dads when they come in to fuck them, or hit them or both? What about the mothers who shag their daughter's boyfriends? What about the kid who watched while his dad gouged out his mum's eyeball and threw it out of the window of their eighth-floor flat?

Thing is, we are our individual personality disorders. That's what makes us human. If we were all rounded, balanced, kind to puppies and all that, then we wouldn't be people, we'd be something else. We'd be sheep. We have to struggle and solve problems. And if there aren't any, then we create them. We climb mountains, go over Niagara Falls in a barrel, lie in a tub of baked beans for Children in Need, fly jets into buildings: whatever it takes to get us away from simply grazing with the herd. That's our thing. That's what we do. We make things and then break things. We put ourselves in the shit and then figure out how to dig ourselves out. And it's not our abilities that make us who we are, it's how we cope with our disabilities. How we deal with our unique disorders.

I'm not saying Mum didn't mess up a bit. If there was an exam in child-raising she'd struggle in some sections. There's her questionable taste in blokes just for starters.

There's the fact of having GCSEs, A levels, degrees and all that – and still managing two unplanned pregnancies.

I was a university baby. A sort of third-year project for Mum. A living dissertation, an alternative to going to careers fairs. Mum didn't talk about it much, but from what I've gleaned I was the result of one too many Bushmills at the Troops Out Soc party. The perfectly logical at the time outcome of Mum getting into a furious row with my dad about things that happened at the Dublin General Post Office in 1916. That, and the seductive power of Leonard Cohen.

In any case I was going to be brought up by the Women's Group, but then they all went off to be recruitment consultants or human resources engineers, and generally knuckled down to making an attempt on Having It All. Which left Mum and Dad struggling in their council flat on Chadwick – the oldest and nicest council estate in town – making friends with all the properly teenage mums, until the inevitable happened, and Dad shagged one of them and fucked off.

I don't blame him for that. He was only twenty-three and some of those teen mums are smoking-hot and not too discerning, I know that. No, I don't blame him for any of that. I blame him for being a prick.

He moved up north when I was seven to pursue his career. His career being getting off with impressionable hippies who mistake his arrogance for intelligence. He lives on a narrowboat and I don't see him any more. It's not the narrowboat so much as the narrow mind I can't stand, though having to share a 29ft living space with your dad and whichever trainee white witch he's managed to tempt back from the pub that week, doesn't help father–son relations.

From age two to eleven it was just me and Mum. I'm not naïve. I know that there must have been blokes; but Mum

98

kept them out of the house, out of sight, out of my life. I'm sure that when I was up at Dad's stuff happened. Back when I was in primary school she lit up the playground. She was the foxiest, youngest mum and it embarrassed the hell out of me to be honest. I always urged her to wear her dowdiest clothes, not to wear make-up, not to draw attention to herself. But she couldn't help it. I always felt the looks she got. And Mum was a laugh too. Quick-witted, quick-tempered, funny. She never tried to impress, with the result that people were always trying to impress her. Everyone always wanted to be part of her gang. Stands to reason that there were always blokes trying to get into her knickers as well. And some of them must have made it. It wasn't just her and her trusty weekend kit for nine years.

She never had a job. Not a real one anyway. In those days people seemed to manage on the dole. Someone was always getting a giro and where we lived people helped each other out. She wasn't proud either. When she got really skint she'd do a bit of cleaning, or get someone to look after me while she worked a few shifts behind the bar at the uni. It's what she'd done as a student and they were always keen to have her back. I guess they sold a few more snakebites whenever she rocked up with her smile and easy banter. That's what I imagine anyway. Occasionally Granny Ann would send us some cash, and so would Dad's mum. Not Dad though. And to be fair Mum never asked him for any. I was definitely her project.

And then, when I was eleven, two things happened: Mum decided to earn some proper dosh. And she met Dean Hessenthaler.

Rosie didn't like it when Aidan started getting interested in girls. Titus encouraged it. Titus set him up with a couple of slags he knew. Aidan Jebb got a blow job when he was fourteen from one of Titus's girls. Aidan had to lie there and pretend to be asleep while Titus filmed this old bird groping him and getting his dick out and waking him up by sucking him off. Titus put it on the internet. *Milf Aunt Wakes Up Her Nephew In That Special Way.* Aidan didn't enjoy it very much. Was that all there was to it? Was that what people paid for?

Aidan wasn't really going to school any more. Sometimes he'd go down to the entrance and just look in and hang around. Sometimes a teacher would call over and say 'Come and join us, Aidan', but mostly they ignored him. And if a teacher's car got keyed then it was Aidan that got the blame, and the cops would be round. They could never prove anything though.

The first time Aidan had full sex it was with a girl called Janie Summers. Janie would do anything for smack and Aidan told her he could get her some. Aidan didn't think she believed him, but she shagged him anyway just in case. And he knew for a fact that she shagged three other lads that afternoon.

A few days after that Aidan's cock felt sore and it hurt whenever he went for a piss. He thought it would get better but it didn't. And it smelled funny and he got really freaked out when there was this greeny-yellow pus coming out. He had a wank just to see, and the spunk was sort of yellowy too. Aidan told Rosie and Rosie was weird about it. She was sort of pleased.

'Told you, didn't I? Told you what would happen,' she said, triumphant.

Titus took Aidan to the clinic in the Lexus. 'You can find your own way back can't you?' he said. 'Take the bus or something. I've got things to do.'

Aidan didn't like the clinic. But then, you weren't meant to. He asked at the desk where he should go and they told him to 'follow the red line to the GUM unit'. He asked what GUM meant and the nurse didn't even look up. Kept writing on a pad. She said 'Genito-urinary medicine' in this bored voice. But then she looked up and when she saw his face she smiled. 'Don't worry,' she said. 'It'll be OK.'

The GUM place had its own waiting room. And there were a few other blokes there. All much older than him. One bloke was flicking through a magazine, but the others weren't doing anything. They were just sitting staring into space. After a while a black guy came in who looked straight at Aidan and said, 'There's a lot of pagan women out there. A lot of pagan women.' Aidan was glad when they called his number.

The doctor was big and Indian and Aidan couldn't understand his accent very well, but he looked at Aidan's cock and laughed and gave him a prescription. Said that he had got away lightly and to be more careful in future. At least, Aidan thought that was what he said. Aidan was going to be careful. Aidan was going to stay away from sex. It wasn't worth all the fuss people made about it.

There was one girl Aidan liked. And not just in a sex way. He just liked to be around her. She had a voice that always sounded like it was sort of laughing. Leanne Gladstone was a girl he met when he was out doing backup on collecting loans. She owed Titus money and sometimes she had her instalment and sometimes she didn't. And sometimes Titus let her off and sometimes he didn't. She had a little toddler – Kai – who was frightened of the dogs and Aidan didn't like it when kids cried. It upset him. Leanne was beautiful. Huge smile, crooked teeth. But crooked in a good way. She could have been a porn star.

She could have been a model. She could've made loads of cash if she wanted.

Titus said, 'You're sitting on a goldmine girl. You might as well use it.' But Leanne just laughed. If she had the cash she gave Titus what she owed. If she didn't she might let him shag her, but she wasn't going to do anything else. She wasn't frightened of him.

Rosie hated Leanne. 'Stuck-up cow,' she said. 'Thinks she's it. Thinks she's special.'

But she was special. Aidan knew it. Titus knew it. Everyone knew it.

And then Leanne disappeared. And then she turned up in the boot of Titus's Lexus.

The car was stolen. Titus reported it and everything. He was calm though. Aidan thought he'd be raging. It was properly insured. Titus was careful about keeping his driving record clean. He kept to the speed limits, didn't drink and drive. He was fully comp, all MOT'd and taxed. No one was going to get him for a crappy motoring thing. That was for mugs. And he bloody loved that car. He didn't even go to the car wash in case it got scratched. He paid people to handwash it, to wax it and buff it. That car was loved.

And then it just vanished. Turned up three days later in Tostock with Leanne naked and dehydrated in the boot. Someone snatched her from her house in front of Kai, stripped her and put her into Titus's car. And left her near Tostock woods in Suffolk.

Titus tried to act shocked.

'Who would do that?' he said. 'Who would do that to Leanne? In my car?' But he seemed pretty calm.

Aidan thought about Leanne's kid. Kai. He found it hard to walk the dogs now. Every time he saw them, he saw the

102

face of Leanne's kid crumpling up and going pink and crying as his mum was taken by the bad men.

Leanne wouldn't say who had taken her, or what they did. But she was different after that. Different in that she was the same as everyone else. Quiet. Scared.

The days move on, Oscar's plane goes up and down but he never lands on the sun. I promise him guinea pigs if he makes it and he brightens immediately. I regret it straight away of course. All the squeaking. It's bound to do my head in, but it's done now. You can't undo promises to children.

The days are still a dull, grey wet background to our dull grey lives and then Oscar is invited to a sleepover by one of the Walking Bus mums. Millie's mum.

It is a fact that nothing is private any more: doctor's reports, school reports, social enquiry reports, court reports, confessions you might make to a priest – all things you could reasonably assume were confidential, right? Wrong. Trust me, there are people out there right now hawking your credit rating round town like the Betterware guy with a new line in plastic food storage. School reports are tagged on Facebook, the neighbourhood priest is blogging about a juicy titbit fed him this very morning by a parishioner. Right now a group of junior doctors are settling down to watch a film of your gran's hysterectomy. They probably have popcorn and cheesy snacks.

This is a world where court photos of tortured children have a Buy It Now price on eBay.

Nothing is sacred. Nothing is secret. Nothing. So it doesn't surprise me that stories of Oscar's supposed emotional abuse and possible personality disorder leak out into the playground. Certainly within two days everyone knows about my meeting with Mrs Bingley. I can tell by the way I've divided opinion in the playground. Some of the mothers lean away from me, or look right through me. I can tell by the way one of the few obviously skint parents, a stone-faced Sumo Mum in jogging bottoms, grabs my arm on the way to school one day, breathes early morning vodka over me and croaks 'Bastards, they're all bastards. Fuck 'em.'

But it's the A-star PTA Walking Bus mums that are the most relieved that I'm screwing up. What would it say about the role of being a mum if it turned out that anyone could do it? That a nineteen-year-old lad could do it?

I remember Mum had to read this thing for a book group once. It was all about how women who had children should be prepared for physical and mental torment. Should be prepared for the death of any joy in their lives. I remember because I was about nine and at that age you remember if your mum suddenly lets out this massive, blood-curdling scream and hurls a library hardback across the room. *Babyshock* it was called or some such. Must have been an interesting meeting. Mum never went back anyway. 'I knew it was a mistake to actually read the books,' she said. 'I only really went for the wine.'

The fact that they are relieved at having concrete proof of my inadequacy as a surrogate parent means that some of these women feel free to start to cluck with all that hideous sympathy again, just as they did in the first days after Mum hit the front page of the *Gazette*. And that's when one of the most groomed and PTA of all the mums asks if Oscar would like to come over for a Halloween sleepover?

'He'll be the only boy, I'm afraid. Do you think he'll mind that?'

'I think he'd love it.'

I'm not sure this is true actually, but it seems the right thing to say. Until I think it makes Oscar sound like a predatory sex-pest. At six. The mum – what is her name? – doesn't recoil though, she smiles that terrifying glossy smile and says, 'Cool. We're going to make it really old-fashioned. Games. You know, apple-bobbing, things like that.'

'He'll like that.'

Will he? I don't know. We don't really do games, Oscar and me. We do movies. We do movies till we fall asleep. We fell asleep in front of *Jason and the Argonauts* last night. This morning Oscar told me that he actually wanted to be an Argonaut when he grew up. Mum did games. Ludo, Uno, Junior Scrabble, all that. All a million years ago, but he seemed to like games back then. Maybe this will be a difficult social situation. Then again, maybe it'll be useful therapy. Maybe it'll help his plane towards the top of the sky.

Chapter Seven

I'm feeling restless without Oscar, and estranged from the house in some odd way. It's the first time we've been apart for a night since the accident. There's a nervousness fizzing in my guts like bad alcohol and I haven't even had a drink yet. Rick and Alfie are meant to be coming round but I can't really be bothered with them. Maybe I should face up to the fact that I'm not a kid any more, not the way that Rick and Alfie are.

Besides, I feel watched. Spied on. He's close by out there, I know it. Part of the weather. Eyes glowing hard and bright and red in the rain. Little septic rubies.

Outside there is laughter and fireworks. Halloween and Guy Fawkes Night seem to have become conflated in recent years. Merged. We're greedy with our celebrations in this country. We want the American candy-fest with its *Scream* masks and polyurethane witches' cloaks, but we also want to continue burning our own sixteenth-century Papist plotters in the same week. How long before we add the Yankee turkeys of Thanksgiving to the good old British turkeys of Christmas? As a nation, we're also well on the way to co-opting Eid, Diwali, Hanukkah and St Patrick's Day into our own celebratory calendar. We could soon become the sort of schizoid country that sees the start of Ramadan as an excuse for an orgy of binge drinking. It could happen.

The doorbell starts ringing at around 6 p.m. Nine-year-old

muggers squeaking 'Trick or treat'. Actually the latex goblin masks are so thick that you can't hear the words but the meaning is clear. 'Give us all your dosh and we might not push burning rags through your letterbox.' And at the end of the pathway you can see shame-faced adults lurking because their kids can't be allowed out to bully law-abiding citizens on their own. The world is, after all, full of paedos and axe-murderers.

Of course I've got no cash in the house. I have to buy off the first three lots of visitors with ice-pops, the all-too-healthy oat bran bars I give to Oscar to take to school as a snack and, most disappointingly of all for one little gang of baby zombies, actual fruit.

'What the fuck is this meant to be?' says baby zombie one.

'It's a fucking pear,' I say and shut the door. As the doorbell rings again, with what I feel sure is a menacing note, I leave the house by the back door and jog painfully down the garden and out into the streets. If I'm not to run the risk of having the house taken apart brick by brick by refugees from *Dawn of the Dead*, then I need a cashpoint very badly.

And so, sixty notes in my sticky palm, I wander through the damp streets until I find myself outside a bar where a cheery outlaw throng are busy smoking and flirting with one another. All the girls seem to be wearing plastic devil horns accessorised with Poundland tridents, which they use to poke the blokes in the arse every now and again. This causes much hilarity every time. Somehow I've found myself outside the Waterside Vodka Bar. I dither.

And then there's a strange sick animal scent, stronger than the usual diesely smell of Southwood town centre at night. And I look up and there he is slouching in the doorway of the Oxfam shop. Of course he is. It's definitely him.

Aidan Jebb. Blue trackie bottoms and a grey Lonsdale hoodie. Like he's a ferrety boxer putting the road-work in. I should go over there and smash his scabby face through the plate-glass window of the shop. I should pound his head against the pavement until it goes pulpy in my hands. I should give myself the satisfaction of hearing his bones crack under my boots. He's nothing.

But I don't.

I look at him, he looks at me and I crack first. I turn and go into the bar nodding at the tuxedoed grunt on the door. He ignores me.

I see them at once at a corner table near a window. Dressed like extras from that Polanski *Macbeth* we watched in GCSE English. Easy for Lucy, she does that all the time, but I wonder about her friends. A blonde witch and a raven-haired witch. And they must have got in early to get a seat because the place is rammed.

I stand behind several sets of broad shoulders at the bar. The Waterside Vodka Bar seems full of huge men with mouths too wide and teeth too big. And they are mostly in fancy dress. There are mad monks and mummies and pirates and vicars. The burliest and beefiest of men have come as tarts of course. Hairy chests and beer bellies bursting free of their satin and tat, their ribbons and bows. Those few that aren't wearing costumes are sporting variations of the same crazily patterned baggy shirt.

I'm not a short guy, but everyone in here is six foot plus with a sleek, successful look. Even the fat bastards in dresses. Everyone seems to be laughing, and the air is full of competing perfumes and facial scrubs. It's a complete horror show.

I'm about to back out of the scrum at the bar, and slip away into the Halloween rain, back to Oaks Avenue, when there's a tug at my sleeve.

'Hello,' Lucy slurs shyly. 'We're drinking watermelon martinis.'

Once the purchase of the martinis has been negotiated, plus Stella for me – I have my standards – I perch on a stool that miraculously becomes free next to their table and am polite but not intrusive. After all, I've made an absolute and unshakable decision – one pint then I'm off.

It's an easy half hour before I make a strange discovery – the shame of turning away from a fight dissipates, evaporates, whatever, and I find I am enjoying myself. Jebb's out there friendless in the rain and I'm in here with the beautiful people. With money and booze and girls telling dirty stories. Who's the loser?

Lucy and her friends are sunshine. Unlike Lucy, her mates don't have an authentic witchy aura. They are not even Goths. They are backcombed just for Halloween, not for life. They are raucous and bawdy. All three of them are teachers, but they're OK. They still have the plastic devil forks. They don't seem to mind me being there as they fizz with filth, telling outlandish tales of sex and embarrass-ment and what wankers blokes are. They remind me of my mum and her mates. They could be just like this when they got together: dirty, filthy – only it's not really filth is it? It's exuberance. It's a kind of joy.

Lucy and her mates attract a lot of attention. And the other two – Heather and Christine – take ages to get back from the bar when it's their turn to go. They get to it fast enough, with a kind of wriggling, side-stepping movement that a rugby coach would admire, but getting back involves negotiating dozens of chat-up situations as beefy ghouls try to get off with them.

'Do you know what he said to me?' says Heather, laugh-ing as she gets back with a tray full of Absolut over ice.

'That one there with the nose.' We look over. A tall, muscular, Latin-looking smootho in a Persil-white grandad shirt accessorised with a noose, raises his glass. His nose looks normal to me.

'Him. Yeah, well he only says, "If beauty is a crime you deserve to be in prison for a very long time."'

The girls laugh, Lucy spitting an ice cube right across the table. Then Christine makes a cross face. 'Cheeky sod. He said that to me too. I'm going to have a word.' They laugh again and Christine says she's going to give Grandad Shirt a piece of her mind.

'Perhaps he's Argentinian,' says Heather. We look at her, puzzled. She sighs. 'In Argentina it's just good manners for blokes to say things like that to women. I read that. In the *Guardian*.'

'He's just a nando,' I say.

'A what?'

'A nando. You know, someone completely ordinary trying to make themselves seem a bit funky, a bit crazee, a bit life-and-soul. Most of the clientele in here are nandos.'

'Ah, like the popular High Street restaurant chain.'

'Exactly.'

'Well, I like Nandos actually. Their piri-piri chicken is to die for,' says Christine, and pouts off to play Build the Sexual Tension with her target and his mates.

'A nando. Very . . . apposite.' Lucy gives me an appraising look. 'There's something about you, Billy Smith.'

Seduction has never been a hobby of mine. I lost my virginity three years ago on a school skiing trip to a girl from Luton called Zamantha. Yeah, Samantha with a z. I've had sex in a Ford Fiesta with a Swedish au pair. In Year Twelve I went out with the three foxiest girls from my AS level drama group – though I only slept with two of them.

Aimee Murray was 'saving herself'. Turned out she was saving herself for this fifty-five-year-old grampie who worked in her dad's giftshop. Caused a right fuss that did.

I do OK I guess, but I admit I'm no stud muffin, no fanny magnet. And Year Thirteen in particular was a long barren spell, which was painful but did allow me to revise for my A levels.

Anyway, I'm no expert, but I think I can tell when someone is interested in me. And Lucy is attentive it has to be said. Sure, she joins in with the banter but she also lets Heather and Christine talk to each other while getting me to talk about the Social History Museum and Mike and Jenny.

I find myself watching her carefully as if she were a case study on one of those body language shows. Is she sitting closer to me than she should, or is it just crowded in here? Are her pupils dilated or is it just dark in here? In what direction are her feet pointing? Is she holding my gaze a fraction too long, or is she just drunk and unable to focus? Did she mean to put her hand on my arm or is she just steadying herself because the gavin in the Ben Sherman top has knocked into her? Is she laughing because I've said something funny or because she wants me to like her? Or because I've said something stupid? God, it's all so stressful. Like I say, some guys do this sort of thing every weekend. For fun. It's not my sport. It's too hard. It's like sitting a psychology exam and your driving test at the same time.

I give Lucy plenty of ways out. Whenever there's a natural lull in our conversation I turn back towards Heather and Christine, but after a few minutes Lucy is asking me about how Lyndon is fitting in at the museum.

And eventually I forget to watch out for signals of interest and properly relax. And at almost that exact second the

111

barman is shouting time, and Christine is dragging over the man who we all now think of as The Argentinian and announcing that we're going dancing.

Lucy says she's just going to go home. Says that she has 4,728 books to mark. Some ludicrous figure anyway.

'Well you're not going to do them tonight are you?' says Heather.

'Yeah, but I want to get up early to finish them all tomorrow. I like to keep Sundays free. It's too depressing to be doing schoolwork then.' At which point it occurs to me that to become a teacher is to continue sixth-form life by other means. This thought is confirmed by Heather's reply.

'Boff,' she says. 'Swot. Nerd.'

'Sticks and stones,' laughs Lucy.

Christine gets suddenly drunkenly serious. 'How are you getting home?'

'Billy's going to walk me back, aren't you Billy?'

'Yeah. I guess,' I say.

Christine holds Lucy's shoulders and looks at her very closely. 'Be careful.'

Lucy laughs again. 'Hey, takes two to tango,' she says and then turns towards The Argentinian who stands puzzled by Christine's side. 'Sorry,' she says to him. 'No offence.'

He looks at me frowning. I shrug. 'They think you're from Argentina,' I say.

His frown deepens. 'I'm from Lithuania,' he says. I shrug again.

He says, 'With women the heart argues but not the mind.'

'Matthew Arnold,' I say. His face lights up.

'You know the work of Matthew Arnold?'

'I'm a historian,' I say. 'Well, going to be. He's on my reading list.'

'I'm a historian too!' he says. 'Well, I'm a builder right now, but in Vilnius I taught history.'

'You're a teacher!' squawks Christine. 'Christ. Just my sodding luck.'

'Sorry,' he says, and then it's all hugs and air-kisses and they move one way – joining a laughing crowd of burly lads feeling fearless in panto clobber and girls tottering on skyscraper heels, still waving their plastic devil forks – and we move the other.

It's stopped raining and the wet streets glisten tangerine under the street lamps. Lucy hooks her arm through mine and we walk in silence mostly, though we stop every now and again to admire the fireworks that flash and pop and fizz over the town. We pass a few other couples who smile and nod as we pass, which I take to mean that we look reasonably right together. That no one is going 'Blimey look at him, he's punching above his weight.'

At the entrance to her apartment block I give Lucy another chance to walk away. We face each other and, ludicrously, I extend my hand. She ignores it and stretches her arms around my neck.

'You know, I was hoping that you might come in. I thought I could give you that table-tennis lesson.'

'What about Milan?'

'He doesn't play table tennis.'

'No, but he is your boyfriend.'

'Milan is in Dublin with his new best mate, Misha, the leading puppeteer in the company. Apparently she has a clit-ring.'

I'm suddenly reminded that Lucy is not all that sober.

'Milan,' she continues, 'is a wanker. He's a nando wanker. And he doesn't play table tennis. Not even on the Wii.' And she starts to cry.

113

And we go inside and we kiss and we touch each other, and then we stop. We put it all on hold for a while. I don't know why.

We do actually attempt to play table tennis, but it's not a game for drunks, though chasing the ball as it bounces around the walls and the furniture is suddenly hilarious. We're no better at doing it than Oscar was.

Then we play Risk, getting that huge board off the wall and plonking it on the floor. We don't play for long, but I'm winning I think. I have a continent. I have South America, so I'm getting two extra armies every round and, as an aspiring social historian, I feel it's my duty to tell her that from that moment on, her war is lost. She should make peace. My extra manpower will wear her down, however inspired her leadership is. That's the lesson of military history from the *Art of War* to Iraq by way of D-Day, Stalingrad, Yom Kippur and the Falklands.

Lucy's answer is to take her dress off. And then her bra. So she's standing there in front of me in her black panties, hands folded across her breasts. She says, 'What about Vietnam, clever clogs? What about Afghanistan? What about the intifada, what about asymmetrical warfare? What about snogging me, you goof?'

And we kiss again. And it gets full-on pretty quick. And it's all heat. Proper fierce. And I'm lost in it. Stroking and touching, all that. Her hand on my cock, mine sliding through the crunchy hair to the slippery inside of her. And her panting breath near my ear. And then somehow neither of us have any clothes on, and then she says, 'No. This isn't working.'

And I'm gutted, because it really is working. For me anyway. And she looks at my face and laughs and says, 'No. Just the beard. It's got to go. I don't want that scratching my thighs. I don't want a rash.' And she gathers it up in

114

her fist and yanks it. And tugs me by the beard to the bathroom. And I sit naked on the edge of the bath and Lucy takes Milan's Mach 3, puts a new blade on, and says, 'Is the beard still sacred?'

And I shake my head. I'm so turned on I can't speak.

Lucy shaves me carefully. I don't know about you but I love having my hair cut, and the best bit is feeling the sulky assistant's hands massaging my head. It's almost sexual, even when it's done by a boot-faced work experience munter in MillionHairs. And this is like that, but better obviously. I watch her face, beautiful and flushed and serious, and I'm worried 'cos she's drunk but her hand is steady, and she seems focused: like a sculptor with a lump of clay. And then she steps back and says 'Voila!' And I stand up and move close to the mirror. I rinse the foam off. And it's weird seeing my old face appear again. The one I'd forgotten I had. Pale and worried-looking. A rat-face, I think. And I flinch at how young I seem. I wouldn't sleep with me.

'Poor baby,' Lucy says. 'What were you hiding from?'

'Everything,' I say, but I feel stupid.

And then she puts her dressing gown on. A thick black thing that makes her look a bit like a monk and she puts her arms around me and says, 'I'm really, really sorry, Billy. You're really, really lovely. But I'm going to send you home.'

I'm pure shocked and I must look it. Lucy laughs.

'I know. It's shit. But I've behaved badly enough already. You've got to go home.'

'Really?' I say.

'Really, really,' she says. 'But call me. If you want.'

And I pick up my clothes, trying to think of something to say. And she smiles and at the door she does a little bye-bye wave and blows me a kiss. And the light in her hallway is interrogation-level harsh and her face is mottled red, her mascara has run in wobbly black streaks and her hair is all every which way. Her lipstick is smeared and her eyes are puffy. She looks beautiful. No one has ever looked more beautiful.

'Cheers then,' I say. It doesn't seem enough, but what else can I say? And I feel the first cold waves of tomorrow's hangover cutting through the heat of the beer and the fooling around. And I leave, my footsteps too loud in the grey concrete stairwell. My own boots feel like they are telling me off.

As I walk back I see an abandoned Poundland devil fork and pick it up. Perhaps Oscar will like it.

I pick Oscar up from the sleepover. Millie's dad is washing the cars when I get round there. His silver Volvo XC90 next to her silver Sirocco. A handsome older man, he himself has a silvery sheen to match the cars. Radio Five is on as I come through his gate and his eyes crinkle with newsreader warmth. He is slim, and has the gym-buffed gleam of a successful American film producer. You know at a glance that here is a life of quiet discipline and order, of racquet sports and fruit juices and jogging and refraining from puddings.

He's not a film producer of course. He's some kind of judge. Not criminal, civil cases. Divorces mainly. This is something I know because Millie's mum is someone whose private life, despite being hugely dull, is relayed in daily instalments in the playground. Thus it is that everyone in the Sir Walter Scott Infants catchment area knows that her Nick has divided up the welcome mat for various minor soap actors, as well as lower-league footballers and their wives.

He grins up from where he squats by the shiny, soapy Swedish wheel-hubs.

'You must be Billy. Come to pick up the little man?'

'Yeah, has he been OK?'

'Oh, you know. Boys will be boys I guess. Go on in, door's open.'

As I step over a torpid tabby and into the substantial porch of their executive family home – a former vicarage I would guess – I think *boys will be boys?* What does that mean? Nothing good I bet.

I walk down a hallway lined with framed originals of work done by Millie in nursery. I know she is the artist because they are neatly labelled underneath as though they were works by a proper painter in a proper gallery. What does it do to you to have your parents treat you as if you were Andy Warhol before your sixth birthday? Has got to be a head-fuck.

I can hear Millie's mum talking on the landline in the kitchen. She has her back to me and, well brought up that I am, I don't interrupt. I stand in the doorway, taking the opportunity to lean against the wall as my skin breaks out in a sudden Stella Artois sweat.

I close my eyes and once again I feel Lucy's hand on my face as she shaves me. I open my eyes at a sudden sharp note in Millie's mum's conversation.

'Mother, it's got nothing to do with that. He's just got an unpleasant personality. End of.' There's a short silence in the kitchen before Millie's mum (what is her name?) crashes in again. 'No, he's cross. He's rude. He's mean. He's a bully. He makes a fuss at the slightest thing. He won't play with the other children. Not nicely anyway. He just wants to play killing games.'

Oscar. She's talking about Oscar. And finally I get it together to do something. I can't bear to hear any more. I cough. Millie's mum (Charlotte? Nearly all the PTA mums seem to be called Charlotte) whirls around, her face a flushing rictus of shame. She is so busted. She shoves a balled fist into her mouth. We share a look but neither of us can form any words. I point upwards. She nods.

I reverse out of the kitchen and round to the stairs. See where manners get you? If only I'd not bothered to seek her out to say bye and thank you for having him, then we wouldn't have this embarrassment between us now. How can there be any way back from this? How do you exchange tiny playground pleasantries with someone who believes your little brother has a personality disorder? I'm allowed to think that – she isn't.

I reach the top of the stairs from where I can hear my little bro giving a lecture on the correct way to hold a lightsabre.

'No. Not like that Millie, you idiot. For Goodness sake, can't you do anything? It's like this.'

I might have got the individual words wrong, but there's no doubting the sense of what he says. He sounds cross. He sounds rude. He sounds mean. He sounds like a bully.

I take a final stride down the Axminstered landing, taking just enough time to note that these walls too are covered with the daubings of the princess of the house, before I'm in the room with the kids.

'Oscar,' I say, 'be nice.' Oscar implodes into wet but noiseless sobs.

'For God's sake. Why do you have to cry at the slightest thing? What would Mum say?'

It's the cheapest of shots. I stare down at the unblinking row of little girls. Millie says, 'We were just playing. God. Stressy.' Exactly like a princess in an American teen flick.

I pick Oscar up and he snuffles into my shoulder. Millie's mum (Julia? Fiona? Felicity? No, it is Charlotte. Definitely

Charlotte) is hopping about at the foot of the stairs, twisting her hands. I wonder if she'll go for abject or brazen. These are, after all, her only real options here. She chooses brazen, but in a surprising and novel form.

'The cat,' she stammers. 'I was talking about the cat. I really hate the cat. Nick got him from the rescue centre. He's always been a monster.' Yeah, right.

As I head down the stairs, my shoulder moistening with Oscar's snot, I think how easy it would be to accept this. We could just have a giggle, turn the whole episode into a little double-act. A little comedy sketch for the enjoyment of the Walking Bus mums. It would probably be my ticket to full acceptance. My, how we would all chortle together. 'The cat,' they would chorus, flapping their painted hands in front of their smooth, unbreakable faces. 'And you thought . . . oh my . . .' What japes. What larks.

Only I'm not having it.

'Bollocks,' I say. She looks stricken all over again. Top. 'And Nick's having an affair, you know that don't you?'

I have no idea where that comes from. Only now that it's out I can see that it is so obviously the truth. That crinkly eyed smile. That sleek charm. That silver Swedish dream machine. How could he not be playing away? Why does a middle-aged man score a top-spec car, if not to try and get laid by younger women? They might not always achieve it, but that is always their intention, their hope. I can tell from the sudden weary look that flickers across her face that she knows it too. Has always known it.

I just brush past her and stride back down the hall/gallery, out of the porch. I nod at Nick who is singing as he soaps the car. Poor sod. I don't think Oscar will be doing many play-dates with Millie in the future.

* * *

I call Lucy and get her voicemail and leave a stupid message. It comes out all wrong. I'm aiming for cheerful and casual but somehow hit retard instead. I press 1 to re-record my message, and it's worse so I don't leave a message at all in the end. Then I change my mind and leave a message that is worse than the first one. Lucy doesn't call me back. I text her. She doesn't text back.

After three days, I stop shaving again.

I get back into Empire big time. It's like a fever. A frenzy. Like being in the grip of a higher power. I drain marshes and tame forests. I subdue the tribe of Amazons who have been plaguing the borderlands for millennia. My cities are all like Dubai – only tidier, shinier, taller and solvent. Each one has a subway and they are all linked by bullet train or monorail. My Football Association lands the continental championships, the average height of the men of my nation gets to one metre eighty-five. We're all as tall and handsome as the Masai. I'm all about growth. I am China, India, Brazil. I am the US in the early years of the twentieth century.

The poor huddled masses flock in and get jobs and houses and find liberation in being part of Billy's dream. There's a place for everyone, especially as I'm pushing into both the great northern deserts and the southern swamps. First the scientists, then the navvies and before you know it, townships and settlements and farms are springing up from the wastelands. It's a kind of magic. I'm on fire.

While I'm at the screen, Oscar sits and scribbles pictures of dinosaurs, or messes about with Lego. Sometimes he looks over my shoulder to see what I'm doing, and murmurs appreciatively. He's such a good kid. Wants to be encouraging. But I don't think he really gets it. Maybe I'll set him up with a little village of his own one of these days. See how he gets on. But not yet. Not just yet.

120

Lucy comes to see me in the museum. We go to Caffè Nero for lunch and she insists on buying my panini, and then she gives me the bad news, like I knew she would.

'I see the beard's on the way back,' she says.

'I let the beard down before,' I say. 'Won't happen again.'

Lucy flinches. There's a pause.

'Milan is the love of my life, you know.'

Yeah, I know.

'Handsome, funny, talented.'

Yeah, I know.

'I just wish he didn't have such an honesty problem.'

But that's the trouble with handsome, funny, talented isn't it? That's the risk you take. Mediocrity is safer, easier to control. Mediocrity is much less likely to shag the arse off a clit-ringed puppeteer.

But it turns out I've got everything wrong, because this isn't what she means at all. For Lucy, the trouble with Milan is that he is *too* honest.

'I wish he didn't need to tell me about it every time. It's selfish. Because once he's owned up then I have to deal with it. Then it's my problem. He can shag who he likes, but telling me about it, that's not fair. That's wrong. That's against the rules.' I laugh.

'And did you tell him about me?'

She looks me straight in the eyes and I can't hold her gaze. Those witchy green eyes would definitely have got her burned a couple of centuries back.

'Yes,' she says.

'And?'

'And he hit me in the face. Twice.' She pauses to see how I'm taking this. I don't know what I'm meant to do. Should I go and punch his lights out? Challenge the brute to a duel? What? She sighs, 'Not really. He just went a bit quiet. Then he played his guitar for a bit. Then he was fine.'

'Oh.'

'Oh is right. Men,' she says. 'Men are rubbish.'

She gives me another hard look. I feel like I'm failing some kind of test. Like I've turned over the exam paper and nothing that I have studied for is on there. Like the questions aren't even in English. Like they are in Klingon or something. She sighs again.

'Thing is: he's my soulmate.'

I look at her face carefully. She doesn't seem to be smiling. She doesn't seem like she's being ironic or sardonic or whatever the right word is.

'I like you,' she says. 'You know I do. But . . .' She spreads her hands helplessly.

Mary Goddard dies fighting. She kicks, shrieks, bites, scratches. She swears. She prays. She cries. None of it makes any difference. She screams that she will be avenged. A fat man hits at her legs with a stick. Her face is pale, her hair red, wild and tangled. Her cheap hat rolls in the mud of the market square. No one picks it up. Her breasts rise and fall. Her full lips stretch wide in a curse, her petticoats rise high as she kicks out. There's a stretch of white thigh. A lascivious, well-dressed, well-groomed type licks his lips. Next to him his wife frowns and purses her lips.

Mary Goddard is twelve but the painter has made her look older with those breasts, those lips, that skin. He knows what he's doing.

As she is finally subdued, her arms pinioned behind her back, each twisting leg secured by eager hands, she is carried, still writhing and twitching, to a cart on which a middle-aged man with a serious but kindly face stands with his hand on the shoulder of a young boy. Unlike Mary the boy stands quiet, head bowed. This is Joe Goddard, who seems embarrassed at the fuss his sister makes. Joe Goddard is ten.

A crowd watch. Some are laughing and drinking, some are sombre. A thin man recites from a Bible. A red-coated soldier is expressionless as he leans on a musket. Another, with his back to the activity nearby, holds out a bucket to his horse.

The army is here to keep order. It was requested that they be on hand to quash any public rowdiness, to put down any riot by an angry public. There's no need. This is a crowd that is placidly curious, rather than inflamed or enraged. This is a crowd with the languid sense of holiday about it. This is an easy gig for the yeomanry. And it must be relief that makes two other soldiers smile as they chat by the town pump. What could they be talking about? Girls? The races? Prize-fighting? The outrageous hikes in the price of beer and bread?

It is 1800 and this is the law in action. Joe and Mary Goddard hung for stealing £30 of books from the shop of Henry Bowker Esq of Crown Street. Mr Bowker himself is here. Well dressed, with his fat hands behind his back, standing in a group with his wife who holds his baby on her hip. The babe sucks on a rusk, while the other three children aged eight, six and three gaze at the struggle taking place a few paces away. They are wearing their Sunday best. This is an important day. An instructive day.

The painting is undistinguished apparently. Written off by art historians as one of a lesser talent's lesser pictures. Dismissed by Wikipedia as 'an implausible Georgian event picture in muddy colours'.

Mike catches me examining it and says, 'That's how to

123

treat villains,' he laughs. 'I bet the local crime rate went down after that.'

I explain to him that within five years of the event the hangman, his wife, the judge, the captain of the yeomanry, and Mr Bowker the bookshop owner, were all dead from a variety of causes ranging from apoplexy to suicide. The painter, Edmund Torrington RA, merely went mad and spent the last ten years of his life in St Luke's. I tell Mike all this and am taken aback when he misquotes Yeats.

'The world's more full of magic than you can understand.'

'What does he mean?' I say later when I recount this conversation to Jen. 'And in any case the line is "The world is more full of *weeping* than you will understand." It's not magic, it's weeping.'

Saturday again and we head out to the crematorium to collect the urn that has Mum's ashes in it. Only we can't because the Nazi attendant wants £39.99 as a release fee and I don't have any money and he won't take a debit card. 'You can pay your respects though.' Which is very big of him and I don't punch him right in his fat jobsworth gob like I should do, but instead we stand and look at Mum's urn in this sort of storeroom thing. And we're quiet for a bit and then Oscar starts talking to it. And I try and shush him but he ignores me.

Oscar babbles on to Mum's fucking ashes about his progress with the plane (second cloud from the top). He talks to that cheap little pot, the pot that makes me think again of Russell Poulter bleeding to death up in Inverness, talks to it like it's really going to respond and I can't bear to listen but I can't get it together to pull him away either. And I suddenly can't see because my eyes are full of tears, which is when Toni calls and she can hear the sob in my throat as I tell her what Oscar is doing and Toni says she'll meet us in the Fun Junction and buy us lunch.

The Fun Junction is an old aircraft hangar on the edge of town just where the old London Road joins the A12. They used to build airships here before the war. British versions of the Zeppelins that the Krauts were so fond of. It's vast. From the 1950s right up until the late eighties, they did secret stuff here involving jet engines and wind resistance and lasers and God knows what. And then it was left empty. A cave of scary shadows on the edge of town.

It used to have the dignity of a major ruin. The awe inspired by a forgotten religion. The sense that, though the old gods had gone, some trace of their power and magic remained. It was the kind of a place where people grew quiet as they approached, out of respect for the ancient mysteries of war and science and craft.

And then, a few years ago, Fun arrived in all its Krazy Kolor, with its shrillness and its shrieks of WTF! STFU! GTFO! LOL! LMAO! LMFAO! The hangar was violated with inflatables of all kinds – not just bouncy castles, but bouncy pirate ships, bouncy space shuttles and bouncy massage parlours.

No, not really. But there is a whole inflatable town. And then there are climbing frames and ball-pools and ropes and swings and slides and fibre-glass animals. Everything in garish colours and soft plastics. And the place is staffed by sullen spotty kids forced to wear stripy blazers, white trousers and straw boaters. And you can always hear a child crying somewhere.

First thing Toni does when she sees us is hand me a note.

'It's from Dean,' she says.

I don't say anything, just shove it in my jeans. She sighs, but doesn't say anything.

125

To be honest Oscar is a little old for the Fun Junction now. And he knows it. But he's excited when I promise that I'll go on the Deathslide with him. This is something that I've sometimes seen dads do, but I've never done it with Oscar before. The Deathslide is a more or less vertical piece of plastic extending from the top of the hangar to a pile of yellow crash mats a metre or so above the floor. It looks both frightening and ludicrous, which is not a good combination, is it?

At the top of the slide you have a brilliant birds'-eye view of the social workings of the soft-play world.

From here you notice just what herd animals little kids are. Random chattering flocks of ankle-biters charging from one zone to another. Like starlings scrapping over worms. Meanwhile the adults sit, squashed on to plastic canteen chairs, folded double over newspapers, coffee cooling beside them, looking up every now and again. Scanning the horizon in the manner of the cavalry in Westerns, looking for some signal that their kids are still about; that whoever they can hear crying, it isn't their Ruby or Pearl, or Harry, or Stanley.

Why did people start giving their kids these War Memorial names? What are they saying about themselves? What is it that they hate about the modern world? What comfort is there to be had from evoking the lost age before the Great War? The only people prepared to embrace the modern are the teen mums for whom having a baby is a chance to flex an imagination not properly engaged elsewhere. A chance to be creative in a world that thinks they should just STFU and work the night-shift in Netto.

So, from up here I can see the bald patches of the middle-aged first-time fathers glancing up from their *Guardian*s to check on their Henrys and Reggies and Berts, while the pierced and studded scraps from the estates shout for Jamelia and Keira and Beckham.

From our special vantage place we can see all the way to Food City. This is the hub where they have collected together the outlets that serve travestied versions of various ethnic cuisines. Food City, the Fun Junction, Southwood. Can there be any more depressing address in the whole world? And then I remember Hessenthaler's note.

Kids, impatient at my pausing to take in the view, have started to wriggle past me to hurl themselves head first down the slide, while I pull the crumpled paper from the back-pocket where I had shoved it. And Oscar, impatient himself, tugs at me just as I've unfolded it, and my balance goes and so we tumble together arse over head towards the cushion. All of which means that I finally read the note in a quivering heap on the crash-mat with kids dropping around me like so many giddy lemmings. It's not ideal.

I half expect the note to be pieced together out of torn newspaper headlines in the way of cartoon ransom demands. That it would have a texture of similar threat. But it's just his normal writing after all. He has pretty neat handwriting. Almost like a girl's.

Billy,
You seem determined to make this difficult. I'm beginning to wonder what kind of message it will take to make you understand how serious I am? I've been patient but I can't wait around for you to see reason. I advise you not to underestimate me. I'm going to do the right thing for my son whether you like it or not. I won't give up. Don't ignore this.

DH

'Twat,' I say to myself, which is unfortunate because the winded tot beside me looks over in horror, and another kid – his sister? – yells 'Mum! This guy called Romeo a twat!' which means that there are a few minutes of delicate negotiating before Oscar and I can get back, sweating, to our table where a waitress is just depositing our order in front of Toni. Pizzas the colour, shape and texture of nuked Frisbees and radioactive-looking blue drinks, exactly what I fancy.

And Toni starts giving me a lecture about being fair and giving Dean a chance, and to cut her off I ask Oscar how I could be a better guardian and he does his special concentrating face as he thinks about the question, turning it over in his mind in the same methodical way he chomps the cardboardy pizza, long strings of cheese hanging from his lip, long strings of snot hanging from his nose too. It has to be said that the kid's a mess.

'Well,' the little philosopher says at last. 'You should send me to bed earlier. You shouldn't let me eat so many chips and takeaways and you shouldn't let me watch so many 12 and 15 movies. And you should get a cleaner in.'

Jesus. So now they're both bossing me about. Why does everyone reckon they're the boss of me? I say, 'Perhaps you should take some responsibility for yourself big man.'

He fixes me with a stern look. 'Billy, I'm six.'

Yeah, yeah, yeah. Victorian kids were up chimneys at six. Kids in the Congo are fighting wars at six.

The crazy logic of LOL has even colonised the bogs in the Fun Junction. The walls are covered in Mr Men and flowers. The colours are the same as the drinks, insanely chemical oranges and blues. And everything is child sized. The urinals are just a few inches off the floor. Naturally this means the floor is damp with mistimed adult piss. The cubicles are half the width of normal ones and require a sort of yogic dexterity to squat down so low while crapping. It makes me think of Mrs Bingley. Maybe this is what her bathroom is like.

I'm standing at the urinal just pissing, not thinking anything, just trying to hit that ceramic flowerpot from this great height when someone behind me speaks.

'She should have just given me the computer. Why didn't she just give it me? Everything would have been all right then.'

I turn my head over my shoulder, my heart lurching painfully against my ribs, a sudden bitterness in my mouth.

Aidan Jebb is standing near the hand-drying machine. I'm close enough to see the spots around his mouth, the freckles across his nose, the stiff fuzz of his hair, the dead, boiled-sweet eyes. But I'm still pissing. I can't move. I lean my head forward, let my forehead touch the cold neon green porcelain of the tiled wall. Just for a second.

When I turn around again he's gone. And when I hurry out of the bogs, there's no sign of him. He has disappeared into the world of Fun. Fun has swallowed him up.

I look everywhere for Jebb, but he's gone and eventually my phone goes. It's Toni, and she's furious.

'Where the bloody hell are you? What are you doing?'

And I'm about to tell her about Aidan Jebb being here and maybe we should phone the police, maybe they could lock down the building, trap him inside. Maybe with any luck he wouldn't surrender and they could shoot him. I'm about to say all this, but I don't get the chance, because she hangs up.

By the time I get back to the table I know that we don't have any chance of catching Jebb and I'm hacked off with Toni and I'm going to let her know about it. She's sitting with Oscar, cutting his pizza into slices.

129

She looks up as I sit down. 'He's been crying, Billy. He didn't know where you were. He was worried. You've been ages.'

I take a close look at her. She's looking good. Not quite A-star, but on the way. Thinner, sharper, like she's been working out.

I keep my voice pleasant as I say, 'You look well, Auntie. Left Frankie yet?' She flushes, but doesn't say anything. I say, 'Have you seen anything of Dean by any chance?' She turns her head, stares away towards Food City.

'You know, we're going to have to sell the house?'

'Oh well, you'll find somewhere else. Teacher's salary and a steady job, you're a safe bet.'

She draws a sharp breath. 'Suzanne's house, Billy. I mean Suzanne's house.'

'Our house,' I say. 'Mine and Oscar's.'

And she sighs again and talks a bit about her role as executor of the will, about debts, about Mum not taking out proper insurance. There's some money, but not enough to cover everything and so on. And on. And on.

'That little job at the museum isn't going to be enough is it? And you're off to uni and Oscar . . .' She tails off.

'What *about* Oscar, Toni?' I know I shouldn't ask. I know I should just ignore it. She hears the danger in my voice, looks down at her hands. Swallows.

'He needs a home, Billy. A proper home.'

Chapter Eight

A big step forward. A bored police voice calls and tells me to watch out for new developments and I do. Turns out Aidan Jebb has lost his official title of youth-who-can't-be-named-for-legal-reasons. Some judge has decided that he can be named, if not shamed, and the hunt is on. Now everyone knows who he is. Not just here in his home town, his turf, but nationwide. There's a window between birds falling out of the sky in Sweden and ten year olds shooting their mothers in Arkansas, so the world turns to us to keep itself going for a while. We're a local phenomenon taken up by the mainstream. We're a sleeper hit.

And so Mum's photo is on the TV. Smiling, elegant and professional. She's part of a proper story. An event. A celebrity. Mum and Aidan Jebb, they are like a celeb couple.

Serious-faced detectives tell us how seriously the courts take perverting the course of justice. They tell us someone must know where Aidan is. They tell us we're making things worse for him by hiding him. The bulletins end with a direct address to the camera. It looks showy, staged. And the cops look like actors. It looks like TV. It could be worse. The cops could look like cops and it could look like real life.

There are rewards too. The *Gazette* offers a grand for information leading to the apprehension and conviction of the main suspect, and is rapidly topped by a national paper offering ten times this. Toni appears on the news, proper distraught, breaking down through her own appeal for Jebb to come forward. I stand behind her trying to focus, trying not to blink as the lights burn my face.

Nice. Well done, Toni. I couldn't do it. I couldn't cry for the cameras. But somebody had to. Kudos.

Oscar and I mostly stay in now. Some days he doesn't go to school. Some days I don't go to work. On those days we eat chocolate. We watch films. We sit in the dark, playing battleships or Snap. Or he watches me play Empire, making suggestions about the colours of my trains and my mobile libraries. I'm a major power now, my people have time for holidays and books. They've never had it so good. I do a speech to tell them so.

We eat takeaways that we don't actually take away, but instead have delivered to our door. Chinese, Indian, Pizza, no one makes us pay. We still don't touch the food in the freezer. We make dens out of the sofa cushions. Unless we've ordered food, we ignore the doorbell. I let the post pile up. A little brown pile of shit on a chair in the hallway. Good news never comes by post. We don't see anyone. We don't speak to anyone.

When Oscar falls asleep, I carry him up to bed and go back down to watch porn, real porn, not the trauma porn – rubbing myself into exhaustion, feeling raw and ashamed and every time promising myself that this is the last time.

If I do go out – to get bog roll or to buy the magazines – then I see Aidan Jebb everywhere. And I've learned my lesson. I'm not spurning any opportunities for vengeance now. I find myself chasing malnourished ragamuffins all over town, hollering at any hooded Year Seven on a bike. My heart pounds every time I see a kid in trackie bottoms.

132

I get up close and can see it's not him, just another idiot in sports kit with tennis-ball hair and a bloodless face. No one starts on me. No one tries to fight me.

'Soz, man,' I say. 'Thought you were someone else.' And they nod and shrug. It's OK, they seem to say, we get it. It's all right. Even when it's a big group, even if they're a bit pissed or stoned or whatever, they don't try and scrap, or take the mick even.

Graffiti has started appearing round town. *Grass up Aidan Jebb* it says. You see it on walls all over. You even see it on the mural on the Co-op. 'Course there's lots of other graffiti there too after all these years. My favourite is across the face of this painting of a young Asian mum wheeling a buggy. 'Niggers are gay' it says. Two kinds of bigotry wrapped up in a surreally efficient package. Very Southwood that. Very now.

No one has claimed the reward yet, but the TV tells us it's just a matter of time.

I go over and over my conversation with him.

'She should have just given it me. Everything would have been all right then.' I conjure up Aidan's plaintive whine, his pinched and scabby face. He's right. I think about inscriptions. *Here lies Suzanne Smith: Died defending her Lenovo Dreampad.* What a waste. Me and Aidan, we agree. We're as one on this. What was the bloody point? Nothing's ever that important.

Ricky calls. 'You hear about Alfie, man? He's been proper done over.' So one lunchtime I go and see Alfie at the hospital.

This is the third time I've been in this hospital since they've built it and I hate it. I hate the clean, disinfected white of it, the bleep and whoosh and whirr of it. The first time was to see Mum just before they made Toni and me decide to switch off the machines. They pretended there was a choice, but there wasn't really. We all knew it. I remember I took one last look at Mum surrounded by all those colour-coded wires and thought the bed looked like an engine with Mum as a battery, like Mum's mix of blood and flesh and gas was necessary to keep all the machinery alive rather than the other way around. Gave me the shivers.

The other time I went to see Mum in the hospital was after she'd died.

Of all the state-of-the-art-departments in the hospital, the mortuary must be the most high-tech department of them all I reckon. The one that most feels like a sci-fi fan's vision of the future. Doors glide open soundlessly in front of you: ambient music plays on a loop. The porter who took me down to the ward of the dead was wearing a Simpsons tie. He clocked me looking at it. Apologised. 'I normally work on the children's ward,' he said. I told him it didn't matter, that the dead wouldn't give a shit. And he looked at me like I was a nutjob, a psycho. 'I'll leave you alone for five minutes, yeah?' But it wasn't really a question.

The rooms of the dead are carefully lit and minimally furnished, but they don't feel bare. They feel like cocoons. Pods taking humankind on a long journey to some distant galaxy. That or rooms in a Bauhaus-inspired boutique hotel chain. Mum looked at home there. Her face resting somewhere between a smile and a frown. Like she hadn't quite decided on what she thought of the décor.

I looked down at Mum, peered at her closely. She actually looked pretty well. Rested. Like she was getting a decent kip.

It was quiet down there, but not silent. There was the

hum and sloosh all modern buildings have, a digital sea lapping at an online shore. And of course there's music in the dead ward too. Sort of sounds a bit like whale song. Ambient wank. Mum would have hated it.

She'd been made up by an expert. Her hair had been done by someone who knew what she was doing. I kissed her on the cheek.

I'd never done that before, kissed Mum while she was sleeping. But I was running out of things to do and there was still an easy two minutes of my five left. And I wanted to feel what she felt like.

She felt like she was alive. That's the miracle of modern air-con systems for you.

As I stood upright again I expected her to wrinkle her nose, to open her eyes, to ask me what I was doing and had I emptied the dishwasher?

Alfie's up on the top floor. A penthouse-type deal. He has a view right across town. He's made friends with his room-mate too, who's asleep when I come in and Alfie tells me about him in whispers.

'He's cool man.' I look over and just see another drooling gramps. 'No really. He was in the war. He got bombed and shit. He was at Dunkirk. He's ninety-four, man. Ninety-four. And, this is the best bit, he's called Alfie too. How freaky is that?'

'What's the matter with him?'

'He's ninety-four, that's what's the matter. He's always falling over and banging his head.'

Alfie – our Alfie, young Alfie – is OK. Better than OK in some ways. I haven't seen him as excited as this for ages. Few days off the grass has done him some good too. He's got some colour in his cheeks and not just from

135

bruising. Looks more like he did as a tiny kid, as a primary school shoplifter.

He's not actually hurt that bad. They're just keeping him in for observation 'cause he was pissing blood when his mum and dad brought him in. He starts to tell me what happened and I think it's going to be the usual – lairy knob takes offence at Alfie's eyeliner, Alfie gives him lip. Lairy knob twats him. That's happened before, several times, though this is the first time Alfie's been put in hospital. But apparently this is a new kind of story.

'There was no conversation. Nothing. Nada. These lads didn't even bother calling me a wanker or anything. Just started on me. But here's the weird thing' – he drops his voice – 'it was like it was a job. Routine. Like I was just the next thing on their workflow.' He leans back against the pillows. Shakes his head, world-weary. 'My friend, the world is out of control.'

'Weird,' I say. But it's not weird. It's Dean. It has to be Dean.

Toni is taking Oscar off for the day. He's going swimming and then to the park.

'Exercise and fresh air,' she says. Oscar makes a cross face, but he's pleased really. Mum always had him out in the park, or swimming, or judo, or disco dancing. Whatever they had going on at the sports centre. 'If you've got a fat kid, you should be locked up. It's abuse.' That was her line. She thought kids were like dogs, needed a good long walk twice a day and I guess it's true we've been at the screen more than we should, me and Oscar. Haven't been out chasing sticks all that often lately.

When they've gone, I phone Lucy and she comes round after work and we're instantly kissing in the hallway. Fierce

136

and frantic. Her coat comes off and seconds later we are mashed together against the wall. Her top is up and my lips find a nipple and her hand reaches down to touch me through my jeans. And my hand pushes up under her skirt searching out the heat that's there and she moans against my ear, and then she pushes me back and smiles. Her face is just centimetres from mine, breaths coming in ragged gasps.

'I bet you thought you were in there.' She smiles, and she takes me by the hand into the kitchen and makes tea. A pot. Two bags of PG to one of Earl Grey.

'We can't do it just because your mum's died,' she smiles again. I root around for biscuits. There's some jammy dodgers somewhere. 'Do you think I'm a prick tease?' she says.

'I guess you are,' I say. 'But I quite like it.'

She laughs and we sit down and drink the tea, which is good, and I tell her about seeing Aidan Jebb everywhere. She just nods. Doesn't say much. And I tell her about what Toni said about the will and selling the house.

'What about if you had a lodger?' she says. I sit quietly and think about it.

'Are you messing with me again?'

'I'm not sure.'

She bites her lip. She looks troubled and then she brightens and she tells me that she would like to clean the place up a bit, maybe paint it. I look around the kitchen and see it through Lucy's eyes. The bin overflowing, the plates stacked up everywhere. The strange beige splodges on the floor. The remains of takeaway meals, their foil containers like so many empty silver coffins. The carcasses of teabags huddled around the sink. The stains on the walls like the contours of small pacific islands. The bottles and the cans. Crap everywhere.

'We could start now.'

'You sure?'

'Of course. It'll be good to be in charge for once. Milan does everything in our flat.'

Of course he does.

'How is old Milano?'

'Fine. Fucking someone else, I think. But at least he's stopped telling me about it.'

'Progress then.'

'Isn't it? He wants us to get married.' And she laughs.

'Will you?'

'I don't know. We might.'

Rosie was out of it one afternoon. Completely wasted. She said Leanne Gladstone had had it coming and Titus knocked her front teeth out. Bashed her face on the bathroom sink till there was a bloody red hole where the teeth had been. Next day he gave Rosie fifty quid and said he wouldn't be round any more.

'You're no use to me now girl, are you? You're no use to anyone.' He shook Aidan's hand as he left. Aidan didn't know what to do, or what to say. Titus looked at him for a moment.

'You're the man of the house now,' he said. And he laughed.

Titus had a new theory. Everyone, he reckoned, was just two tricks away from the gutter. Not just prozzies. Everyone. Bankers. Government ministers. Judges. Police chiefs. Plumbers. Dealers. Everyone was just two pay packets from living on the street. He'd noticed it over many years of observation and calculation – prostitutes had two tricks' worth of savings. And prostitutes were as good a barometer of the temperature of the world's economy as anything else. Watch the comings and goings on the street and you don't need to watch the news, or read the papers.

All of us are just two tricks away from dereliction, my friend. Titus Cooke always liked the sound of words. *De-re-lick-tion.* He turned the syllables over in his mouth to savour them.

Now there was just Rosie and Aidan at home with no one else to organise things. Titus had made it very clear that he was not to be contacted. *You a liability girl. Deal with it.* No one to organise things and Titus had made it very clear they weren't to call him, or try to contact him in any way. Rosie tried calling him once, shouting at his voice-mail in the street till the neighbours called the police.

This was a low. What Titus would call a bad weather time. A steady, depressing drizzle of bills and fines and summonses. Of rows and headaches and people shouting up at the windows. Rosie in bed, sending Aidan to the shops for booze, to the street for ten pound wraps. Aidan didn't want his mum clucking in bed. He didn't want her pissing herself and messing the place any more.

Aidan was calling in all the favours he was owed. Using up all the credit he had. And he was working hard too, trying to keep the pair of them. He was in and out of Cash Converters every day. Phones, bikes, videos. He took a chimney pot in once. A chimney pot was worth the same as three phones.

He was too big now to get in through bathroom windows and skylights the way the younger kids did. Often he was too unsteady to trust himself on the leap from roof to garage. He was at the mercy of the rusting brackets that held drainpipes to the wall in a way that he had never been before, his life depending on his declining athleticism and speed of thought. And it was too hard. Just too hard. When

Titus went, some of the gang disappeared too. Aidan was exiled from the court and it was felt unwise to hang with him too much.

It made him angry to think about the easy life his mum was having. He hadn't really liked it when she was a rock star, but he'd liked hanging with Titus. He'd liked walking the dogs. All that straining muscle under his control. He was a power. A superhero. King of the world. Those dogs, Cassius and Cocoa, they were like living, breathing glocks. Twenty stone of muscled terror, his to unleash whenever he got the word. Whenever he wanted practically. With those dogs, he was God. Without them, he was just Aidan.

And now Rosie was pissing in her bed, moaning and whining. Clucking and scratching and watching telly. She was lazy. No other word for it. A disgrace. He wanted to smack her. And then, one day, he suddenly wasn't wanting to smack her any more. He *was* smacking her. Over and over and she was crying and he was ashamed, enraged. And in his rage and shame he wanted to kill her, but he didn't.

He left her crying, adding salty self-pity to the other fluids on that bed – the blood and the spunk and the piss and the shit and the spit and the booze and puke and God knows what. A disgrace. And he went down to the magistrates' court, which was a good place to meet the right connections, and later he sat in a room for hours somewhere with Mr Happy, so called because he never smiled, and without ever once talking they passed the crack pipe and the weed and the bottle back and forth.

And when everything was done, when everything was used up and empty, they hauled themselves up. Aidan sort of almost laughed at gravity's attempts to hold him down. Mr Happy didn't, but when they were both upright he bumped knuckles all the same, acknowledged the difficulty of the task.

And they were out down the narrow chute of the hall-way, stepping over the bills and the legal threats and leaflets from the council and the make-up catalogue and into the street, where Aidan laughed again, this time at the audacity of the wind and its attempts to push him around and Mr Happy croaked at him. *Laters, blood.*

And then Aidan was crossing the Royal Insurance car park where a lady who looked a bit like how his mum used to look was standing by the boot of a Golf GTI. She had something in her hand. Saleable goods. *It'll be OK. One hard pull, down to Cashcon and the job's a good 'un.*

And he came up behind her and grabbed the strap of the laptop bag, and the lady, this tart, this slag, wouldn't let go. And he tugged and she tugged back, and she was shouting and he let go of the bag and she fell and hit her head and he ran. Ran through the traffic, cars swerving, horns going, people shouting and up the alleyway into the Institute where they teach cooking and joinery and hairdressing and music technology and stuff like that, and where it's easy to get lost.

Aidan really needed to sleep when he got back. It had been a tough few days. He lay down and closed his eyes but he kept hearing the thunk as the lady's head hit the pavement and he needed something to block it out. It was stopping him sleeping and he really needed some kip.

Aidan Jebb went to his bag. All his stuff was in there. He emptied it out on the floor. Somewhere in there, with the socks and the pants and T-shirts and the trackie bottoms, was an old CD. Burned at home years before from the master they'd made at school. The primary choir singing. Track three, Aidan singing 'Here, There and Everywhere'.

On his own, almost. The rest of the choir just sort of humming behind him. Aidan listened to the whole song and then skipped back to it. It didn't make him feel better. It made him feel worse. But he needed to feel worse. It felt right to feel bad. *I want her everywhere/and if she's beside me I will never care* . . . Maybe there was still time. Not to become a classical singer, not for Fame Academy and things like that, but maybe he could do something. Music technology at the Institute. Something.

Aidan turned the music off. He got a pen and paper and made lists of all the people he owed money to. That made him feel better and it should have made him feel worse. He was in the shit, but he still felt better about things. He went into the kitchen. *Christ, the state of this place.* Aidan didn't know why they had to live like this. He looked in the fridge, then in the cupboards. Nothing. Aidan punched the wall and shouted. A wordless bellow.

Rosie appeared, her face swollen and bruised. The sight of her made Aidan sick. Not just her face, but she was wearing this flimsy nightie thing and he could see her tits and the dark cloud of her pubes. *What was wrong with her?* She didn't say anything, just ducked her head like she was saying sorry and went away. Aidan could feel the sweats starting, he could feel the shivering starting and he went into the dark of the living room and lay on the busted sofa. He closed his eyes.

Aidan thought of Leanne. She'd kissed him once. Not a sexy kiss. A brother-kiss, on the cheek. She'd smelled nice. She'd smelled of soap. Not perfume or anything, just soap like they used to have at primary school. Aidan tried to remember when that was. How long it was before Titus's Lexus had got stolen.

* * *

142

Lucy's round and she's talking decorating. 'Radiccio,' she says. 'And arsenic.'

'What?'

'For the walls in here.'

She hands me a slim catalogue. Farrow and Ball. Radiccio is a deep, rich red. The colour of arterial blood. Arsenic is grey. Blood and poison. Why not?

'Yeah,' I say. 'Let's paint the house red.'

Oscar has his own ideas. 'Can I have my room like Bernard's?'

'Who?'

He sighs, a sound which contains a whole world of weariness. A sound that tells me that God I'm thick sometimes. 'Bernard. You know in that book.'

'*Not now, Bernard*?'

'Yes.'

Not now, Bernard. In this classic kids' story a child tries to get his parents' attention but is continually rebuffed with the phrase 'Not now, Bernard'. Eventually the little lad takes himself off to the garden where he is eaten by a monster. The monster then tries to attack the parents but he too is fobbed off with the same line, the parents not noticing that Bernard's place has been taken by a fierce and hungry beastie. The monster ends up eating Bernard's tea – in front of the TV of course – and being put to bed in Bernard's room. The last scene sees the monster sitting in Bernard's bed, surrounded by Bernard's toys muttering 'But I'm a monster' in a baffled tone. Bernard's mum switches off the light with the book's pay-off line, which is, of course, 'Not now, Bernard.' It is a heartbreaking little morality play about the psychological dangers of neglecting your kids. See Bernard – now there's a kid that's properly emotionally abused. And this unsubtle sub-text has spoken to Oscar.

143

Thing is, Bernard's room in the book is a zany mix of lime-green walls, turquoise carpets and pictures of space rockets on the walls. It will look disgusting.

'Can I have my room like that, Billy?' He's found the book and he's pointing at the relevant page.

'Of course you can big man. You can have your room any way you like.'

Toni rings, she sounds nervous. And she does lots of chat, small talk. After we've done how Oscar is, how I am, we go on to how the house is, how her work is, how the museum is, I wait. And I wait. I'm cool, neutral. I am polite. I am not sarky, facetious, flippant or angry. I'm practically a saint. It's hard work though. And I wait some more.

Eventually she comes out with it. 'I've left Frankie.'

I wait some more. She waits too. She cracks first. 'What do you think?'

What do I think? I think that Frankie is an idiot but I have a sudden rush of sympathy for him. He's not going to cope well on his own.

'I think it's none of my business. How do you feel?'

'Exhilarated. Nervous. We've been together eleven years.'

'How's he?' I say.

She goes quiet. There's a long pause. 'Crying all the time.'

'Where are you living?' Another pause.

'With a friend.'

'A friend from work?'

'No. Does it matter?' She sounds irritable.

'I guess not.' I ask her if she wants to stay here with me.

'Your house? With all Suzie's things in it. I'm not ready for that yet.'

I can feel her shivering down the phone. 'God, we're in a mess aren't we, Billy?'

144

Yes, we are. I'm a step further forward than her though. I can sit in my dead mother's house. I can sleep in it even. Not well. Not for long. But I can do it.

Mum's cash card stops working. I knew it had to happen, but I'd managed to both know this and rely on the money simultaneously. Weird how you can do that kind of double think. So now there's just my wages and my post office account. And Oscar's pig. Not a whole heap of cash it's true.

I spend an evening making calculations and manage to work out a way of surviving. Basically, I'm not going to pay any bills. Everyone knows that it takes ages to get cut off. These big companies have to go through loads of legal shit before they can turn off the water and the gas and the electric and all that. I'm already ignoring the stuff from the credit card companies.

And if it comes to court I'll hold Oscar up in the dock. He can do his pale little Oliver Twist face and no judge is going to make us homeless then. Something will turn up. It always does.

And there are always people worse off. In *Life! Death! Prizes!* I read of two sisters, 16 and 19, who died of cystic fibrosis *on the same day.*

'I was just pleased my angels reached heaven together,' said their mum, Christine, 38, of Corby, Northants. Of course Christine, 38, of Corby, does have the advantage of believing in angels and heaven and all that. Even if I had had the benefit of her belief system, another magazine I once picked up in the hospital would have cured me.

It was just before Mum died, we were in the hospital. Oscar was having his quiet little war with his plastic knights and Mum was not doing much, obviously. I picked up a magazine left by another visitor. *Best Friend.*

145

Best Friend has all the *Life! Death! Prizes!* stuff that other trauma porn has. But it's for dogs. There are heart-warming stories about surviving freak accidents, there are funny pics of puppies wearing hats, and there are problem pages and a page written by a canine spiritualist, Paul.

A typical letter that Paul has to deal with: a reader, JG from Ayrshire, writes in saying that he's racked with guilt because he had his three-year-old hunter, the sadly ill-named Lucky, euthanized. Unlucky Lucky had been taking a while to recover from a cruciate ligament injury and then he strained the other leg. JG was told that he'd need another expensive two months of cage rest. So JG had him put down. Lucky was, after all, 'miserable anyway'. Why, JG wanted to know, did he feel so guilty? He'd had other dogs put down and not lost sleep over it.

Luckily for JG, Paul can give instant peace of mind. Paul can offer absolution. Paul doesn't say, 'You are feeling guilty because you are a murdering scumbag who puts your own convenience before your duty towards your pets.' No, Paul reassures JG that young Lucky will be gambolling after rabbits in the afterlife. He has, says Paul, found his true, free self and that JG should let Lucky's freedom enter his heart also. The way Paul tells it, JG deserves some kind of award for releasing Lucky from the shackles of this dreary mortal coil. Lucky was lucky to have such a caring owner.

Paul seems to have absolute proof that everything you heard about heaven is true. If you're a dog anyway.

To hear Paul tell it, every euthanized mongrel gets seventy-two virgin bitches. And this is why I don't believe in an afterlife. If Mum is not rotting in the ground, but is instead cheerfully picnicking in the hereafter with Elvis, then Lucky is there too, pissing on lamp posts. And not only Lucky – every wasp, every fly, every I don't know, every syphilis germ that there has ever been is also enjoying a blissful eternity. Lucky is dead, Mum is dead, and the rest of us will be following them soon enough. Read the papers. Didn't you hear? 5000 blackbirds fell out of a clear blue Swedish sky the other week. The whole fucking planet is dying.

Milan is at a theatre festival in Glasgow and so now Lucy is round every night working on the house. We don't kiss, we don't touch, but she must know that I really want to. For one thing I let her talk. I listen to her tell me what horrors 9E4 are, and how lovely 7Y3 are and how parents have abdicated responsibility and expect schools to teach kids how to be decent citizens as well as all the GCSE business.

'A lot of them can't tie their own shoe-laces. At eleven.'

And she rants about declining behaviour only just stopping short of arguing for the return of both conscription and the birch.

'You sound like Mike at the museum,' I say. 'Maybe you should be a Tory politician. I don't think they've got any Goths on the front bench yet.' She smiles, but thinly.

She says, 'You have to work hard at not turning into a fascist working in schools. You start out as a liberal feeling sorry for kids and end up taking so much crap that you start wanting capital punishment for defacing library books.' She pauses. 'And they're so apathetic, even now. Even with the world that's being planned for them.'

I remember a Smith family outing. Mum, Oscar, and I marching against the rise in university tuition fees. Mum's organised it all. Booked us tickets on the Red/Green Alliance coach. Made sandwiches, brought a flask of hot

147

Ribena, made a placard with Oscar. It reads 'This Crap Wouldn't Happen at Hogwarts.' People chuckle over it, though it causes an all together too spirited argument about just how Hogwarts is funded, about whether it qualifies for charitable status and whether it should be replaced by a truly comprehensive wizard training school with intake decided by a lottery rather than the current unacceptably opaque admissions policy.

'Is Hogwarts a real school?' says Oscar, confused.

This sparks a heated debate about the nature of reality which takes us all the way from Southwood to Ongar, where people start to get excited about getting close to the big bad city. Southwood is fifty-one miles from London, but most of us have never been.

My own sign gets left at home. Mum says it lacks wit. I say I don't think marches are about wit, more about visibility and impact. Mum says she's the expert on demos not me, but if I can explain my slogan to Oscar then I can take it. So the placard stays behind. It reads 'Don't Suck Tory Cock.' A simple but effective message, but it might be tricky to get a reception kid to appreciate all the nuances. There'll be other occasions to use it over the next few years I'm sure.

Oscar takes to activism like he's done it all his life. Five minutes off the coach and he's seen how it works. I see him looking about, drinking it all in, and pretty soon he's confident enough to feel able to add his voice to the first tentative chants. 'They say cut back. We say fight back,' he bellows. He's definitely the loudest and sounds the most committed to the cause. The students around him giggle and he gives them his gravest look, shaming them into redoubling their own vocal efforts. 'They say cut back. We say fight back.' Pretty soon the whole rally has taken it up and Oscar

148

flushes pink with pride. 'Good work, comrade. Fresh blood, it's what the Left needs,' says an old boy marching next to us. Oscar smiles.

Mum's in her element. She starts chants, she strikes up conversations with everyone, from the old socialist worker next to us to the high school students on their first march, to the peelers escorting us. And her radicalism is only slightly undermined by a tendency to say 'Ooh, there's a great little vintage shop down here' as we pass some back alley in Shoreditch. She learns everyone's names, and pretty soon she's swapping reminiscences with other veterans of the poll tax riots, anti-apartheid and the miners' strike.

'The miners' strike, Mum? Are you sure? You must have been about six.'

'I was fourteen actually, Mr Social Historian. And it was my punk rock, my Woodstock. A defining moment. Made me want to change the world.'

'Via the medium of Event Management.'

'Yes, well it took me a while to realise that you do more good by being happy, than you do by being dutiful. And running my own business makes me happy. Being in charge of my own little world works for me. I still want to make things better for everyone.'

'They also serve who help conferences run smoothly.'

'Exactly.'

We decide not to go back to Southwood on the Red/Green Alliance coach, but instead round off our day of action with spaghetti at Bella Pasta and a trip to see the musical version of *The Railway Children*. And then we stay over in a family suite at the flash new St Pancras hotel.

'All revolutions should end with dinner and a show,' says Mum.

* * *

As Lucy gets on with the decorating I make her tea. Earl Grey and normal teabags in the same pot. I feed her wine in the hope that she'll get pissed. I buy biscuits. I heat up some of the many lasagnes and casseroles that still fill our freezer. I do all the boring jobs. I generally act like her slave. Sometimes I just rub and sand and prepare surfaces, while she sits on the floor marking, moaning about kids and telling me where I've missed a bit. And of course I want to get her into bed. Of course I hope she'll let me see her appendix scar again along with the rest of her – but even just chatting, this might well be the best time of my life.

And she's pure sunshine with Oscar too. She makes stencils of spaceships to go on his walls to try and get the authentic *Not now, Bernard* look and lets him use the spray can. She plays hide and seek and makes up games with his stuffed toys. She watches *MI High* with him. This is a spy programme where teen agents battle the forces of darkness in a vaguely comic way. Oscar takes it very seriously and Lucy takes it very seriously with him and they discuss the finer points of the episode afterwards.

She also explains about maps and orographic rainfall, Oxbow lakes and migration of peoples, rehearsing Key Stage 3 geography units on a very receptive Key Stage 1 audience.

'If Oscar gets it, then surely to God 9E fucking 4 can get it too,' she says.

Everyone's got used to having Lyndon Bowers around in the museum. He's helpful, easy with both the lawnmower enthusiasts and the primary school kids who make up our principal client groups. He also does all the menial tasks without complaining, often without even being asked. He's far harder working than the rest of us. He doesn't waste time moaning about how everything is going to hell (Mike), or doing wordsearches (Jen) or staring into space (me). He's also become a bit of a social history expert himself in that he's painstakingly worked his way through the selection of *Horrible Histories* we keep in the Gift Shop. Truth is he probably knows at least as much as I do now.

He has stayed shy of me – mainly because I ignore him – but still, it's a surprise when he tells us that he's leaving. We have a hurried whip round. Jen and I contribute a fiver each and Mike puts in a tenner. We rack our brains to think of something we can buy. As the resident teenager I'm meant to be the expert, but I suspect that Lyndon and I don't really have any tastes that coincide.

In the end we gather up a selection of souvenirs from our gift shop – I'd love to see that Southwood Museum iron-on transfer on his favourite ball cap – and put the money in an envelope with a Purple Ronnie card, chosen by Jen.

Lyndon is proper touched. I swear I see his eyes well up. He hugs Jen and Mike and, after a moment's hesitation, he does the same with me. I can feel his muscles beneath his jacket. I close my eyes. He smells of kids' bubble bath. Like the stuff I get for Oscar. He smells like Matey.

He's also got us a box of Roses chocolates to share. And as we dive in I point to the opened envelope from where the notes peep out. 'Twenty quid. It'll buy you quite a bit of White Lightning, that will,' I say, and there's a sudden hush and I think I've ruined the mood. Thrown the cold piss of reality over everything. But Lyndon just grins and nods.

He doesn't make a speech exactly, but he says, 'I like it here. You're all sound, you know. I've learned a lot.' And he promises to be back to visit.

We leave the museum together me and him, which is something that has not happened before, and, as we get

151

to the gate, he stops and hovers. I'm thinking that surely he can't want another hug, when he seems to make his mind up.

'Billy,' he says, 'I know where he is.'

'Who?' I say, though of course I know. I can feel a hard icy lump forming under my ribs.

'Jebb. He's not in Southwood no more, but I know where he is.'

He's not looking at me, he's staring hard at his trainers.

'Thought about telling the police?'

He looks at me now. Yeah, right. As if. That's what his look says, and I feel like apologising. I feel like saying 'Yeah, sorry, stupid thing to say.' He produces a bit of paper and holds it out. If I take it then I've got to do something with it. I'll have to take action. I close my eyes. Lyndon loses patience. He leans forward and shoves the paper deep into my pocket. He looks up at our church tower.

'You know, before I worked here, I never even noticed this place. Walked past it a million times and never even saw it. It's been here like for centuries and it'll be here for centuries after we're all dead, but I never even saw it before the day I started here. Weird.'

It's the longest speech he's made to me. Mike was always his confidant. It used to piss me off a bit, the way they would chat about football, the way Lyndon would nod and mutter encouragingly as Mike went off on one about the old days – the golden age when you were allowed to fit up known crims.

'The ordinary decent criminal knew it was an occupational hazard of the life they'd chosen. Took it as part of the job. Not like now. Now it's all human rights and all that crap.'

It used to get on my tits having to listen to all that, but

152

once Lyndon was the new favoured audience, I found myself getting sort of jealous. I got over it – I'm not that sad – but still, my nose was a bit out of joint I admit.

Lyndon says, 'Look after yourself.' And turns, hunches his shoulders and mooches off into the Friday shoppers. I lean against the railings and watch him go. I close my eyes again. I feel rain on my face. I think I could just throw this scrappy piece of paper away. I could screw it up and drop it on the street. Another bit of litter blowing around the town centre. I'd be letting something go. I'd be letting some bitter part of me free. It would be therapeutic. Healing.

Chapter Nine

I ask Lucy how she got together with Milan. This is stupid. It's like when you've got toothache and you keep sticking things in the nerve to make it hurt.

She smiles and says, 'What? Apart from him being like, totally hot, able to play a million instruments and being a really talented artist?' She pauses. 'And totally hot. Or did I say that already?'

'You might have mentioned it.'

Then she gets serious and says, 'I don't know if I can tell you. How grown up are you feeling?'

'How grown up does anyone feel?' I say.

She laughs. 'What does that even mean?' Then she says, 'All the time I was at school I never felt like me. Never felt like anyone really got me, you know?' Of course I know. Everyone feels like that.

I'm obscurely disappointed in her, but she doesn't notice.

'And when I got to uni I changed. New hair, tattoos, everything. Had different kind of friends. Didn't join sports clubs. Not even Table Tennis Soc. Started smoking. Had drinking mates, druggy mates.' She stops. Fiddles with her hair, adjusts the biro that holds it up. 'But I still felt like me. Still felt like no one really got me.'

Yes, that's because everyone always feels like that.

'And then one day I'm in this pub in Nottingham – The Bell – with some mates. It's the afternoon but we're all getting off our tits because . . . we're students. Because we can. And I notice Milan looking at me. It's hard not to notice Milan with him being so tall and handsome and with those eyes and everything.'

God, I despise this bloke.

'But I'm not thinking about him. I don't even fancy him. I fancy this other guy, this lecturer actually.' She pauses to think about this other guy, this lecturer. She seems almost surprised at herself. As if she had completely forgotten this other guy, this lecturer, and is staggered to discover that he can find his way into her head after all this time. 'Anyway, I go to the bogs and Milan is waiting outside when I come out. Like he's been watching me, waiting to see when I'd need a piss.'

'Sounds sinister,' I say. 'Sounds like stalking.'

'You are so transparent, Billy Smith,' she says, smiling. 'And he stops me and he goes,' – and here Lucy leans into me, stares right into my eyes and hisses – 'Get on your knees.' I feel my heart twitch.

'What?'

'That's what he says – "*Get on your knees*" – just like that.'

'What did you do?' I say, though I know the answer.

'I got on my knees. Right there outside the bogs in The Bell. I didn't know what else to do. And he looked down at me for a few moments, and then he told me to go back to my table to get all my stuff and to meet him outside. He said I had exactly two minutes or he'd be gone. And that he'd be counting to 120 slowly. And he walked outside.'

And she could have stopped there, but no, I had to hear the rest of it. How they took a cab to his bedsit, which she paid for. How he made her strip. How he tied her up. How, in a flat, dead voice, he described exactly what he was going

155

to do to her. How he described how he was going to beat her with his belt and fuck her and how she was going to cry and how that would make him feel very, very good.

'And it's funny but when it came to it, when he smacked me and everything, it was pretty gentle. Like it was a performance, like a sort of show. And I felt safer with him than I'd ever felt before with a lover. He was calling me an animal, calling me all sorts, and he was telling me what I'd feel and how I'd be crying and begging him to stop and everything. But it was like he was giving me a script really. A sort of guide about how to behave. It was serious, but like a game too. In fact he could have been a lot rougher. I sort of wanted him to be. It was ritualistic, that's what it was. Like it was from some secret, magic book. It was definitely sex, but sort of religious too. A ceremony. Do you know what I mean?'

'And you could have stopped it at any time?'

'Well I could have started laughing, that would have stopped things pretty quickly I imagine. It normally does with boys I find. But I didn't want to stop it. I liked it.'

I tell her that I could do that kind of thing with her. Do S&M and all that. I'd like to. I say it like a joke but I mean it and she knows that. And she smiles, but looks a bit sad with it.

'Billy, if I have to teach you how to be dominant it sort of defeats the object doesn't it.'

The house is more or less finished by the time the Social Service Stasi descend, noses twitching like dogs trained to sniff out perverted satanic practices involving, I don't know, virgin's blood and goats. My assigned handlers are called Zara and Penny. Neither even offered up a surname, it's all part of creating the illusion that we're friends, mates. That we all simply have the best interests of the child at heart. A unit. Buddies working together on a community project.

We don't know that they are coming of course, so while on the Friday I'm moaning at Lucy for hiding a well developed protestant work ethic behind all that pagan war-paint, three days later I'm offering up silent prayers of gratitude for her determination to finish the Oaks Avenue makeover before Milan gets back from his Scottish jaunt. If Zara and Penny had seen the place as it was, before she took it all in hand, then I'm sure Oscar would have been in some state-sponsored kennel somewhere in no time. As it was, by the time they come round the place is gleaming and sterile. You could practise cannibalistic rites on the kitchen floor without fear of infection. And of course, the fridge and the freezer are both bulging with healthy meals and will be till the end of time. Zara and Penny both approve of that, though in their different ways neither look like they go for healthy options much themselves. Penny is a mountain of blancmangey flesh, while Zara is emaciated and scabby. Mum read *James and the Giant Peach* to me when I was little and Zara and Penny are Aunt Sponge and Aunt Spiker basically. Younger maybe, but with none of their playful charm.

Oscar plays his part too. He reads and plays and smiles and shows off his bookbag like a regular CBeebies kid. If it were me, I'd have been well suspicious: but the kinds of people who go into social work aren't too bright. They can't be, or they wouldn't do it.

It's an insoluble paradox that has defied some of the brightest government thinkers. Social work is a job so difficult that you need the cleverest people doing it, but because it's so difficult no remotely clever person will consider it. Only the dumb and the depressed even think about it.

Social workers are the goalkeepers of the public services – people only ever remember their mistakes. You've only got to lose one piece of paper, mislay one file, fall for one well-worked parental lie and there you are, named and shamed in the press, hounded from your home almost as if you were a baby-killer yourself. It's no wonder that the social service operatives are bitter, and less clued up than the average Netto till-bot. What is a surprise is that councils still find recruits wanting to do it.

This is the other thing about social workers: they must have the sickest imaginations behind those threadbare professional smiles. They can see criminal thoughts and perversion everywhere. This part of Essex has a long tradition of witchfinding – we have an exhibit or two in the museum commemorating it – and Zara and Penny are part of that heritage.

Oscar and I high five as they leave. We're clean. Once they are both safely back in their council-issue beige Punto, I make a Hitler tache with my index finger and goose-step around the freshly radiccio-ed and arsenic-ed living room muttering, 'Vere are zey hidink ze emotional abuse? Ve know it is here somevere.'

Oscar giggles. It makes no sense to him, but a comedy Kraut accent and a silly walk is always amusing whatever age you are. And after his bath I do the drying machine at Quadruple Maximum Explode and he squeals as he somersaults through the air and bounces on to the bed.

I'm a reject in the playground now. All the A-star PTA mums know what I did to Charlotte's marriage. How I busted it wide open. She had to take action. She had to confront her husband. And now he's moved out and there's the dreary guerrilla war over money, access, houses and all that shit. I've spread an indelible and unsavoury stain across the smart white PTA blouse of her life.

Listen, I tell them all in my head, if it wasn't me it would be someone else. When he chucked his girlfriend, she might have forwarded his texts and emails to Charlotte. She might have sent her the photos and the phone recordings of their dirty talk.

Or she might have got pregnant: a split condom, a forgotten pill, a hasty tumble on the stairs before the cap was inserted.

Or Charlotte could have walked in on them. Nick's eyes widening in horror as she pushed open the bedroom door, the unsuspecting girl on her hard-working knees, giving it her all and thinking his sudden gasp signals approaching climax rather than simple shock at being discovered by his wife.

Or maybe it would be nothing quite so dramatic. A credit card bill opened in error, a hotel receipt, Nick punched in the face by the man he was cuckolding. Everything spills out eventually. Like Mike says when he's talking about his time in the Met, 'Nothing stays buried for ever.'

This should be a golden age for Charlotte. A dream scenario. The marriage is dead, and she has the moral high ground all to herself. In another year or two maybe she would have been playing Lady Chatterley with some suburban Mellors, and then it would have been Nick getting all the playground sympathy.

You don't fool me, Charlotte. The twenty-something window cleaner. The unexpectedly hard-bodied Baron Hard-up in the am-dram panto. That dad you nodded at in the library, the one with sad eyes, who you just knew would be up for it if you weren't married and he wasn't married . . . All of them fuses waiting to be lit. Right now, you're emphatically in the right. You're a Wronged Wife with the privileges that come with that. That's something to be celebrated. Milk it. Why all the hairy eyeballs in the playground? Why snub the messenger? Not that this messenger cares particularly.

Mrs Bingley's being nice however. She almost seems apologetic, though perhaps I'm fooling myself. But her bracelets jangle cheerily and her voice chimes along with them. Exclusion is not mentioned. Emotional abuse is not mentioned. Avoidant Personality Disorder is not mentioned. Instead Oscar's efforts to reach the sun are highly praised, despite him not actually managing to get there yet. Perhaps this is the lesson: being good, being *appropriate*, is a life-long journey and we never actually reach the final destination. We are forever working towards the target of inner grace and in the act of striving without hope is the pure A-star virtue to be found. Seems the sort of thing a church school would go for. Proper depressing though.

But things are improving. Oscar doesn't seem to have threatened to eviscerate anyone recently. And he gets given a part in the Christmas production, a surreal take on the Nativity called *The Grumpy Snowman*. The basic plot is that a snowman, renowned for his misanthropic nature, is called upon to attend the birth of Jesus in Bethlehem. Despite the heat and his clear mobility issues, he travels there, whereupon he is overcome by joy at the sight of our little saviour and throws off grumpiness for ever and ever amen. Mad, isn't it? Oscar is a shepherd, a perfectly respectable cameo part. Millie, I notice, has been cast as the Christmas Pudding which, together with her parents' painful and messily imminent divorce, should ensure some severe anorexia earlier rather than later.

* * *

Milan is back so I don't see Lucy for a bit. I text her once or twice. *How are you?* I say. Seconds later my phone pings and, despite myself, my heart races. *Fine* she says. No kiss or anything. She's fine. Just fine.

I'm still finding it hard to sleep. Drink helps a bit and porn helps, but all the pornography on the web is getting to be like the music on my phone. I'm using it all up. It's getting boring. I reckon that pretty soon I'll have seen everything that you can get for free that isn't actually weird. And sometimes I find myself drifting off. Not to sleep, but into inconsequential thoughts. There can be a hardcore amateur orgy happening centimetres from my nose and I find myself thinking about human swine flu or whether tomorrow is the day the bin men take the plastic, or whether it's the day they take the food-waste.

I determinedly make the effort, trawling through the internet, cock in hand, looking for something exciting, a guaranteed turn-on. And in the end it's usually girls kissing. Not licking, fucking, lactating or tying each other up. Just two ordinary girls kissing with their clothes on. It's the kind of thing I can't tell anyone. But I watch and come and afterwards sometimes I sleep and sometimes I have to do it again. Drink. Girls kissing. A desperate orgasm and, finally, finally, uneasy dreams until it's the morning and Oscar crawls into bed, damp and smelling of piss. He still hasn't sorted that.

One night I get out the screwed-up scrap of paper that Lyndon shoved in my pocket. I smooth it out, half hoping that I won't be able to decode Lyndon's handwriting. It's an outer London address, not too complicated, and then I throw the paper away. I don't put it in the bin, I just fling it out of the front door. As I open it, I half think I might see him lurking across the street as he has before. Wouldn't that be weird? Letting the wet night breeze take his address

161

into the kingdom of nowhere, while he stood and watched me do it.

But he's not there. No one's there.

The night is cold and wet and everyone is asleep. There are no lights in the houses of Oaks Avenue. Just the street lamps standing guard over the hedges, and the family saloons, and the general brooding semi-detachedness of the road. And I wonder if the address can be right because if I've been seeing Aidan here in Southwood – in the Fun Junction, in Oaks Avenue, across the fucking street – how, exactly, is he managing that commute?

It hurts my head to think about it, and I go back inside and have another drink and think that maybe I will have forgotten the address by morning.

I haven't. I haven't.

The letter arrives on a Saturday. A big brown bulky rectangle stamped important and confidential, and I ignore it at first because I assume it's more legal crap about gas and electricity and all that.

But it sits there on top of the pile radiating malignant energy. It sits on the hall chair like a tumour. Blind and evil and killing me. In the end I tell myself that hey-ho it might not even be from the utilities, it might just be stuff from Sussex. Probably is, in fact. Harmless crap about lectures and half-price veggie burgers and student discounts on the slot machines on the pier, and so I force myself to open it.

It isn't anything like that. 'Course it isn't. It's a tumour after all. It's a pack of stuff from the family court and when you boil it all down it's telling me that Toni wants custody of Oscar. It also tells me that Essex Social Services will be supporting her application based on the report written by the social workers assigned to the case, which took evidence from all parties concerned with the welfare of Oscar, including the school. And including Dean bastard Hessenthaler who has been concerned with Oscar's welfare for about a minute. So it turns out that Mrs Bingley's recent warmth wasn't contrition: it was guilt and shame. Zara and Penny too – all smiles and nods when they left the house, knowing they were going to stitch me up back at the office later.

I phone Toni and get the voicemail. I phone the social services number, knowing that there won't be anyone in but needing to do something. I get halfway through an abusive message when I realise that it will no doubt be added to the ammunition to be fired at me in court, so I apologise and hang up even if the damage has almost certainly been done.

I phone Lucy and get her voicemail too.

I phone Alfie and he's sympathetic. Ish. But I hear him choosing his words so carefully, like a guy picking his way through a minefield, and I guess that while he might sympathise with me, he agrees with them. Alfie thinks Oscar will be better off with Toni. I try to tell him what a tosser Dean is, but I find myself getting confused and I can hear Alfie getting bored. I can practically feel his shrug down the phone. He's no help.

I take Oscar into town and buy him new socks and pants and stuff like that. I buy him an England football shirt 'cos it's reduced in JJB. Oscar himself is dubious. He's torn.

'I don't think Mum would let me wear this.' His forehead crinkling. But he wants it anyway, I can tell.

'Mum's not here is she?' I say, and then wish I hadn't. I take him off for a pizza and an ice cream.

Someone cracked. Someone heeded the graffiti. Someone grassed up Aidan Jebb. The police said it would happen.

163

And the someone in question was his mum. The first person to phone in and claim the community action trust award was Rosie. And once the first call was in the floodgates open. Pretty soon the hotline was swamped, ringing off the wall as a stream of mates, fellow gang members, drug-taking associates and casual acquaintances felt a sudden urge to do their civic duty. It was like Children in Need for a while there.

But Aidan wasn't stupid. He was already gone ghost. No notes, no nothing but he was off. He took a rucksack and his mum's handbag and when Rosie went into his room she found the CD in the player and played it over and over. That old Beatles tune. *If she's beside me/I will never care . . .* And she cried and thought about the day he'd performed it live. His shining face. His wonky-toothed smile. The way he'd winked and given her a thumbs up as the choir were shuffling into position. Like a little Macca himself.

He hadn't been nervous. Rosie was. Rosie had been shitting herself, even though she'd calmed herself down with a couple of Kronenbergs. There had been some humming to get the note and then he'd just opened his mouth and out had come this magic. And afterwards he'd just grinned and sat back in his place like he'd done some-thing ordinary. Like he'd just had a piss or something. And afterwards Rosie had got cross because he just accepted all her compliments with a shrug and when she'd asked him how he'd wanted to celebrate he'd just said, 'Can we go home and watch TV, Mum? Just me and you?' Which was taking the mick because he knew that Titus was meant to be coming round and Titus would want to celebrate too, wouldn't he?

Rosie had been a shit mum, she knew it, and it was too late for Aidan. Maybe if she had another one . . . And then she was crying again and she couldn't have said whether it was for herself, or for Aidan, or for Titus or for all the children she hadn't had, or the ones that she might have had, or the ones she might still have, or the state of the fucking world. Aidan had weighed two pounds. He should have died, like Callum. He should have died.

I keep Oscar off school for a few days. I can't face Mrs Bingley, or the playground. I try and get hold of Toni but she's avoiding me, and so I just send a couple of emails to Dean. I've got to do something and I know they'll get back to Toni, so I say exactly what I think about her and him and their scheming, and I make it very clear that they're not going to get Oscar, or any of Mum's money come to that. And I go and see Mr Waddington.

Mr Waddington looks even more tired than he did the last time and he explains that he's not a family law specialist, but that he will give me some professional advice anyway pro bono. He takes a deep breath and runs his hand over his head, smoothing back the long, wispy and unruly strands of hair back in place. Mr Waddington must be the last person in Britain to have the full Bobby Charlton comb-over. It looks ridiculous, but it does fit the image of the steady small-town lawyer. It fits the look. Mr Waddington wears a quality made-to-measure, dark navy, herring-bone three-piece suit so maybe the comb-over is part of the look. Maybe it's actually good for business, part of a deliberate style put together by an image consultant to shout: Boring. Unimaginative. Old school. Trustworthy.

Mr Waddington looks at me steadily and says, 'I feel that on the balance of probabilities, the court may very well award residency to your aunt and that in the light of this perhaps your interests – and those of your brother – will be

165

best served by coming to some private accommodation with her.'

I trash his office.

There is something about the way those grey eyes blink behind his glasses, something about the deliberate, careful modulation of his voice that just makes me flip. The red mist descends and I begin by sweeping all the papers and books off his desk. Then I kick the glass out of this bow-legged Victorian cabinet thing that stands against the wall, and smash the decorative plates that are stored inside.

It only takes a couple of seconds and Mr Waddington doesn't stop me, and I'm starting on pulling the books from the bookcases and chucking them on the floor, but his secretary rushes in and starts shrieking and then some other solicitors run in and some bloke gets me on the ground, and holds me down with his full weight. He's breathing hard and I can smell the sour industrial max-pax office coffee on his breath, and suddenly I feel exhausted, and Mr Waddington must have said something because the bloke gets off me and I stand up, feeling stupid. And everyone shuffles away from me, but they look sort of wary and on edge in case I kick off again, but Mr Waddington just puts his hand on my shoulder and leaves it there. I want to shake it off, but I don't. Something about those soft grey eyes stops me.

'Billy,' he says. 'Call me if you need to talk, OK. Or if you think I can help.' His voice is as grey and mild as his eyes, and he maintains a professional, neutral modulation. He puts a little card in the pocket of my shirt.

Everyone watches in silence as I turn and leave the office. Outside, I put my face up to the inevitable rain and shout as loud as I can to an indifferent sky. 'Fuckfuckfuckfuck.' The sky doesn't care. How many stupid human performances

166

has it seen? Billions upon billions. The sky has seen it all and it's all boring.

Lucy comes round. She's got a new look. She's gone bobbed. The biro has gone from her hair. And the hair is a sober brunette. She's wearing sixties girl-group jeans and a dark denim shirt that contrasts with the milky whiteness of her skin. She looks unbelievably wholesome. Good enough to eat.

Her eyes widen when she sees me.

'Christ, Billy,' she says. 'You look terrible.'

I shrug. 'Feel all right. I like the hair.'

'A change is as good as and all that,' she says. 'I'll make some soup.'

And Lucy nips to the shops and comes back with vegetables and makes soup and then she insists on putting Oscar to bed. She reads him AA Milne and my heart cracks as she reads about James James Morrison Morrison Weatherby George Dupree, the kid who disappears because he went down to the end of the town on his own.

I can hear Oscar giggling, but I'm sure no children's poet would be quite so flip about child abduction these days. And now we all know, don't we, about the emotional abuse that Christopher Robin suffered? How he was forced to stay in the bluebell woods of childhood with Tigger and Pooh and fucking Piglet, forced to grow old without growing up. Kept by his dad's readers in the cellar of the whole country's imagination. A reluctant national treasure, now and for ever six, forced to drag around the sandy-haired, button-nosed, freckle-faced ghost of himself from his sixth birthday till the day he died. Unable to get on or get laid because Christopher Robin and Pooh bear were always looking on.

167

Not his dad's fault. Not anyone's fault. But abuse all the same.

And Lucy runs a bath and makes me get in it and she soaps me all over, taking as much care and time on my back and my shoulders as she does on my straining cock.

And when I get out she dries me, and makes me lie on my front on my bed and massages me, and when I think I can't take any more, when I think I'll explode, she turns me over and puts me in her mouth and it could be a short time or a long time, I don't know, and then I empty myself into her. And when I finish, she laughs and she has a pale pathway of my spunk marking a route down her chin which she wipes off with the back of her hand.

And then she says, 'I'll make a cup of tea, shall I?' and when she comes back, I'm almost asleep but I open my eyes and say, 'What was that all about, Lucy? Pity fuck?'

And she purses her lips and then I can see her decide not to be annoyed and she smiles and shows all those teeth.

'More a sympathy blow job. Big difference.'

'You still did it just out of kindness,' I say.

'Just nothing,' she says. 'What you've got to realise, Billy Smith, is that kindness is all right. Kindness is good.'

Chapter Ten

A man walks into the expansive, airy lobby of his Tudor farmhouse in the village of Barton-in-the-Beans, Leicestershire. Crazy name, crazy place. It's the quietest, darkest hour, just before three in the morning, but he's not the only one awake. Upstairs in her attic room his daughter, his only child, Teagan, is MSN-ing her mates and it's all OMG, he didn't, you didn't and LMFAO and smiley, smiley faces and all that. It's so still that the man can hear her pecking at her keyboard from downstairs.

He looks up at the CCTV. He doesn't smile or wave, but he gives it a hard stare. He sighs, looks around the hall. He's had this place three years, poured a fortune into it. It's been here since 1639, seen civil wars and world wars and plagues and crop failures. He rescued it from dereliction and now it's all en-suited up. It's been a magazine feature. Not *Life! Death! Prizes!* though it will get there. It's been in *Living etc*.

The man runs a sweaty hand through his grey hair. He's a handsome man, everyone says so. Carrying a few pounds, but generous and a good neighbour. And a laugh. Only today he was at a barbie and in cracking form, telling stories laughing, joking. He brought a case of beers. Quality lager, none of your crap.

This man is David Fairweather who took over his dad's crappy little handyman business and turned it into the biggest building firm in this part of Leicestershire. He works hard, plays hard. Doesn't take losing well. At the tennis club, he'll chuck his racquet about, cheat about line calls, huff and puff and swear. Most of the members think it's funny.

David Fairweather picks up his shotgun, the one he uses when he hosts shooting parties on his estate – he's a man with aspirations – and he goes up the polished stone of the staircase. He goes along the carpeted hall. He goes up another set of twisting, spiral stairs, up to the big attic room where Teagan sits typing ☺ ☺ ☺ to her mate Olivia Horsfall. Livvy Horsfall has just confessed that she has done it for the first time, just that night with Ian Baker. Teagan thinks that's cool. Ian Baker is fit as fuck.

David Fairweather, 44, pauses outside her room and reads, for the last time, the note hanging from her door-knob. It's a sign taken from a Prague hotel and shows a sketch of a sleeping baby and underneath are the words *Prosim, Neruste!* And to this Teagan has added in lovely schoolgirl italics: *AKA Get Lost!!!!!!*

The sign is a souvenir from the county youth orchestra tour to the Czech Republic. Teagan plays clarinet. She's good. Could get grade eight next year if she keeps up with the lessons and the practice.

The sign twists a bit. There's a draught somewhere, but that's OK – these old houses need ventilation.

David Fairweather puts his hand on the door-handle. Teagan Fairweather, 15, has time to type *OMG! Pops alert* before her father takes a quick step inside and fires both barrels into her chest as she turns to face him. Teagan is blasted off her chair and against the wall, smashing the PC off her desk as she does so. A mile away, Livvy smiles. She types *T you are so in the poo. You'll be grounded for a week*. Teagan is dead before she hits the floor. Or at least we hope so.

No one hears the shots. The house is a mile and a half from any neighbours. Ruth Fairweather, David's childhood sweetheart and wife of twenty years, is in the house, but she was strangled as she slept just over an hour ago.

David knows what he has to do now. He has to shoot Teagan's horses, Muffin and Sheldon. He has to splash petrol around the house, make sure it goes everywhere. He has to park a tractor across the lane to the house. He has to barricade the doors. He has to shoot his dogs, Barley and McGrew. He has to start several fires. Last of all he has to go back up to the attic room and lie down next to Teagan and then he has to wait.

And as I read about it I can see it all happening. A disaster movie in my head. I see the paint shrivelling, the walls blackening, the glass fizzing into tiny shards like cava bubbles. The bodies turning to ashes and dust. It's an option for me. It's a viable plan B.

In *Life! Death! Prizes!* going down in flames is a common reaction to the prospect of losing everything. Perhaps the most common reaction of all. If I can't have it, no one else will either. A blazing fuck you to the world. David Fairweather owed half a mill to the taxman. Well, the bastards want it, they can have it.

Every week I read of lovers killed, babies gassed, houses turned into blackened ceremonial pyres, all because a big boy was asked to share his toys. No one wants to share toys. The British Empire clinging on to its colonies, Hitler playing Risk with real countries and real people, flipping the board over when he loses. Goebbels laying out his babies like dead blue tit chicks. It's the law of the playground. No big psychological mystery behind it.

171

In the scheme of things, taking Oscar with me in this way would be pretty mild. That urge to lay waste to everything around you rather than lose what you love. I get that. I totally get that. Basically no one – no man anyway – ever grows up. That's the message from *Life! Death! Prizes!*

One lunchtime I'm nipping out for a burger – it's the fuel I need now – Big King double whoppers, bacon double cheeseburgers, Tex-Mex onion rings, the works. I always go large. The first mouthful is a sort of ecstasy, but after that it's kind of disgusting but I make the effort. I persist. Persistence, after all, is everything.

Mum was always quoting this guy Calvin Coolidge. I can hear her now, banging on, fixing me with a laughing eye. Declaiming.

'Nothing in the world can take the place of Persistence. Talent will not; nothing is more common than unsuccessful men with talent. Genius will not; unrewarded genius is almost a proverb. Education will not; the world is full of educated derelicts. Persistence and determination alone are omnipotent. The slogan "Press On" has solved, and always will solve, the problems of the human race.' Yeah, yeah.

But I agree with her. It was persistence that kept me trying weed, when the first few drags made me feel like puking. It was persistence that kept me drinking Stella, despite thinking it tasted like toilet cleaner when I first tried it. And, now, I press on at BK every lunchtime, chewing through the plastic cheese, the strange hot sweetness of the meat. Crunching through the special southern-recipe fries and generally getting myself addicted. By eleven every morning I start craving high-fat, high-salt fried meat with all the trimmings.

I do vary the diet. It's not always BK, sometimes it's KFC,

sometimes I go to Kev's Kabin, the little shack near the bus station, which will do you an all-day Truckers' breakfast for £3.40. You've got to support small businesses where you can.

It's in Kev's Kabin that I meet Toni's ex, Frankie. He's cheerful at first and gives me the full-on buddy-buddy stuff. The friendly punch on the arm that is a little too hard. The laugh that's a little too loud. He ruffles my hair, like I was six.

'Hi Frankie,' I say. 'How are you?'

'Never better my friend, never better.'

Then he starts crying. I look around and I know that everyone in Kev's has noticed by the way they are all suddenly staring into their tea or their *Daily Star*s. By the sudden hush. By the way a kid gets slapped for saying, 'Mummy why is that man crying?'

It turns out that by 'Never better', Frankie means 'Total crap'. He has fallen apart without Toni. He can't sleep, he can't eat. I can't help myself – I look at his plate where the remains of the full English smear his plate. He follows my look. 'I don't eat for ages. And then I eat rubbish.' He says that he can't understand it, that he thought they would be together for ever. That he thought the world of Toni, that he would do anything for her.

And yeah, I think, anything as long as it didn't inconvenience you. Anything except make her feel easy about herself, anything except let her have a baby, anything except compliment her in public. Anything except tidy up, stop watching TV, or drinking. Anything except anything really. But what could you do? You couldn't stop being Frankie, could you?

But he does look terrible. His teeth are yellowy, his face pale and papery and he has dark circles under his eyes.

173

Shadows that fail to mask the lines. He seems to have lost more hair. He has grey stubble. He has egg yolk on his shirt collar. He is not looking his best.

I try to sympathise.

'And Dean's a bit of a wanker isn't he?' I say.

He looks stricken. 'Who?' he says.

Oh shit. He doesn't know. I stare into my mug. There's a tiny fly struggling in there. I watch the fly persist. I watch it press on. I watch it give it up and die. I don't say anything else. I don't need to.

'Dean Hessenthaler? Suzanne's ex?' And he slumps in his chair. 'Dean Hessenthaler. Christ.' He looked utterly defeated before, but now he's discovered a whole new universe of pain.

'Are you sure?' he says at last.

'Not really,' I say. 'But it's a possibility. Sorry mate.'

He gathers himself up. 'Yeah well. You better not be lying, that's all. You better not be messing with me.' And I look up and meet his eye. He hates me. He hates me for seeing him crying. He hates me for knowing about his weakness and sorrow. He hates me the way that all victims hate all witnesses.

Frankie blows his nose into a napkin. He makes a stretch for dignity. Grabs for it. Almost gets hold of it.

'Did you see the football last night?'

'No,' I say. 'Who won?' His face crumples again. He doesn't know. He can't remember.

Lunchtime in the Social History Museum. I'm on the desk while Jenny and Mike are taking lunch out together. They do this more and more these days. This leaves me on my own with a party of primary school kids. They want to know everything. And it occurs to me that schools do a

174

good job of knocking enthusiasm for learning out of kids. Take any kid Oscar's age and they are desperate to learn. They want to know how the whale became and all that. Why the sun is and who put it there. Not to mention who dreamt up the concept of the lawnmower, which I am able to tell them of course.

By age eleven half those kids are still putting their hands up, straining to get smiley faces stickers on their sweat-shirts, while the other half are practising the ancient folk crafts of rolling doobies and sniffing donkey tranquillisers. By sixteen, there's an elite squad of mummy's little darlings learning dressage and the oboe, while the majority swallow their rage and their boredom and dream of high-school berserking sessions. Some of them graduate to coshing grannies outside the post office on pension day.

Musing on all this means I almost miss him. Aidan Jebb standing like a twisted saint amid happy and inquisitive cherubim. He's standing with his arsenic face, his arsenic eyes and his dead hair, staring over. I think I can smell the vermin reek of him from here. I can taste it almost. There's something in my mouth anyway. A rancid scalding that makes me heave and gag. My stomach cramps. I have to remember to breathe.

I get myself together. I ease myself off my high stool. I have no plan. I'm going to rely on pure instinct and then a voice says, 'How much are these?' I glance down. A moon-faced girl – round face, round eyes, round specs, little hoop of a mouth – is holding up one of the speciality iron-on badges. 'You can have it,' I say. But it's too late, by the time I look back Jebb's gone, leaving just an extra chill in the church and a watery bubbling in my guts.

The girl speaks again. 'Cor, thanks ever so much,' she says, like she's in the fucking Famous Five or something.

She even has a little round voice to go with her glasses. And then she says, 'Gosh, are you all right? You look like you just thought of something ever so bad.'

'I wonder what he wants,' I say and there's something in my voice because the little round-faced girl suddenly turns around and jogs back to her teacher and spends the rest of the visit to the museum swinging from her hand and sucking her thumb. I spend the rest of the day lost in fantasies of murderous violence and am so useless that Mike virtually begs me to go home.

It had to happen, so it does. There's an invasion on my northern shores. Some jealous fuck, no doubt pissed off at his life as a call centre drone in downtown Lahore or wherever, is after a slice of my Empire action. Well, I'm ready for him. I've prepared a flexible defence. And I have reserves to rush there. I have my best generals, my most fanatical and loyal guards. All of them desperate for glory and ready to die for their leader. These guys are like the SS, only less sensitive. Less inclined to do small-talk and social niceties. Shock and awe. If this guy drops a hundred bombs on me, I'll drop a thousand on him. If he drops a thousand on me, I'll drop a million on him. This little slumdog will rue the day. I'll have his people eating mud before the end of the week. Bring it on.

In the museum Mike is mourning the absence of Lyndon. He doesn't say anything, but he's more grumpy and argumentative than ever. Irascible, that's what he is. He complains about everything all the time, whereas before it was just most things most of the time. He gets into rows with management over little things. An email comes round to all employees from the Chief Executive's office suggesting that in these cost-conscious times we all be that little bit more aware of pressures on budgets. Perhaps if we're arranging a meeting we could bring our own Hobnobs. I think this is funny. Jen thinks this is funny. Mike doesn't think it's funny. He thinks it's an outrage. A bleeding liberty.

'The guy who dreamt up that email, he's on £90K a year. That's quite a few packets of Hobnobs right there. The council tax has gone up eleven per cent in the last three years. Eleven per cent! But we only get our rubbish picked up once a fortnight now instead of once a week. Pathetic.'

And whereas once he would have just moaned to us and we'd have had a laugh and forgotten about it, now he has to phone the Chief Exec's office and give the man himself a piece of his mind. Jen is worried. 'He'll get himself fired,' she says. I'm not so worried about this. Anyone who talks to Mike is in no doubt that here is a man who knows his rights, who is more than a match for any disciplinary tribunal. No, I'm worried he'll give himself a heart attack, a stroke, an embolism. Something nastily cardiovascular anyway.

The day after the Hobnob email we get a visit from the Cultural Services Manager. This is a rare event. Normally we are left alone by management. Free to quietly do our own thing. This is what Mike's new found belligerence has led to I think, we've popped up on someone's radar. We're on someone's to do list, someone's business development plan.

Anna Mabbutt is a vivacious thirty-five-year-old with unruly hair, who seems delighted by the museum.

'This is great,' she says. 'This place is like a little secret. We should definitely make more use of it. What an asset.' She congratulates us on how well everything has been kept. I show her round and she shivers with delight at the Viking skin and gasps at the story of Mary and Joe Goddard. She loves the crypt with our witch-finder models and is charmed by the lawnmower. 'And you still sell these iron-on badges!' she exclaims when we get to our little gift shop area. 'I used to collect these. This place is just so, so great.'

And she shakes her mane of curly, cavalier hair and dips her Hobnob into the fair trade decaff we've made for her.

Mike produces the biscuits sort of like an offering, like it was a religious thing. He says, 'I brought these from home you know.' But Anna, she wasn't phased by that. She just laughs again and says, 'You got that email too? Mad wasn't it?'

Now she's all businesslike and saying, 'What's your yearly footfall like? Roughly. To the nearest thousand.'

And we all look at each other because we don't know, not even roughly, though it can't be massive. Nowhere near even a single thousand.

Anna says, 'Don't worry. I can look it up later, when I'm back in my office.' And she starts up again singing the praises of our 'fantastic resource', which has 'such potential'. We are all of us convinced that this enthusiasm can't lead to anything good.

We're chilling one evening, Oscar and me, watching a bit of *Pirates of the Caribbean* before bed, when there's a fierce knock at the front door. The bell died weeks ago, so everyone has to knock pretty fiercely to be heard over the telly or the music, but this is way too fierce to answer. Oscar looks at me and I smile back. 'Hey, big man. Don't worry. If we wait long enough, they'll go away.'

I already have an idea who it might be. I've had that British Gas on the phone, and Npower, and the District Council and American Express, and HSBC. People ringing

178

from India and from Belfast and God knows where else about a few quids' worth of unpaid stuff in a little Essex town, a million miles from them. You can't pay bullies anyway. That's the first thing you learn in the playground. Give the bigger boy your bun money on day one and you'll never ever get to enjoy a bun of your own. And Oscar and me, we need our buns. Our little comforts.

The Saxons all knew this. They tried to buy off the Vikings and ended up having to nail their skins to the church door in order to be left alone.

Whoever this bully is, he's imbibed Calvin Coolidge's advice and just keeps going. Knocking, knocking, knocking. It's like GCSE *Macbeth* all over again. And the gasman or whoever, ain't waking anyone either.

'Wake Duncan with thy knocking I would thou couldst,' I whisper and Oscar looks at me like I'm mad. Of course he does. It is a bit mad I guess.

'Who's Duncan?' he says and then, 'Maybe we should open the door, Billy.' He's got his Being Brave voice on.

But we don't have to because just then there's a splintering, tearing sound and we have to do something.

'Upstairs Oscar, now,' I say, and he scurries off and I race down the hall and get there in time to see the door come open with a bang and I stare at a tiny woman in her mid-twenties I guess, who blinks back at me from behind protective eye-wear.

'What's going on?' I begin and the girl holds up a little plastic wallet.

'British Gas,' she says. She's doing OK, sounding tough enough, but I know she's got her Being Brave voice on too. 'We sent a letter. Several letters.' She takes a breath. 'I've come to cut you off.'

Since we're both play-acting here I put on my most

179

furious I Know My Rights voice and say, 'Like hell. You need a court order. So fucking fuck off before I call the police. Coming here frightening people. There's a little kid upstairs you know.'

The girl swallows hard. Her long, white throat ripples like some kind of weird cloud formation. Like some kind of smoke signal.

'I have a warrant Mr Smith, and we have exhausted all reasonable means of contacting you. And I must tell you that if you attempt to refuse me entry then I will be calling the police myself.' She doesn't sound convinced by any of this. She also sounds miserable. Excellent. Sunshine.

'Enjoy your job do you?' I say, and I walk past her and walk down the drive into Oaks Avenue. I can feel her eyes on me all the way. As far as I can tell she doesn't go into the house and begin twisting knobs and sawing at pipes, or whatever these gangsters have to do.

When I'm in the road I start shouting. Proper yelling.

'THERE'S A WOMAN HERE WANTS TO CUT OFF MY GAS.' This is something I've learned from reading the welfare rights leaflets we stock in the museum. Make a public fuss. And it works because I hear a panicked stumble behind me.

'You can't do this,' she hisses.

'CAN'T DO WHAT, MISS?' I bellow. 'CAN'T TELL THE WORLD THAT THE AUTHORITIES ARE HERE TO LEAVE ME AND MY SIX-YEAR-OLD BROTHER WITHOUT HEAT, OR ANY MEANS OF COOKING IN THE MIDDLE OF WINTER. WITH CHRISTMAS COMING UP?'

'We sent you letters.' She has raised her voice a bit, but she's going to come off second best in this game and she knows it. I don't think she was a GCSE drama girl at

180

school, though I can see her doing stage management, she has that kind of nervy efficiency about her.

This is suburban England, so there is no sign that anyone in Oaks Avenue has taken any notice. Our only audience so far has been the blind hedges and the sleeping cars. If this had been one of the rough estates, I'm sure a little lynch mob would have gathered by now. That won't happen here, but she doesn't know that. I wonder if Aidan Jebb is watching all this. I feel sure he is. Little chicken-shit. I raise my voice even more. Maybe I can flush him out.

'I CAN'T BELIEVE YOU PEOPLE,' I begin again, shouting so loud I feel a rip in my throat.

'Stop it,' she says. And she looks like she's going to say something else, but she doesn't. She opens and closes her mouth silently, like a big stupid fish.

Oscar appears and clings to my leg. I see him through her eyes and see how frail he seems, how thin, though I happen to know that he's as tough as old boots. But it's a useful look right at the moment. He's got that whole Oliver Twist thing going on. She takes a long moment and then says, 'Mr Smith, if you are having difficulty paying your bill I can give you the number of our helpline who will explain your options. It's a freephone number so you won't . . .' And she stops again. Her voice sounds watery and wobbly, all trace of Being Brave has vanished. She squats so she's on a level with Oscar.

'What's your name?' she whispers, but Oscar just holds tighter to my leg. And gas girl sighs as she straightens up. 'Mr Smith,' she begins again, but she's interrupted by more shouting. Not from me this time.

'Hey! Hey there!' It's Mr Khan from next door who comes jogging over, cheque book already open. He's out of breath. 'How much do they owe?'

'Mr Khan please, there's no need.'

'Be quiet please, Billy.' Very forceful.

'No, honestly, I'm going to phone this number and sort it all out.'

He doesn't look at me. He keeps his eyes on gas girl. 'How much?'

Gas girl looks embarrassed. 'Er £457.39 for both gas and electric,' she says at last.

'I'm writing you a cheque for £550,' he says, 'so they will be in credit.'

'Can't take cheques,' says gas girl miserably. 'I have a debit card machine in the van though.'

'OK,' says Mr Khan, and they repair to the little pink van parked twenty metres or so away, far enough to have been out of view had I looked out of my window when the knocking first started. A transparent tactic for catching householders by surprise. Something she's learned on some training course. They really are proper bastards these people.

I don't know whether to follow them or stay where I am and in the end I opt for ushering Oscar back in the house and up to bed. I wonder what I'll do about the bust door. Locksmiths cost a fortune don't they?

Mr Khan appears hovering on the doorstep.

'Thanks mate,' I say. 'But you really didn't have to.'

He waves his hands dismissively. 'And I have called a locksmith,' he says. 'I have let him know it's an emergency, but even so he says he can't be here until tomorrow.' Now that is very easily the longest sentence Mr Khan has addressed to me. It's a world record by some distance. He shakes his head as if in sorrow at a country where the locksmiths put off work for twelve hours.

'And Billy?'

182

'Yes, Mr Khan.'

'Umar, please. Billy, your mum was . . .' He stops. Starts again. 'She was . . .' Stops again. Spreads his arms out, palms up. Lost for words. I have to rescue him. 'Yes, Mr Khan she was. Completely. I hear that a lot.'

He smiles. Then he says, 'Sort yourself out, Billy. For Oscar's sake.' And he trots off back to Mrs Khan and his perfect lawn. Sort myself out? What does he mean? I'm fine. We're fine.

The bloke who comes to fix the door in the morning is an unbearably upbeat life and soul kind of guy. Talkative. Inquisitive. Friendly. Wanting to know my views on the premiership, on immigration, on the state of the world today. And generous with his own thoughts naturally. I can't bear it. I make him a cup of tea, and then explain that I've got to get ready for work. I leave him chattering to Oscar. He seems fine with that. They both do. I can hear them gossiping away merrily while I look at my face in the mirror and think about shaving. The beard is pretty thick again and itches a bit. In the end I leave it.

He finishes up and I hear him opening and closing the door a few times to show Oscar what a fine craftsman he is, and then he shouts a cheery goodbye up the stairs.

When I come down Oscar says, 'He's a very nice man.'

I agree with as much enthusiasm as I can muster, which isn't much to be fair. And then Oscar says, 'He left me this. In case we need him again.' And holds out a little business card. I take it and put it in my pocket. It is only later, when I'm rooting around for cash in KFC, that I dig it out and look at it.

It's an undistinguished piece of flimsy card. Just black Times New Roman 12-point on white. Nothing fancy. No

183

graphics. Just a number and the name of the business. *Total Security Solutions*.

The happy locksmith guy works for Dean. Dean Hessenthaler is just another small businessman. Another entrepreneur scuffling about in the shallow end of the service sector. I almost laugh. There was me thinking he was now something big in the arm-twisting, leg-breaking business.

There's no doubt about it now. Aidan Jebb is not in London. He's here in Southwood and he's following me. I see him everywhere, always just at the fringes of my vision. Keeping almost, but not quite, out of sight. And now I know for sure it's him. It's not my mind playing tricks.

I come out of the museum and he's there lurking outside Primark, or Next, or H and bleeding M.

If I go to the park with Oscar he's often there by the bandstand or the caff. And, of course, quite often he's in Oaks Avenue watching, waiting.

He's always wearing the same stuff. The same clothes he was wearing when I saw him in the bogs at the Fun Junction. He's always hunched over and staring at the ground. When he feels my eyes on him – when he's got my attention – he straightens up and mooches off. He seems unhurried but he's quick all the same. One minute he's there, the next he's gone before I've had a chance to call the peelers or anyone.

I tell the cops about him. About being stalked. And they send someone round to take details.

The cop they send is pretty set three to be honest. PC Harding. Heavy-set and slow moving. I can picture him at school. A steady kid but none too bright, working his way through the textbooks. Doing his homework, doing what he's told. Diligent but thick. Useful as a full-back in the school football team. Solid, impassable, able to hoof the ball upfield. Getting a full set of Cs in his GCSEs and everyone being pleased with that. He's probably got an allotment.

He notes down everything I say and then says, 'Thank you for all this, Billy. I'll update our records.' How come I'm Billy? How come I'm not Mr Smith to you? That's what I think.

Then he hem-hems a couple of times. 'I have to say though, Billy, all our information points to Mr Jebb having left Southwood. Probably for one of the major urban centres, or abroad even.' *Jebb's* a fucking Mr, I think.

'I'm telling you he's following me around. He's outside in the bloody street some nights. He's harassing me.'

'You've been mistaken before though, haven't you Billy?'

'It's him.'

PC Harding sighs. Jesus, I think, how much sighing can one kid take?

'Has he approached you at all? I mean apart from the time you saw him in the Fun Junction?'

'Not really. I told you. He just stands and stares.'

PC Harding nods and puts his notebook away. 'We'll keep a look out and just phone us when you see him again.' He takes a long, slow look around the living room. 'Look after yourself, Billy,' he says.

Mike comes back from a phone conversation with Anna Mabbutt. He is not happy. 'We've got to do an event,' he says. Mike doesn't like events. They disturb the placid surface of our cosy little pond. 'Some young German artist. Uses the iconography of the English country church in his work. Not that you'd know it seeing as his work is all abstracts.' Jen and I share a smile at the easy way Mike has with the word iconography.

Turns out that Hartmet Muhl has an exhibition in the Town Hall Gallery and Anna Mabbutt would like him to give a talk at the Social History Museum.

Mike scowls. 'She wants to raise our profile. Wants us to make the best of ourselves. Wants us to let people know we can sort all their edutainment needs.'

And it's bollocks of course. No one works in museums because they want their profile raised. No one is interested in making the best of themselves. It's a ridiculous idea. And who the fuck has edutainment needs?

The week before the day of the family court hearing, Toni rings keen to sort something out. 'It's not just about Oscar, Billy. This is about helping you too. I don't understand why you're being like this.'

'I'm not being like anything.'

'Listen, Billy. You're off to university in September. That's just nine months away. You're not going to take Oscar with you, are you? Have you thought about that?'

'Why can't Oscar go to Brighton?'

'Oh behave, Billy.'

'He's going to Brighton. 'Course he is.' And I have a sudden picture of me and him roller skating along the front. Playing the machines on the pier. Mountain-boarding on the Downs. It'll be pure total sunshine. The students will love him.

'What about school? What about accommodation?'

'I believe they have schools and houses in Brighton.'

'You know what I mean.'

'I'm not sure I do, Toni. What do you mean?' I hear her take a breath. I imagine her catching Dean's eye and shaking her head. He's probably massaging her feet or something gross. *He's not playing ball. He's being difficult.*

186

'You'll still see Oscar, you know,' she says, finally. 'All the time. No one is trying to steal him. He just needs to be in a place where he has clean clothes. Where someone gets him to school on time. Makes sure he eats right. Gets him to bed at a reasonable hour. Helps him with his reading and his spelling. He needs to be looked after. And so do you.'

'So why don't you move in here?'

'What?' She sounds panicked.

'The house is all painted and lovely. You should see what I've done to it. It's very contemporary. Radiccio and arsenic. You could have Mum's room. We could take turns cooking dinner. You'd have space to work. We could share the bills.'

'Billy, I've got to tell you. I'm seeing Dean.'

I keep my voice level. 'Has he popped it in yet?'

'Don't be disgusting.'

'I'm not being disgusting. I'm not the one shagging my sister's psycho ex-boyfriend. The father of my nephew. Has he popped it in yet?'

But I don't think she heard me repeat the question. The phone is buzzing in my ear. I use 14713 to call her back.

'I saw Frankie the other day,' I say, before she can hang up again. 'He's in a right state.'

'You never liked Frankie.'

'I like him more now. Now that I know what he had to put up with.'

'Why do you have to start fights, Billy? You used to be such a nice boy.'

'See you in court, Toni,' I say.

Steve Mantel comes into the museum. He is more pissed than I have ever seen him. He's reeling, doing the drunk's waltz all over the place. You know that dance. That old one-two-three. Two wild lurches forward, followed by one

187

tottering sway backwards until you're convinced that the dancer must collapse on his arse, but somehow he pitches forward again to repeat the process. Highly edutaining, but Mike has strong views about the possibility of vomit in the museum and so he rushes to grab one arm and, knowing the routine, I move to catch the other.

Mantel makes a token effort at resistance, but he's proper feeble. He's like a big, clumsy child. His bones feel as light and as fragile as Oscar's.

As we get him to the door, he turns and fixes me with a bright, fierce eye and spits out, 'I've got grade eight piano.' And, as he spins and whirls off into the endless drizzle, he whispers it again. His voice filled with old, old pain.

'I've got grade eight piano.'

Later I say to Mike, 'Has he?'

'What?' he says.

'Steve Mantel. Has he got grade eight piano?'

'I've never known him tell a lie,' he says.

I'm rehearsing with Oscar when Lucy comes round. Not his lines from *The Grumpy Snowman* – we've got those down – but what he's going to say in the family court. We're working up quite an act, me and him. I'm proud of it and he's a natural.

Lucy is all dressed up. All blacks and whites again. She looks like a diamond-hard star. She shines.

'Night out with the girls. Thought I'd pop in here first.'

'Time for bed,' I say to Oscar.

He purses his lips, frowns. He looks like a disapproving old man.

Lucy plays a rousing sword-fighting game with Oscar and then gets him ready for bed. Does his teeth, reads to him, explains to him about nomadic tribesmen in the

Kalahari and everything. He teaches her all about the drying machine and she does that and I tidy up. And then she comes back down and we watch a bit of telly and do some old chat – catch up and all that – and we smoke a joint and have some wine. And we finish one bottle and I go and get another, but when I come back into the living room, she's standing up and putting her coat on.

'Got to go,' she says. 'The girls are waiting for me.' And I'm about to beg and plead for her to stay but she stops me. 'Don't,' she says. 'Billy, don't.' And then the space between us evaporates and she kisses me and strokes my face. 'Tell you what,' she says. 'I will do one last thing. I'll give you another shave. Could you cope with that?'

I tell her that I think I can cope, and when my face is smooth and naked I tell her that every time I shave I will think of her. I won't be able to help myself. That shaving will be something I will look forward to for the rest of my life. Lucy laughs.

'You idiot,' she says. Then she kisses me again. Then she leaves.

Chapter Eleven

I have a burst of energy and take a day off work to fill in
the tax credit forms and to register for benefits. It feels like
a victory just digging the forms out of the kitchen drawer
where I had stuffed them. See, I tell myself, it's not hard. By
the time I've got to go and collect Oscar I have just about
finished page one of form one. These forms are designed to
suck the life out of the claimant. I am not a stupid man but
these forms make me feel like I am. Reading them gives me
the mother and father of all headaches. I haven't read
anything more complex than *Life! Death! Prizes!* in yonks.

I do question one and I go for a walk. I make a mistake on
question two and I read a couple of magazines. I finally
complete question three and I tidy the house. Top to bottom,
including Mum's bedroom and Mum's office. That's how
desperate all this makes me. This is what I'm driven to.

We didn't decorate these rooms when we did the others.
Lucy wanted to, but I wouldn't let her. Now I wonder why.
They are just rooms. And not really rooms that I'm
connected with any more. In fact they don't look like real
rooms at all. I could stick little laminated cards up in the
hallway labelled *My Mother's Bedroom* and *My Mother's
Office* and they would become what they are: exhibits.

I have a flashback to Dean's stuff scattered across the
front garden. I shiver. Death has turned Mum into a sort
of performer in my memory. Everything she ever did is

now framed and frozen. Every action now looks to have had some conscious significance. Her life is a series of concepts. If I try and concentrate on the human memories of her as a person, all I get are gestures. Sets. Stages. Dialogue. Concepts. Installations.

In the bedroom I pull sheets off the bed. They still smell of Mum. They smell of Chanel and sleep. Mum was traditional in her choice of fragrance. 'Good enough for Marilyn. Good enough for me,' she said. More lines.

Unlike with Marilyn Monroe, however, Chanel wasn't all she wore in bed. Underneath the pillow are her favourite pyjamas. Tattered, Paisley men's pjs that used to hang off her. When I was younger they used to annoy me in the way that anything weird about a parent is annoying.

'Get a nightie, Mum,' I'd say. 'Get something decent.'

And she did have other stuff she wore at night, but she never got rid of the paisley pjs.

'They were a present,' she'd say. 'From someone special.'

I make a start on question three of form one and then the forms all go back in the drawer. Another day won't hurt.

And I watch *In Which We Serve* on Channel Four until it's time to pick up Oscar. The film is an old black and white one about a working class family that sticks together through the war. I keep wanting the main characters to die. And some of them do, but not enough and when they do go it's quietly and off-screen.

Curtis Hughes is arrested. Possession of a firearm. I see his pinched cartoony face staring out of the *Gazette* one Wednesday. I'd recognise it anywhere. I also recognise the gun. It looks very like the pistol that was the personal weapon of Captain Terence Mayhew MC and Bar, who

191

was killed at the second battle of Ypres in 1917, and which was presented to the Social History Museum by his grandson Philip Mayhew in 1995.

When I get to work on Thursday I check the display case labelled *Southwood and The Great War*, and sure enough we are one Smith and Wesson six-shooter light. It's gone and so has the little card giving us all the details of Captain Mayhew's short but glorious military career. Lyndon. It has to be Lyndon.

I tell Mike and it looks like his faith in humanity is finally broken by this little act of knavery. Thirty years in the Met and it's finally some ordinary work experience kid that makes him see that people are kind of crap. He goes white. Then red. For a second I think he's going to keel over. He looks like he's going to have a heart attack. He sits down heavily behind the desk.

'The little sod,' he says over and over. 'The little fucker.'

Obviously I was hoping to undermine Mike's fondness for Lyndon. Yes that was part of my aims and objectives in telling him. But now I feel like a shit. Does it really matter?

'Hey Mike,' I say. 'The gun was ancient. Ancient and bust. There's no way it would have fired, even if he could have got ammo for it.' Ammo? What am I? Nine years old?

Mike isn't comforted and he's still in shock. 'I trusted him. The little sod. I trusted him.'

'Well, that's the thing, Mike. You can't trust people.' But he's not listening to me. Of course he isn't. His heart is breaking.

My phone goes in the middle of a long headachey museum afternoon.

'He's dead, Billy. He's dead.' Alfie.

'Slow down mate. Who is?'

'Alfie Campbell. The other Alfie, the one who was in hospital with me.'

And he subsides into a generalised, liquid murmur, the sound of snot, of a tongue suddenly too big for the mouth, of words that refuse to hold any regular shape. He swallows and sighs. I'm that relieved I almost laugh.

'Billy?'

I don't know what he wants me to say.

'It's sad, Alf mate, but he was ninety-four.' Ninety-four. I feel my mouth getting old just saying it. Alfie hangs up. But I don't know what he's so mad about. Mr Campbell had a proper life. He fought Jerry on the beaches. He packed up his troubles in his old kitbag. He had an affair with a mademoiselle from Armentières, watched bluebirds over the white cliffs of Dover with the future Mrs Campbell. He saw his kids grow up. He saw his grandkids grow up. Fucking hell, even his great-grandkids aren't exactly babies any more. And he had the respect and reverence of those around him. This is all guesswork but one thing is for certain, Alfie Campbell at least had a crack at all of this, a chance. Who knows whether he lived his life well or badly, but he got his share of it and a bit more besides.

I think for a moment about the people left who lived through the war and I wonder what will happen if the last ever veteran turns out to be an unrepentant Nazi. What if he's a former concentration camp guard? What if the very last person left, the actual final indisputable winner of the war, turns out to be someone who shot a Jewish baby just to see how long she would take to bleed to death in the snow?

What if the very last Vietnam vet turns out to be that guy who's shot all those kids at My Lai? Will he still get a parade back in Motherfuck, Nebraska, his coffin draped in Old Glory? Probably.

Anna Mabbutt calls and asks for me. Mike hands the phone over with a suspicious look. Turns out that Anna wants me to host the artist guy's lecture.

'I can't do it,' she says. 'Promised the family a day out. And you'll be brilliant.'

'Mike should do it,' I protest. 'He's team leader.'

Anna laughs. A kind of snort really. 'Mike has made it very clear what he thinks of modern art. And what he thinks about Germans. I'm not sure he'd deliver the most, er, diplomatic of welcomes. No, you do it. You're good with people. You've a pleasant, friendly manner. You'll be great.' I find myself filling up. It's been a bloody long time since anyone told me I was good at anything. Anna's voice becomes serious, confiding. 'Look, Billy, museums have got to change. They've got to become more interesting to more people. They need to be relevant. And having audiences seeing fresh faces and hearing young passionate voices is part of that. We've got to re-boot the museum brand. And you can help.'

I get it. She wants me to provide the LOL. And how typically blind of the middle-aged to fall for the myth that all young people are top to toe full of the sparkliest vitality. She needs to get out more.

She tells me I just need to prepare a little speech about how lucky we are to have this Hartmet Muhl in our humble museum. Make sure everyone has a glass of wine, and get everybody out the door after an hour. Simples.

The day of the court hearing. Oscar and I in our funeral suits. I was all for him wearing a different uniform to be honest. Cords and that Next jumper Mum got him just before she died. His sensible, well-looked-after, middle-class boy look. His PTA look. But he sees me in my suit and wants to wear the same and I give in.

We have a big breakfast. Coco Pops, bacon sarnies, the works – breakfast is, after all, the most important meal of the day – rehearse for an hour or so and head off to the bus stop. We go into the Spar on the way. I want to pick up a newspaper. I have no real experience of the court system but if it's like any other kind of bureaucracy there will be quite a bit of waiting involved and I want to be prepared. As I pick up a few copies of *Life! Death! Prizes!* and *The Times* for if I get really bored, Oscar starts banging on about getting a Chupa Chups. I could easily say yes. I normally would say yes. But something about his tone annoys me, and I also wonder about what it'll look like at the hearing if the first time the authorities lay eyes on Oscar he's got candy stuck in his gob at 9.30 in the morning.

He doesn't let it lie.

As we leave the shop he moves the whingeing up a gear. Mum would have let him, he whines. Mum let him have a Chupa Chups every time they went to the Spar, it was a little treat. This might be true because Mum hardly ever went to the Spar, so it was a rule she could invent knowing that she was rarely going to have to succumb to its conditions.

When this doesn't work, Oscar switches tack. Chupa Chups are healthy he argues. They have no artificial flavourings or preservatives. To hear him tell it a Chupa Chups is a health food recommended by the Food Agency and a potential cure for the woeful state of child nutrition throughout the world. He's passionate, absurdly articulate, and it makes me laugh. And my laughing just enrages him.

The thing about Oscar is that he never has tantrums. Not outside school anyway. Not like me. Apparently I was terrible as a child. If I didn't get my way I'd shout, scream, roll on the floor. On one famous occasion I started wailing, 'You're killing me! You're killing me!' at Mum in the centre of town and someone called the police. I guess it was lucky for Mum that when two motorcycle cops appeared, looking all *Terminator*ish in their helmets and their leathers, I yelled at them too and they were too pissed off to investigate further. But Oscar has never had a tantrum. He can be moany and grumpy and clingy. He can sulk a little bit. And obviously he can needle the occasional Princess Smartypants on a sleepover, but Oscar's general response to life is to blink back the tears and get on with it.

His mum's dead. He can cope with not getting a Chupa Chups. Except today apparently.

It's like a siren going off. An inhuman scream that sounds like someone being tortured. It's a single sustained note of pure pain that makes me want to kill him. But I don't. I ignore it. My shoulders go tight and I can feel the tension settle in my stomach like a hard weight, but I swallow it all.

'Don't Oscar. Not today.'

I whisper it but in any case he's already moved rational thought. I don't think he can hear me now. His face is purple with fury and I have a sudden flashback to the moment of his birth. The moment when we all thought he was born asleep as the gravestones say.

The bus arrives and Oscar stops screaming and rockets up the stairs while I get on with paying the driver.

'Cheer up bud,' he says. 'Might never happen.'

I go upstairs and I can't see Oscar at first. He always likes to ride at the front of the top deck, likes to imagine that he's the driver. But he's not there now even though those seats are free. I scan the bus and an old lady smiles gummily at me – she looks about a thousand years old, her face a crumpled, tea-stained tissue. She points to the space next to her. Oscar is curled up there, trying to hide.

The seat behind is free and I smile back at the old lady and make my way down the aisle of the bus as it lurches into its drunken motion. As I pass Oscar he springs up and makes a dash for the front of the bus. I catch his arm. He swings at me wildly with his free hand.

'I'm not sitting with you!'

I am sensible, reasonable, as I explain that I don't mind where he sits on the top deck, but I have to be able to see him and once he's chosen his place he has to stay there. I keep my voice calm, even and pleasant as I explain that the bus will stop and start and throw him across the aisle if he's not sitting down.

I could be an air hostess calming a minor celeb high on fear and free first-class fizz. I could be a special constable explaining directions to an Alzheimered tourist. I am patient. I am good-humoured. And while I do all this, Oscar keeps trying to punch me with his balled and bony fist and yelling wordlessly to block out my speech.

Still patient, still calm, still reasonable, I stoop, pick Oscar up and haul him on to the free seat with me. His scream goes up another blood-curdling notch, his whole body thrashes spastically and he spits, though I'm not sure it's deliberate.

I can tell that the rest of the bus is deeply disturbed by what's going on. I can tell this by the way they stare straight ahead. Not talking to their neighbours and ostentatiously not watching our struggle. Only the old lady turns and smiles encouragingly at me, before turning back to face the front. Thank God for England where 'Don't Interfere' is the guiding principle of the nation.

The tightness in my shoulders is physically painful now,

197

but you wouldn't know it as I keep up a soothing stream of words. They are not really for Oscar's benefit. He's far, far beyond reason now, lost in a supernova of rage. He's a firestorm that just needs to burn itself out. My job now is to hold him tight on my lap to stop him getting free and doing himself an injury. My words are partly a mantra to keep myself calm, and partly propaganda for those on the bus. Whatever the actual words I'm supposedly addressing to Oscar, the actual message goes out to my real constituency, the fellow travellers on the bus. Don't worry, I'm saying. It's fine. We're OK. This is just a blip. You can carry on ignoring us.

God, I'm being reasonable. I deserve a medal. Really.

Three or four stops in through the morning gridlock, I'm aware of someone looming over me. Huffing and puffing like he's just run a long hard race. I look up. The figure is tall, slim, with a shaved head. Youngish, thirty maybe, he's carrying a laptop bag and wearing an M&S smart-casual jacket that has seen better days, so I guess he's not the skinhead thug his number zero haircut would suggest. His look actually says struggling writer, or trendy teacher, or – God help us – social worker. Inner city curate maybe. Something caring and/or creative for sure.

He speaks to me. At first I can't catch what he's saying – Oscar is still bawling and still twisting like a dying fish on a hook – the curate-type guy repeats himself, louder.

'Will you leave that child alone?'

'What?' I can hardly believe what I've heard. I've been Mr Patient. Mr Nice. Mr Reasonable.

The curate guy takes a sharp intake of breath. I can't hear it over the screaming, but I see his diaphragm flex. He's very tense.

'Will you leave that child alone?' He's like one of those

retro toys where you pull a string and they say a sentence. My First Key Worker or something. He puts his hand on my arm which is aching with the effort of holding on to the wriggling, squirming, incandescent bundle of wet noise that is Oscar.

And I lose it.

The red mist comes down and I shove Oscar off my lap on to the space next to me and I'm up and swinging at this interfering fuck. My first couple of punches don't connect. I hear them whistle through the air. But then I'm smacking this guy hard, and his hands are up trying to protect his stupid face as my fists land on his head and shoulders and forearms. He retreats steadily, head down and when we're near the front, up near the stairs, the bus staggers to a halt and I stumble forward into him. For a moment our faces are a centimetre away from each other. We are close enough to kiss.

'Leave my family alone,' I say. I'm panting, suddenly knackered and it comes out as a breathless hiss.

He's calm, despite the thin worm of blood that slinks from his nose into his stupid interfering mouth.

'Your family. That's a big joke.'

I move back. The mist has lifted and I don't feel angry any more. He heads off down the stairs and I turn and face the bus. It's so clear that everyone thinks I'm a nut-job. I am The Nutter On The Bus. The guy you avoid, the guy whose eyes you don't meet for fear of getting a knuckle sandwich. I can see fear and loathing on every face. Every face except Oscar's. He is silent now, looking at me with astonishment. Astonishment and awe. Love, in other words.

I shrug to the other passengers, trying to convey apology and the fact that I am, you know, actually just a reasonable straight-up geezer provoked beyond endurance. And maybe it works. Or works for a few people. As I retake my seat, the gummy old lady turns and says in a reedy but piercing soprano, 'Well, serves him right. You don't get involved with other people's children, do you?'

I don't answer. I can't. I'm too full of weeping.

The family court is designed to be as unthreatening as possible. From the outside it resembles a large, detached, retirement bungalow. And there's a preponderance of retro-chic in the car park – all those bubbly remodelled versions of vintage classics. What you could call the New Past, I suppose. All those Beetles, Minis, Fiat 500s – all telling us that this is another female domain. Another place that is all about emotional intelligence testing. My heart sinks. One thing strikes me though. These new versions of old motors, they are all much bigger, more muscular than the ones they are replacing. Just that bit more aggressive. The real past was weedy and got worn out early. Packed up after 80,000 miles. The New Past is, for all its sleek lines, much more butch, and will keep going forever. We've reinvented the past in our image, made it colder, harder, tougher than it was.

Inside it's as though we're in a thoroughly modern hospice. It's all pot plants and walls in soothing greys. Arsenic. Geometrical abstracts on the wall. Rothko. The sense of muffled murder going on in secret rooms. We could be in Switzerland.

And the family court is, after all, meant to be a neutral zone for the settling of disputes. This is where we come to have the human heat taken out of *Life! Death! Prizes!* and have it replaced by an institutional dream of head-nodding and low murmurs. Tepid battles fought with rustled papers instead of fists and teeth.

200

We're early and I'm glad because it means I can sit in a waiting room armchair and recover, let my shoulders relax a little. Oscar seems happy now. His inexplicable supernova forgotten. He's brought along a couple of unhorsed knights and they are doing the usual bow-legged hand-to-hand combat on the coffee table.

I pick up some random trauma porn mag. I've brought my own of course, but I always like to see what's lying around. This one turns out to be *Best Friend*. Of course. Family courts are a great place for dog lovers. I'm thinking of all the teen dads with their weapon-hounds who wind up here, but even though the cover story is of a woman who loves her pit bull puppy so much that she breastfeeds it, I find I can't concentrate. I'm all shaken up after the battle on the bus. And something is nagging at me about it. It's not just the fact of the fight. Or Oscar wigging out in such uncharacteristic fashion. There's something else too. Something is whispering malevolence underneath my thoughts. Something crap.

While we're sitting there a guy comes through laden with ribboned files. He's a handsome dude, looks like a TV lawyer. He greets the whole room with a smile, which freezes when he notices me and Oscar. I can't place him but Oscar notices the sudden cooling of the emotional temperature and looks up.

'Billy, look. It's Millie's dad. Hello Mr James, how are you?'

He sounds genuinely pleased to see him. Nick smiles at Oscar despite himself – people can't help smiling at that boy – and he takes a pace towards me. I close my eyes. I'm sure he's going to smack me. Go on then, I think, pretend I'm to blame. Pretend the death of your marriage was about me not about your unfaithfulness, your cheap betrayal, your shoddy lies.

What happens?

Nothing happens.

When I open my eyes again Millie's dad is gone and Oscar is frowning hard at me. Maybe that's blown it. These judges, these lawyers. They are bound to stick together. Karma. That's what Mum would think. I'm just reaping as I've sown.

When Toni arrives she is wearing her best teaching trouser suit and fiddling with her handbag. She's lost weight and the jacket hangs off her a bit. She looks nervous, stressed. Her skin is blotchy. Good.

'Hello boys,' she says with a lop-sided attempt at a smile.

'Hello Aunt Tonia,' says Oscar and moves to hug her. I've anticipated this and my hand is light on his shoulder. I squeeze and he stops. Stays where he is. 'How are you?' he says instead. Formal. Polite. Cool. Just like we've practised.

Mary and Joe Goddard's trial was quick. Mr Henry Bowker asserted that Joe Goddard had distracted him with an apparent opportunistic theft of an item – a popular novel in a cheap edition – from his window display. He had momentarily left his premises to pursue this thief, who had proved far too fleet-footed for him, and was returning breathless and disconsolate, when he had seen Mary Goddard fleeing the shop cradling several weighty volumes. Mr Warton had raised the hue and cry and the crowd had eventually cornered Mary in Chapel Lane by the Old School House. In her desperation to escape her pursuers Mary had dropped her haul, causing the volumes – which were expensive, leather-bound editions of works of much scientific interest and value – to become damaged by the mud and ordure of the gutter.

Upon hearing of his sister's arrest and incarceration

202

within the town lock-up, Joe Goddard had returned and offered himself up to the constable. Several witnesses attested to the facts of the case and neither Mary nor Joe disputed them. In fact reports made at the time spoke of the impudent silence which both maintained throughout the proceedings.

Mr Bowker pressed for an example to be made of these children who he believed had plainly planned this assault on his shop with a meticulous thoroughness that spoke of a truly ingrained wickedness.

He spoke of Mary having gone after books of particular value, thus suggesting that this was no spur of the moment theft necessitated by hunger or want. Mary must have spent several days at least assessing his stock. He further argued that many other honest traders had suffered from similar attacks and that these two were well known in the town as nuisance-makers, vagabonds and sneak thieves. A succession of worthy citizens attested to the accuracy of these remarks. The court also heard that Mary in particular had a vicious tongue and a sharp temper, and had also sold her virtue many times over despite her age. Taken together the two of them were a disease within the body of the town. A spiritual infection.

The judge – Sir Dalton Shields – had asked if any were prepared to speak up in defence of, or in mitigation for, the accused and was plainly struck by the unwillingness of any of the townsfolk, no matter how pious, to excuse the activities of these young criminals. Taking into account their history of criminality and sin, notwithstanding their tender years, the justice declared himself satisfied the children were old enough to know right from wrong and had set their hearts against honest labour, preferring instead the easy charms of the immoral life. To allow these children to scorn at justice was to weaken the whole society and he would therefore pronounce the most dreadful sentence possible. He did this, he said, with a heavy heart and with the hope that God would have mercy on their immortal souls. At which point it is said that not one but two ladies, only recently witnesses against the prisoners, did faint dead away. Mary Goddard and Joe were silent however. Mary still and pale, while her brother flushed red and looked at her seemingly for guidance, all the while chewing upon a trembling lip.

As the children were led away through the silent courtroom Justice Shields asked that the Captain of the Chelmsford Yeomanry be instructed to attend the carrying out of the sentence with his troop. Sir Shields felt they should be on hand to ensure that the will of the law be expedited without public outcry or interference.

Chapter Twelve

Our courtroom could be any room in any institution anywhere. Long table, plastic chairs. Flip-chart at the end, left over from a Health and Safety workshop judging by the spider diagram that remains marker-penned in purple on the grey of the recycled paper. The judge himself is similarly informal. Smart-casual. Top Man jacket, pale blue shirt with top button undone. Chinos. Hush puppies. We look over-dressed, Oscar, Toni and Me. Zara and Penny are there looking like keen sixth formers with their pencil cases and notepads in front of them. The other person in the room is the clerk to the court, a youngish woman in jeans and a Middlesex University Rowing Club hoodie who smiles at me and Oscar as we sit down. Pity? Sympathy? Good sign? Bad sign? My rune reading skills are rusty and there's no point speculating but I do anyway. I decide it's a good sign. Surely the clerk to the court will know which way the wind is blowing, and she's smiling.

The judge does a generalised low-wattage smile to the room, carefully avoiding turning its weak power directly at anyone in particular. He makes some crack about the weather, clears his throat and begins.

He explains that the court is here to decide primary residency rather than custody and that he is sure all parties agree that the welfare of the child, of Oscar – and he pauses to smile at the boy – is absolutely paramount. He runs through the various acts that govern the care and control of minors. He sets out the rules of engagement. He's after Queensberry rules. He wants this scrap calm, dignified, quiet, reasonable.

Zara begins. She reads her report, word for word, in a tight, stretched monotone. She describes the concerns of social services about my maturity, my ability to put Oscar's needs before my own. My apparent lack of interest in the future, my inability to plan. My refusal to accept, or even acknowledge, professional help. The fact that Oscar appears to lead a chaotic life with no structured routine. She mentions that he eats odd things at odd times and is allowed to stay up late watching movies instead of being tucked up in bed with the *Young Person's Guide to the Orchestra* or whatever.

Oscar listens to this. I know he does. He might seem to be sat oblivious, recreating the tales of King Arthur with his bandy knights, but he doesn't fool me. He's drinking it all in, this slagging of his big bro. I can see it in the stiffening of his stick-figure shoulders under that suit jacket. You wouldn't notice unless you knew him well. But I see it, and I wonder if Toni does.

The judge asks if I want to respond and I'm suddenly so tired that I can hardly be bothered. The hill seems all at once too high to climb, too steep. What's the bloody point?

Despite this, I think I demolish their arguments pretty damn effectively. My future's planned already. We're going to sell the house and then me and Oscar, sorry my lord, Oscar and I, will relocate to Brighton where I have a place at Sussex Uni. The resulting degree will enable me to get a job that pays enough to support both Oscar and myself and build a career, et cetera et cetera. While I'm at college we'll survive through a mixture of loans and benefits just like thousands of young single parent students already do. I have supportive friends and don't need professional input because, as far as I can tell, the professionals are backstabbing robots who wouldn't know emotional abuse if it chained them up in a windowless cellar. Or words to that effect.

Zara and Penny look at each other and swap 'I told you so' nods. Toni doodles on the pad in front of her. The clickety-clack of the clerk's shorthand machine is suddenly dominant. It's been chattering away beneath the talk but I only notice it now. And now that I do notice, it seems proper loud. Like someone firing a machine gun into the room.

It's Penny's turn now as she outlines the visit to Toni's place. She describes furniture, carpets, light and air, well-tended gardens. She talks recipes. It sounds less like a formal report and more like a lifestyle feature.

'For fuck's sake. Did you discuss shoes as well?'

Too late I realise I've said this out loud. But I swear the judge smiles and Penny flushes hotly and continues to recite St Toni's many and various virtues. Chief among which seems to be her stated desire to work as a partner with the social service department in developing a long-term strategy for Oscar's development.

'What about Dean?' I say. 'What about the violent, ignorant boyfriend?'

Penny looks at the judge. Clearly she expects action. Maybe she thinks it's going to be like school and that I'll be sent out if I disturb the lesson. The judge stares blandly back. Penny shuffles uncomfortably.

'Mr Dean Hessenthaler is Ms Smith's current boyfriend.'

'And is he violent and ignorant?'

'We have no grounds for believing so. And he is also Oscar's natural father.'

'And does he have access at present?'

'We believe Billy has denied Mr Hessenthaler access to Oscar despite repeated requests.'

'You,' – I point at both Zara and Penny – 'You can both call me Mr Smith if you don't mind.'

The judge looks at me. You can tell that he thinks he's landed slap bang in the middle of *Life! Death! Prizes!* with all its sticky muddle and mess. The depressing stain of it all is getting him down. You and me both, your honour. You and me both.

'Have you denied access, Mr Smith?' The light stress on Mr makes it sound sarcastic, insulting.

'Yes,' I say.

'Why is that?' the judge asks coolly.

'Because he's a dick.'

'Being a, er, an idiot isn't yet a criminal offence, Mr Smith. Nor does it disqualify one from the rights and responsibilities of fatherhood. Have you any concrete grounds for believing your aunt's partner – your brother's father – will harm Oscar?'

So many grounds. None of them concrete. Just a feeling that it is wrong to disappear for five years and then waltz back into your kid's life like a hero. Just a feeling that a bloke who will blast a football into a kid's face just because he was enjoying himself, is generally bad news. Just a feeling that someone who will get off with his dead ex-girlfriend's sister just to get access to the child he abandoned years ago, is somehow dangerous. But articulating all this is beyond me right now. Especially as I've worked out what was bugging me about the guy on the bus.

'Dean just can't be trusted,' I say. 'He's got a personality disorder.' The judge scribbles something.

Then it's Toni's turn. She says that she is sure her sister would want her to have care and control of Oscar. She also says that she'd be willing to have both of us with her: that she feels I'd also benefit from her support and guidance. She's a tad defensive about her relationship with Dean, describing it as being in its early stages but that yes, she does feel that Oscar should be given a chance to know his father and that she would like to be able to facilitate this in a safe environment. She describes her pain at seeing Oscar suffering and being so brave, such a good little soldier. And she talks about her worries over my mental health. *My* mental health.

We break for tea and juice and biscuits which we take in a strained silence. After a minute or two Toni picks up a spare knight and begins to play with Oscar. This is such a naked attempt to curry favour with the judge that I laugh. But in the sterility of the family courtroom my laughing comes out harsh and fake and everyone stares at me with wide, scared eyes, so I stop. I leave them to it. It's so transparent a ploy that the judge is bound to see through it. I close my eyes.

The git on the bus. There was something clipped and foreign about his voice, and there was something about the way he was dressed. A struggling writer look had been my first thought. But now I'm thinking European artist. I'm thinking Hartmet Muhl. I'm thinking I've just twatted the honoured guest I'm meant to be introducing to the public tomorrow.

When the court resumes, the judge is very keen to let Oscar have his say and I'm proud of him. My performance might have been ropey so far, but the little man is magnificent. He remembers his lines perfectly and also makes them sound natural. Makes them sound like things that just have to be said, rather than things we've learned. He talks about all the cool things we do together, the regular games of junior scrabble, the children's classics I read, the games of football in the park, the trips to the pool and to stately homes. When he answers a direct question of the judge he is both polite and fluent. He says that yes, he often watches films but he talks about Pixar, about *Toy Story*, *WALL-E* and *The Incredibles*, rather than *Saving Private Ryan* or *The Road* – both of which he has also seen.

The judge smiles and nods and jots the odd word down on the yellow pad in front of him. Zara and Penny stay impassive, while Toni fidgets and wriggles and sighs. She knows it's not looking easy for her.

I had worried that Oscar's meltdown on the bus would mean a meltdown in court, but I needn't have worried. Oscar parries and fences like a pure total lawyer himself. He talks about the nighttime routine. Bath, story, bed. He talks about learning his spellings after he's had his Cheerios. He tells us about his friends at school and he improvises a riff about how I'm going to start taking him back to Judo on Saturdays.

The judge nods and smiles through it all. And I relax finally, begin to feel the tightness in my shoulders ease off.

There's a wait while the judge retires to make his final decision and we're back in the waiting room performing our own separate silences. Toni is flushed and restless. Zara munches on some fishy sandwich and Penny sits, head in hands, thinking, I guess, of the damage to her career this whole episode has done. Then again, maybe she's not thinking anything at all.

I ask Toni to keep an eye on Oscar. She looks surprised but nods, and I go outside to call Anna Mabbutt. I ask her what Hartmet Muhl looks like. I've only seen one, pretty

210

crappy, picture on the flyer advertising his talk. And to be honest, it's so smudged and shadowy it could be anyone. The in-house reprographic team you see. The council-tax payers no longer tolerate forking out for anything decent done at a proper printer's.

She says, 'Oh, you know. Very German. Tall. Blond. Always looks very stern.' I ask her if it was at all possible that he'd be on the number 7 bus. 'I suppose he could be. He's staying in a B&B near the park.' Right, that settles it. It was definitely him.

'I can't do the thing tomorrow. The talk.'

'Why not?' She sounds concerned. Like she thinks I'm ill.

'Because I've just punched Herr Muhl in the face. Several times,' I say this flip, like it could be a joke. But she makes me go through the whole story and then she sighs.

'I bet you haven't but I'll come in. I should probably be there anyway. I was only going to the Fun Junction with the kids. No big deal.' That's what she says, though somehow, behind the professional briskness I get the sense that she's very pissed off indeed. That it is a big deal.

I picture a whining husband arguing that she takes her poxy council job too seriously, that she's never home. That she never makes time for him and the boys any more, that she's always thinking work, work, work. I imagine her promising that they'll do something special as a family very soon. Promise. Cross her heart and hope to die.

We're in that dead room for over an hour before the judge's clerk calls us back in. She's not smiling any more.

The judge does the usual chat about it being a sad case, said that he hopes common sense will prevail and that all parties will work out a compromise. He says that he was most struck by Oscar's testimony, which showed that he loved his brother

211

very much but also backed up the report sent in by Mrs Bingley at the school who had expressed concerns about his silence and his secretive behaviour, and her worries that Oscar wasn't being allowed the space to be a happy, normal child. And so on and so forth.

The judge gives custody – sorry, residency – to Toni with the further order that I get frequent access and a demand that the social service team monitor the situation. And there's more. But I don't really listen. Toni cries and Zara and Penny cry. Sisters doing it for themselves etc. Oscar doesn't cry. He just looks at me frowning. Maybe he doesn't take it all in. And the judge sets a date of three weeks for the handover to be completed. And Toni tries to talk about dates but I'm not having it.

I turn my back on her and call a cab. We're not going by bus again. Three weeks. Over my dead fucking body.

That night I wake coughing on the sofa. I sit up. The room is smoky with the weed-haze. And I squint into it. There's something wrong. Everything's wrong. My scalp prickles. I'm sweating. My shoulders are stiff and tight again. There's an ache in my stomach. I feel adrift in some bleak and name-less ocean. Suddenly conscious of all the suffering there has ever been in the world.

And then I see him.

That grey Lonsdale hoodie, those blue trackies, almost but not quite melding in with the crenulations of the wall. Standing still as a sentry. Aidan Jebb.

Hatred pours off him, almost visible amid the shadow and swirl of the room and I gag into the blanket I don't remember pulling over me last night. I feel a looseness in my guts and I fight against a need to shit. Christ. Oh Christ.

Jebb takes a shuffling step out of the gloom. His face is

212

mostly hidden by his hood but I see his tongue snake out and flick across his lips.

'Why didn't she give it to me? Why didn't she just give it to me?' He sounds pleading, whining, angry, bullying, all at once. His voice thin, breathy, rasping. He sounds desperate. I feel sick. There's blood roaring in my ears.

I'm ready for him. Ready for the knife or whatever. He looks frail enough in this darkness and he's not getting near Oscar.

I open my mouth. They say that you should try and make a connection in this sort of circumstance. Make your attacker see that you're a person, rather than a victim. But I'm not a person. I'm a collection of noisy fluids. I feel liquid, barely contained in my own skin. I'm in no shape for fighting.

'It would have been all right. Why didn't she give it to me?'

I close my eyes, take a breath, consciously slow my racing heart. I'm thinking. Go nuclear. Go nuclear. Kill him. Smash his murdering skull against the wall. Let's have that radiccio stain pooling on the floor. Let it all be over.

I open my eyes.

He's gone. There's nothing. Not even that smell. I stand up, switch on the lights. The room is innocuous in its everyday mess. It's just a room.

I go upstairs and check on Oscar, who purrs softly in my old cabin bed. I watch him, sleeping easily. I check the rest of the house. Leaving all the lights on. After all, my bill's in credit thanks to Mr Khan. I check the doors and windows. Everything's shut, locked and bolted. I sit heavily on my bed. I can't think about it any more. I don't want to think at all any more. I know what I have to do. It's late and it's not responsible, but while Oscar sleeps I take all the

213

remaining money from his pig and I take a PDQ cab out to the twenty-four-hour Tesco and buy the stuff I need. The essentials.

Twelve bottles of firelighter fluid for the price of ten: £22.59. A box of Cooks long matches: 79p. Some fire-retardant gloves: £5.99. And a top-of-the-range, proper sharp kitchen knife: £6.30. I get ID'd for this and have to show my driving licence. The old girl behind the check-out scrutinises this for a while. She clocks my name.

'I was sorry to hear about your mum,' she says. 'How's the little one doing?'

And I don't even know her. Small towns you see. Always someone prying and nosing about and thinking they can ask you how you are.

'He's fine,' I say. 'As well as. Top really.'

'That's great,' she says. 'Resilient, aren't they? Little ones.'

I'm back within the hour and Oscar is still sleeping easy. Nothing bad happened while I was out.

I get fired from the museum. I go into work and Anna Mabbutt is in looking both defiant and smiley, while Mike is looking so grim that at first I think it's him they're getting shot of. But no. At least not today.

Mike and Anna see me in the office. Anna does the talking. Mike just sits there, scowling.

Restructuring. Reorganising. Rethinking. Stable team. People with commitment. Cutting back on casual staff. Council-wide drive to be lean as well as green. New initiatives to make the museum a dynamic part of Southwood's robust and broad-shouldered leisure portfolio. Appreciate what you've done. Goodbye. It takes a bit longer than that. But not much.

I don't say, 'What happened to re-booting the museum brand?' I don't protest much at all, except when Anna tells me that I needn't work until the end of the month, end of the week will be fine.

'How about the end of the day?' I say. Turns out she's fine with that. In fact, it's a bit upsetting to discover just how fine she is with that.

'OK,' she says. 'And we'll still pay you up to the end of the month.'

Big woop-de-woop.

Afterwards I say to Mike, 'Thanks for sticking up for me mate. Appreciate it.' He sighs. I wish they'd all stop all that. All that sighing. It really does get on my tits. I hate it.

'Billy, you've had a scrap in the museum while a school was visiting. You've attacked a guest speaker.' So it was old Hartmet then. 'More importantly, you don't do anything while you're here. You sit around daydreaming. You're a passenger to be honest. And quite often you're not here anyway. And I don't mind actually. You've had a bloody rough time, we all know that. But we're on management radar now.'

'Yeah, because you took offence at being asked to buy your own Hobnobs.'

He ignores me. Just keeps steamrolling on. 'Anyway, they're getting rid of me too.'

'Bollocks.'

'It's true. Jen and me, we've both got to re-apply for our own jobs. And I'm sixty-six, Billy. I don't think Ms Mabbutt sees me as the future.' He sweeps his hair back. He looks exhausted. He looks old. Impossible now to imagine him going toe-to-toe with the Krays. Or strong-arming Hessenthaler come to that. And that was just a few weeks ago. He looks done in. 'Don't worry about me

215

though. I'll be OK. I've got my police pension. My golf. My band.'

'You're in a band?'

He laughs. 'Don't sound so shocked my friend. Yes, I'm in a band. The Rave-ons. Rock and Roll. Sixties stuff. We gig a lot. You should come and see us.'

Which is how I find out that Mike saw all the classic bands back in the day. The Beatles, The Stones, The Kinks, The Who, all of them. He usually saw them for free too. Standing at the back in his copper's uniform, making sure the kids didn't riot.

'Best gig I ever saw was The Faces at The Roundhouse. Brilliant show and then I came out and some toerag was trying to nick my bike. Got an arrest out of it. A good night that was.'

Later I think how wrong we are about old people. They're not the past, they are the future, whatever the Ms Mabbutts think. Old people know where the rest of us are headed. They're sending us back these clear, explicit messages about the dark and loveless place we're speeding towards. But we're just not listening. Our fingers are in our ears, our eyes are shut and we're la-la-la-ing to drown out the bad news.

At the end of the day I get the exact same send-off as Lyndon Bowers. All the anorak badges; a crisp, ATM-fresh twenty; a handshake (Mike); and a kiss on the cheek (Jen).

'Keep in touch,' she says. I nod. Maybe. Maybe not.

Mike says, 'Chin up. Remember . . .'

I interrupt, 'Yeah, yeah. Nothing fazes the A-team.'

Lucy is getting married. She comes round to tell me especially.

'So no chance of a sympathy shag then?'

216

'Not this time, Billy. At least let me get the honeymoon out of the way first. And the baby.' Not only engaged, you see, pregnant too.

'Milan's over the moon,' she says. 'And it's definitely his by the way, so don't get any funny ideas.'

'I know that you can't get pregnant from a blow job,' I say.

Lucy blushes. 'No need to be crude,' she says. There's every need, I think. But I don't say this. I say something else instead.

'Just because he's the daddy now, doesn't mean he'll always be the daddy.' And she asks me what I mean. And I tell her being a father is not about who put what where. It's about the other stuff. It's about Fireman Sam wellies and dinner money. It's about snakes and ladders and all three *Toy Stor*ies. It's about love, not spunk. Mostly, however, it's about time. About putting the hours in. That, and having £295,000 – because that's what it costs to raise a child now apparently.

'How much?' she says and does a shocked face. And then she laughs and lies down full length on the sofa, hands behind her head like someone who doesn't need to worry about anything. God, she's beautiful. What a waste.

Here's what I'm reading when the police come round. A girl in Hull pushes a bloke off the Humber Bridge. Jeremy Philip, 27, of Beverley, had been threatening suicide and Kayla Bosleigh, 17, of Anlaby, sick of him holding up the traffic, helps him along. Gets out of her car, climbs up alongside him, like she's going to try and talk him down. And gives him a huge great shove. Other people waiting in their cars cheer, and she gives them all a wave.

Meanwhile, in Motherwell, a guy gets eight years for

poisoning his children in an attempt to claim compensation from Baxter's soup. For that he gets two years for assault and five years for making false claims. Meanwhile sextuplets are born on a kitchen floor in Belfast, apparently without the help of either IVF or a midwife. And none of this is in *Life! Death! Prizes!* This is in *The Times*. The fucking *Times*.

The police are two girls: PC Loyd and PC Bone, though they introduce themselves shyly as Chloe and Rhiannon. Both in their early twenties, middle-class accents with the fresh, grassy scent of uni hockey teams still hovering around their well-scrubbed B+ faces. They have a difficult brief. It's not one which Hendon Police College or any episode of *The Bill* or *Holby Blue* could prepare you for. Yes, they are breaking the news of a death, but the script is a weird one. A bit left-field. What if I start whooping, cheering and breaking out the fizz? What do they do then? Do they accept a glass or what?

They're here to tell me that they've found a body that fits the description of Aidan Jebb. A member of the family is on the way to identify the corpse and they'll have final confirmation then, but they thought they should inform me in case I heard it from other sources. More delicately, they want to eliminate me from their enquiries. Jebb's death isn't exactly suspicious, but it is unexplained and they hope I'll understand that they have to talk to anyone who might have wished Jebb ill.

'That's gonna be a lot of talking,' I say. 'Tea?'

They look around the living room and I see the room through their orderly plod minds and yes, I can see that 86 Oaks Avenue has been more sanitary than this. I can also see them clocking the roaches stubbed into the earth in the yucca plant pot. Who gives a shit? Weed is barely a drug at all these days. If anyone really cared about it they wouldn't sell king-size Rizlas in Waitrose would they? You only use king-size Rizlas for spliffs. No one gets a sudden urge to make a really long ciggie do they? I imagine there's a decent mark up on those giant skins too.

Chloe and Rhiannon decline the tea, but I tell them that I fancy a cup and I go through to the kitchen and start clonking about with cups and shit. One of the girls – Rhiannon, I think – follows me in.

I'm keeping it together, but the honest truth is I'm proper shaken up by this news. I try and think when it was that I saw him in my bedroom. All I know for sure is that I haven't slept properly since. I've become a right Lady Macbeth, checking the doors and windows every twenty minutes, prowling from room to room, unable to put the lights out. 86 Oaks Avenue is a constant, blazing beacon of light if not hope. Maybe O and R know about Jebb's movements and this is some kind of fucked-up peeler trap that I am busy falling right into.

'When did he die?'

'The body we've found is about eleven weeks old. But the cold weather might have delayed the normal process of decomposition. It's one of the things that makes identification harder.'

No, that's not right.

I have to look at Rhiannon to check, but I'm pretty sure I haven't said this aloud.

'We believe the deceased died by hanging.' I can feel her eyes on me, watching, in a textbook GCSE policing kind of a way, for any unusual facial reactions. I concentrate on filling the kettle. Rhiannon coughs out another little nugget.

'Some personal items belonging to Mr Jebb were found at the scene, close by the body.' I don't say anything. I don't care about Jebb's personal items. If they are Jebb's. She goes on. 'The body was discovered in a derelict factory in an industrial park in Havering.' That someone, anyone, could wriggle and choke their last, and kick their legs in that spastic dance on their own, and then hang dead and unmissed in a factory unit in East London for nearly three months, makes you think. Makes you think what a long way we've come from stringing up a pair of book thieves in the marketplace. Now the kids have the decency to find a quiet spot and do it on their own with no fuss and bother. Progress. And, as for going unnoticed, unwanted, unclaimed. Well, like I say, the dead don't give a fuck do they?

At this point I'm trying to stay pretty flip about it all, but I can feel the beginnings of that ice-shelf below my ribs again. My arms itch. I can feel the stirrings of an uneasy sickness. A premonition.

Sure enough, Rhiannon takes a call as I'm showing my cop girls out. There's some nodding and murmuring. Wordless affirmations. She hangs up.

'That was the station. They have confirmed it. It's definitely Aidan Jebb.' She still doesn't know whether to console me or congratulate me. Hug me or high five me. She goes for a demure handshake. 'Let us know if you think of anything that might be helpful to us. Or if you need anything.' And she escapes.

I watch them chatting and smiling as they get into their Focus. I can't hear the words, but I can guess at them.

'That was a strange one,' Chloe is saying. 'That kid gives me the creeps.' And Rhiannon replies, 'Did you notice him staring at my tits?' 'Cos I've noticed that about women in authority positions. They always think we're looking at their breasts. But we're not. Not always.

* * *

220

Aidan Jebb took a train to Liverpool Street. It was the first train journey he'd ever been on. He bought a coke and a Twix and stared at the countryside. Fields. Cows. Sheep. Aidan hadn't really thought about these things since he was in Year Three and went to the rare breeds centre in Dedham. He didn't want to think about them now. He put his head on the table and listened to the thump of the train over the track. It was like a song, he thought. A weird, never-ending tune. He couldn't sleep, but he dozed and after a while he couldn't even do that, so he raised his head and looked around him. Everywhere people had stuff. They had headphones on, iPods, iPads, laptops, Netbooks, Nintendos, PSPs, books, dog's-bollocks phones, magazines, sandwiches, crisps, children. Stuff. Stuff that was fizzing and ticking, bleeping and singing. And people were talking about crap. Work and weather. Holidays and houses. Crap.

The train was rammed, but still he had a whole table to himself, which he was pleased about but also made him angry. Why wouldn't they sit next to him?

And then the crowds in London. Aidan imagined them all gone. He imagined a bomb that cleared the people and left the buildings. He had an idea that someone had come up with a bomb like that. They should use it. Clear the streets a bit. He was bumped and jostled and squashed and he didn't like it. And the underground: more people with their perfumes and their aftershave, their morning minty-freshness, their shiny faces, their papers. More bumping up to suits and overcoats. He was too tired for all of this. And people did this every day.

Aidan had an address and a phone number. Havering. One of Titus's old mates. Someone he used to get stuff for. But when he texted there was something not right about the text that came back. It was well friendly for a start. Aidan

221

knew what that meant. It meant they were going to grass him up. Well, fuck that.

Aidan knew what to look for. There are plenty of empty factory spaces now, and no one checks them. Some security guy might shine a light around them now and again. But security guys are all lazy fucks. And they don't want trouble. It took a while, but Aidan found the perfect spot. A place that used to make special floors for offices that needed lots of cables. A place with a little office where you could keep a bit warm, a place with a 2007 Year at a Glance Planner on the wall. Little coloured dots still attached. They were still in here making stuff, moving stuff, five years ago. Aidan crawled into his sleeping bag and waited to see if his imaginary friend would remember him. He waited to see if Jesus would come. Waited for a sign as to what he should do next. He sung himself to sleep. A thin and fragile whisper. '*I want her everywhere . . .*'

Chapter Thirteen

Empire. Situation report: fucked. Big time. It's my own fault. I went charging in. Got suckered. Done. I wouldn't have been caught like this in the playground in Chadwick Primary. My mind's not been on the developing situation. I've let my attention wander and now it's too late.

Flushed with success, drunk on blood, I let my soldiers rush over the borders in pursuit of the enemy and it's clear that that is what was expected. That was what they – the Kwoks, the Chungs, the Chens – were banking on.

And now I'm finished. The very stones of my nation are in revolt. See in Empire, it turns out that needn't simply be soldiers and tanks and steel and shells that can do you harm. If they've stockpiled enough points, if they have found the ancient spells – the cheats that trump the mere physics of bullets – then you are in big, big trouble my friend.

Get the wizards and the wolves and the faerie battalions conducting an insurgency against you and you have major problems of command and control. You're snafued big time.

So it is that my air force find themselves fighting kamikaze crows, are torn apart by eagles as big as houses and impervious to rockets. The navy is overwhelmed by waves and whales and nameless deepsea monsters. Meanwhile, the ordinary Tommies are in a war against fast-moving divisions of volcanoes. Eviscerated by ghosts. The very soil rises up against them. My enemies even control the weather. And I didn't know about this, didn't know the passwords and pathways and secret codes that enable the gifted virtual world leader to make himself Lord of Everyfuckingthing that creeps upon the Earth. To return the living world to the void and see that it is good.

And my enemies are many as well as various. It's clear that all over the world from Dhaka to Kursk, Tehran to Bulawayo, the nerd-massive have been conferring. The internet cafés of Ventiane and Port-au-Prince and pretty much every other third world dust-bowl flea-pit, or jungle shit-hole, have been hosting conferences on how to deal with Billy Smith. How to bring that arrogant, decadent Western imperialist to his knees.

Paranoia? You think so? So how come I get the same message – 'Cry Havoc' – coming into my Empire inbox thousands of times in a twenty-four-hour period, and from IP addresses all over the world? Except England. And there's fuck-all English students would be dropping Shakespeare references into their victory roll. It's only the foreign kids do that.

Takes just two days for my people to move from the late twenty-first century to the stone age. I have led them to disaster. The population goes from 100 million productive citizen-consumers to 311 savages incapable of written language and prone to terrible genetic mutations that leave them howling with agony through the long nuclear winter nights. My people spend their days scavenging amid the snow for the means of suicide.

It's a weird feeling thinking just how hated I must have become. How a random alliance of geeks from the ass-ends of the world has found satisfaction in knocking over my puny sandcastle. Of course it's not about me, it's about all

224

of us in the old world. They want us all dead. It's over. The new masters want us to get off the highway. To stop lying down in front of their bulldozers and just let them get on with things. We get on their tits with our continuing refusal to face the fact of our own redundancy. And their patience is wearing thin as our time runs out.

And it doesn't matter. It doesn't matter. It doesn't matter. It doesn't matter. I say this over and over. And when Oscar comes to ask if he can make himself a butter sandwich, he says, 'Why are you crying, Billy?'

He sounds awed, like he's witnessed a miracle. I didn't even cry at Mum's funeral.

And I would laugh, except that I can't. It feels like my mouth tastes suddenly of burnt books and barbed wire. He's quick on the uptake as usual is Oscar. He's suddenly the lying voice of the whole world. 'It's just a game, Billy.' He knows it's a lie as he says it. It's never just a game. Nothing is ever just anything.

Later, I'm sitting smoking with Alfie. I haven't seen him for weeks and I wouldn't be seeing him now if I hadn't come home with Oscar to find him camped on the doorstep. And Oscar was ridiculously pleased to see him and Alfie bathed him, Brothers Grimm'd him and maximum exploded him. They've always got on. Oscar is impressed by him, thinks Alfie is a style icon. The day after he's seen Alfie, Oscar always does something weird to his hair, tries to replicate the spikes and twists and turrets of Alfie's painstakingly manufactured tresses by rubbing in Vaseline and soap.

Alfie's got Oscar in bed, and now we're listening to his current love, a Brazilian rap-metal band called Granny Scarecrow and he's talking irrelevant stuff about some music festival in Serbia, and I interrupt to ask him if he believes in ghosts. And he thinks for a long while. It's such a long pause that I think he might have nodded out. 'Your mum,' he mutters. Another pause, longer if anything. 'She's not coming back.' Which wasn't the question. And why do people feel like they need to tell me things I know? And in that second I'm decided. After tonight I'm really, really, really not going to see Alfie ever again.

I look at him now. Alfie with his hazy eyes, his L'Oréal poll, all shiny and black and because-I'm-worth-it. I look at his black combats, his Bundeswehr jacket, the fucking real live medal he bought at a charity auction at the British Legion and that he's got pinned to his chest. Like he'd last even a minute in a shooting war. I look at him with his sulky spoilt face, the soft face of a kid who did bassoon lessons and youth theatre.

We've done all right. The accident of sitting next to each other in Mrs Manton's reception class sparked a friendship that has done solid service, lasted well, but now it's time for an upgrade in the mates department. When Alfie talks about girls and bands and, especially about weed, I don't really get it. I feel a pang for a lost world, but that's all it is: a pang. As worlds went it wasn't such a good one. A waiting room where no one's name ever gets called. I can hardly believe I spent so long there.

And I realise that he hasn't changed at all. The kid I went nicking sweets with, the one I played Action Man with, he's with me now in the room. And that's the problem. Alfie is still one half of that pair of nickers. He hasn't moved on at all. He's still playing with Action Man, only he's his own doll now. Indie Action Man with a special punchable face.

I'm not going to see Lucy again either. She felt like what I needed for a while, but she wasn't. What will I miss? Her smile? Her kiss? Her soft hands as they held the Mach 3 to my chin? Her lips? Her eyelashes scratching like insect wings against my cheek? All her careless beauty? Her thoughtless cruelty? Of course. I'll miss all those things, but it feels good to know that things are finally getting sorted. Coming to a head.

Granny Scarecrow whinge on. Giving it the big one. In Portuguese. I cough and stub out my joint.

'You're a waste of space, Alfie,' I say. 'You're proper boring. And this music's like cancer.'

His face. He looks like I've slapped him. Yay. LMFAO. He gets up and turns the music off. He says some stuff. I don't listen. He leaves. He goes out into the world of rain and noise and bars and girls and dog shit and music and puke. And I sit in my room and try to listen to nothing. Only you can't listen to nothing, can you? There's always something. Always someone shouting. Someone weeping.

Aidan Jebb stopped breathing, finally. Within three minutes his brain cells began to die. That's three minutes of choked agony. More than a lifetime. More than Callum got.

His heart stopped beating and his body cells were unable to receive supplies of blood and oxygen. His dying blood migrated from the capillaries in the upper surfaces, which paled while the lower surfaces grew dark. Calcium ions leaked into his muscle cells, preventing relaxation. Those muscles stiffened until decomposition began.

As the cells died they lost the capacity to fight off bacteria. After twelve hours he was cool to the touch. Not that anyone was there to touch him. After twenty-four hours he was cold to the bone.

At this point he still looked fresh as he twisted slightly with the air currents that ambled around the factory.

Inside however, the bacteria that were feasting on the

227

contents of the intestine – that Twix – were beginning to feast on the intestine itself. And the insects were also hearing the call. With no defences such blowflies and houseflies that were toughing out the winter were able to get in and find the openings they craved to lay eggs. The mouth, the eyes, the anus. It took a long time for the maggots to hatch. It was winter after all and the factory was chill.

After four days the bacteria had broken down the tissues and cells. Fluids dribbled into the body cavities. Respiring anaerobically, they produced hydrogen sulphide, methane, caderverine and putrescine. These gases attracted more insects and from further afield. Ten days after his death the build-up of gases created pressure within the body, inflating it and forcing fluid out of cells and blood vessels and into the body cavity.

Because it was winter and the insects were slow, grave wax formed over Jebb's face. Do you know about grave wax? This is the tougher animal version of the fur that grows on rotting fruit. A blanket that protects it a little from nature's vandalism.

Eventually sleepy winter maggots moved throughout the body, secreting digestive enzymes and tearing tissues with their mouth hooks. They moved as a mass, benefiting from communal heat and shared digestive secretions. They moved as an ordered, heaving, seething, society. Working together. No 'I' in their team.

Their effort and industry attracted the predators, the beetles that fed on the maggots as well as the decaying flesh.

Seventeen days after his death, Jebb's bloated body burst and the exposed parts of the body were black while the internal flesh was turning into sludge. A Halloween slush puppy. Only nourishing and protein-packed. A hearty stew if you happened to be a worm.

Three weeks after he kicked and choked, Aidan's body had lost most of its flesh and what remained had dried out. Beneath the trainers a thick tarry stain spread. The map of a country no one ever wants to visit.

Fifty days after his death and the body was dry and decomposed slowly. Micro-organisms moved in to start work on the hair.

Fifty-three days after his death, a six-month-old Alsatian called Felix led a private security guard called Ross Elliott through an exciting playground of abandoned factory units and retail opportunities, and together they found what was left.

Jebb had been dead fifty-one days when he appeared in my room.

I'm not telling anyone about this. And already I'm not sure that even I believed it happened. I was doped up, drunk, mad with grief, dreaming. All of these could be true.

I go and stand where Mary and Joe Goddard were hung. There's no blue plaque, nothing marks the spot at all. The square itself was hit by a stray Luftwaffe bomb in 1940, a pilot lightening his load as he sprinted home for ersatz Kaffee und Kuchen after a hard day blasting the crap out of the East End.

Market Square was further vandalised by the Urban District Council wanting to maximise the retail experience for the diverse shopping communities of the borough, or whatever the council jargon was back in the 1950s. Anyway, they knocked down some of the small, crooked buildings that the Luftwaffe hadn't managed to get to, widened some of the narrow alleyways that every generation since the Romans had quite liked, and then surrendered the space to the first generation of popular family saloon cars.

What delusions people had then. What dreams. What hopes. All those model cars called things like Corsairs and Consuls, Zodiacs and Zephyrs. Names meant to make you think of pirates and judges and Gods. Superhuman names. The history of the car is like a journey of social history itself. It starts with Gods and Kings and Empires and moves to the place we're at now. Where cars need to shout 'STFU' or 'LOL'. Or else they simply have a number, like they are a special chemical compound. A 'here-comes-the-science-bit' on wheels. A secret weapon. A new gun, or a face cream. Something like that.

So Market Square is now a car park, except on Sundays when it hosts a car-boot sale, which means it kind of looks the same but with the vehicles surrounded by the detritus of a not-quite-modern life. All that antiquated stuff. All that social history. Vinyl records and VHS tapes and books. Board games and road maps. And it's not just the past that gets flogged off for pennies here. It seems to me that the future is being dumped too. Microwaves, mobile phones, desktop PCs, memory sticks and computer games. We're using up the future so quickly now. Things start to putrefy the moment they are out of the packaging.

The place where the gibbet stood is in front of Primark. And I stand and try to imagine the last moments. Joe quiet, acquiescent, wishing his sister would stop embarrassing him in public with her cursing and her spitting and her vengeful howling. Mary, her mind a boiling sweat of hate. But however hard I try and call it up, there's no power in this place. No sorrow big enough to stretch across the centuries and clutch at our hearts. Impossible even for Mary, with all her anger and noise, to make a dent on this bit of the future. Then again, she saw off the hangman and his wife and Sir Dalton and the captain on duty. So maybe she was satisfied with that. Maybe she doesn't need to battle with the Primark shoppers too. Her work is done.

The Grumpy Snowman is tomorrow and then I have to hand Oscar over. I get all the receipts for the stuff I bought in Tescos and I put them in an envelope and post them to Toni. She'll get them tomorrow. I want her to see them. I want her to read them. Read them and weep.

It's one of the days where Oscar is at Scotties, the after-school club, so I spend the afternoon in the court building. Aidan Jebb's inquest. And that's when I hear the true story of his wasted and pathetic life. And I'm wrong on everything. Big surprise. There's no Vladivar stories, no mother turning rock-star tricks. 'Course there's no music either. No singing. No *Here, There and Everywhere*. There's just a kid determined to break his mother's heart. And succeeding. Being A-star at that, if nothing else.

There's not many in the court. There's me, there's a bored reporter – a girl about my age, showing off her shorthand by scrawling in her pad at dizzying speed. Slow down, I want to say to her, no one's watching. No one cares. And then there's a woman in her thirties with a nice, round face and plasticky hair the colour of processed cheese. I wonder who she is. She doesn't look like police or social work or council. She doesn't look bored enough or angry enough. She looks tired and anxious. Then it comes to me: this is Aidan's mum. Suddenly I can't imagine her selling blow jobs. I imagine her asking if I want cash-back and do I have a Nectar card? She looks like she works in the Sainsbury's Local. I have to re-frame. Come up with a new story. A whole new world.

She doesn't cry. But she does shake a bit. A police officer runs through the stuff Chloe and Rhiannon told me. A pathologist, a nervous girl in an M&S trouser suit, runs

231

through the injuries Jebb had, ending with the opinion that they were entirely consistent with hanging. Another police officer – a detective who obviously fancies himself in top to toe Paul Smith – tells the court that Aidan Jebb, aged seventeen, of no fixed abode, was wanted in connection with the murder of Suzanne Smith, aged forty, of 86 Oaks Avenue, at the time of his death and that case was now closed.

Finally, a Zara-slash-Penny stands up. She's neither fat nor thin, this one but she has the same my-puppy's-just-died look, the same slightly hunched and resentful demeanour. The same way with words. It's Zara-slash-Penny who describes the 'poor lifestyle choices of the deceased despite the best efforts of Aidan's primary care giver'. In other words, your honour, the mother here tried her best but hey-ho. Sometimes your best can still be a bit shit.

When I get back from the court I take a long slow walk through all the rooms of the house, and it depresses me how grubby they are. There are hammocks of spiderwebs hanging in the corners, balls of strange unidentifiable detritus on the sills and on the carpets. I'm embarrassed that I haven't even noticed the forces of fluff and dust and dirt gathering and infiltrating everywhere. Doesn't take them long. Doesn't seem two minutes since I last cleared up. I go and look for our hoover, our Henry.

I find him in Mum's office, lurking under her desk. How did he get there? But it's a good place for him. Mum always used to talk to Henry like he was real, like he was a dim but placid child. 'Come along now, Henry,' she'd say as she tugged him along the hallway, or bumped him down the stairs. 'Don't hold us up, we've got a lot to do today.' She'd be chuntering on to him between rooms, or using him as a

232

dancing partner as she blasted Abba or the Bad Seeds over the noise he made.

It always delighted Oscar. As a toddler he used to follow Mum and Henry around, trying to catch the vacuum answering back. I think perhaps he was happy to think there was someone younger and smaller than him in the house. And actually, I'm not sure that Oscar doesn't still half think that Henry might be a real, living, breathing creature. Some kind of irrepressibly cheerful dwarf.

Once I've located Henry, I can't be arsed to actually use him. It seems like too much effort all of a sudden. Like everything.

Oscar is thrilled when I say he's going to have a special magic dinner. He thinks it's because his plane has finally reached the top of the sky.

'And we can have guinea pigs now, Billy. You promised.'

So we go out and get them from Petworld. Two Peruvian guinea pigs of impeccable pedigree. They cost £39.99. Or, to put it another way, they cost exactly the same as getting an urn full of your mother's ashes from the crematorium.

We have Oscar's favourites for dinner. Gypsy toast. Häagan-Dazs. I've had gypsy toast at other people's houses. They always call it eggy bread. I always thought it was emblematic of Mum's difference, the way she was better than other people's mums. They had eggs and bread. We had gypsies. They had prose. We had poetry. They had their mums, we had Suzie. They had black-and-white, we had colour. Not just a common-or-garden Milf, but a mother you wanted to fall in love with.

Maybe all kids feel that way about their mums.

If they do, they're wrong.

We play football on the Kinect, Oscar and I, which I haven't done for ages. I let him win, but I make it close so he doesn't suspect. He's pretty sharp about that sort of thing. Hates being patronised.

We watch the original *Star Wars* film. I say he can go to bed as late as he likes, but he doesn't look so thrilled about this.

'I have my play tomorrow, Billy. I don't want to be tired for that. I don't want to mess that up.'

In the end he insists on practising his lines one final time. And rehearsing his little shepherd dance. And he's word perfect, move perfect. And then he insists on bath and bed. I let Oscar have a long time playing in the bath until he's complaining that he's gone all wrinkly and that it's time for the drying machine at Quadruple Maximum Explode.

I could drown him. There would be no need for the knife then. I could just grab him by those skinny shoulders and force him under the lukewarm water. He'd be too shocked to resist. It wouldn't take long. But I hesitate, and Oscar gets himself out and wraps himself in his favourite towel. The one with a shark on it.

Then I carry him into my bedroom. He's so light. Even wet through he weighs almost nothing. I take a photo of him on my phone and send it off to Toni. He does a goofy face for her. A proper gurn. Good. She should have something to remind her of Oscar's last moments. A picture of him looking happy.

Seconds later my phone pings. Toni's text says *ah what an angel.*

Intelligent people can be so dumb sometimes.

After the drying machine I say he can have whatever story he likes. He can have a long one if he wants. He can even have a Postman bleeding Pat or a Thomas the bloody Tank Engine, both of which I normally avoid because those stories are as long and rambling and as boring as Pat's route. And as flat as the island of Sodor itself. To my surprise he chooses *Can't You Sleep, Little Bear?*

Can't You Sleep Little Bear? is the story of a bear who can't sleep because he's scared of the dark. His dad (Big Bear, of course) gathers an array of lanterns to try and keep the dark away. He starts with small ones and ends up with a humongous burning tree of a thing, a full-on bonfire in a box. Still Little Bear can't get his head down. In the end Little Bear has to learn to live with the dark. In fact the title of the book should really be *Get Over it, Little Bear*. The truth is that you can't ever keep the dark from the little bears.

The dark will find us all if it wants to.

I check my emails. I haven't done this for ages and there's loads of shit to wipe off. The Viagra sellers have been busy. The Viagra markets never sleep. And there's tons of bollocks from my mates which I delete. And some stuff from Mum's mates, which I also delete. I don't bother with Facebook, or Tumblr or Twitter, or Arena or xScope, or any of that shit that Mum liked.

And then I sit and I drink the vino I got in earlier and I surf PornHub looking for stuff that's not weird and that I haven't seen before. There's not much. Not enough.

If were done, 'twere best done quickly. GCSE *Macbeth* never leaves you if you have a good teacher, and I had the best teacher in the school. Jones the Vein we called him. Anyone simply overhearing would be puzzled because Jonesy was a bloke with absolutely no vanity at all. He dressed in the same old chalky suit day in day out., but he was cursed by the way a vein in his forehead would start throbbing if he thought one of his students was taking the piss. And one of his students was always taking the piss. He was the one who said I should try for Cambridge. I gave him a cheery no, I don't think so, Jonesy. You should have seen the vein throb then. I thought it was going to burst. He never spoke to me again. Not unless he absolutely had to.

Now. It has to be now. I can't put it off any longer.

I soak all the tea towels in white spirit. And spread them through the house. I splash whatever is left all around pretty randomly. The fumes make me a bit headachy.

And I get a drink and lie down on the living-room sofa. I'm not scared. I know the smoke will get me before the flames do. I'll cough and I'll choke for a bit, and then I'll sleep, while outside neighbours will try and smash their way in. They'll be beaten back by the heat and the smoke, and later these same neighbours will appear soot-smudged but excited on *Look East*. They'll describe their efforts to rescue the kids trapped here – they won't know that Oscar was dead already of course – and they'll grow tearful as they talk about the sparky little boy, the lovely lad, who lived in with his brother. They'll rehearse once again the tragedy of their lost mother.

And in a month or two maybe Toni will sit down with a young journo and dictate her story of how she was robbed of sister and nephews, all in a few short weeks. And then she'll spend the cash she gets on a holiday or a makeover. It's a sick world. Maybe she'll call Dean her rock. Maybe she'll say, 'I couldn't have got through it without him.'

The bottle's empty. Then the second bottle is empty and then I have to do it. I have to get my £6.30 vegetable knife. I have to place a pillow over the dreaming face of my little brother and then, quickly and gently, I have to cut his carotid artery. I should have drowned him. Should have done it while I had the chance. It's going to be harder now. I can't even be sure my hand will be steady. What if he wakes up?

It'll be OK. It has to be OK. It'll be over in no time, and then it'll be white spirit on the radiccio and arsenic. Fire on the new curtains. Fire blistering the rockets of the *Not now, Bernard* themed room. I'll put those soaked and stinking towels everywhere and especially near the doors in case I panic and try and force an escape at the last minute. I imagine the newsreader's sombre voice, the meaningful look he'll give the viewers when he reveals that an accelerant was used.

And, as if in a strange waking dream, I get up off the sofa, let the blanket that covers me – that covered both Oscar and me during *Star Wars* – fall to the floor and allow myself to be pulled into the hallway. But it has to be now. He's asleep. He's safe. He's dreaming of guinea pigs. There is no better time.

And then Dean Hessenthaler is in the hallway with me.

I'm not even surprised.

That's how dislocated I am. I'm stumbling through a landscape of horrors. Quicksand sucking at my feet. Pushing through air that seems to be solidifying around me. Making me push hard to get through it. There is the insistent skeletal blues of a train coming from somewhere. Anything could happen here and so of course Oscar's dad has to be swaying in my hallway. His face puffy and red. Radiccio. An exhausted dying glitter in his eye.

Dean is even drunker than me and he trip-traps up the hall, carefully. It's like he's dancing on ice for the very first time. He's a big man and he no longer trusts his legs to hold him up. His own body is deserting him.

'Well done, Billy boy,' he slurs. 'Bloody well done.'

He sways backwards. And forwards. A ship tossed on vicious and unforgiving seas. Seas that want to break it and drown the crew. And so we sway. Our eyes locked together in the hall. Two gunslingers at the end of a shit afternoon movie.

'What have I done to you, eh? What the *fuck* have I ever done to you?' He sounds like he wants to cry.

It's enough. The spell that I wrapped around myself falls away like that blanket we wore during Star Wars. I'm standing in the hall with a knife. I have matches and lighter fluid. I feel a nausea of relief. The sweat breaks out across my neck and under my armpits. I feel dizzy. Black insects swim past my eyes and I lean against those grey walls. Just a shade of grey, not arsenic after all.

'Come and sit down, Dean.'

'Have you got drink in, you little bastard?'

'Yeah, Dean. Yeah, there's drink.'

Would I have done it? Could I have done it? Could I have looked at Oscar's perfect little face, listened to the snuffling, guinea-pig noises of his dreams, and still been able to do it?

Yeah, probably. People do.

Then again, maybe I conjured Dean up myself. Maybe I drew him to Oaks Avenue with my psychic powers. Maybe it was that.

It's four in the morning as we sit there, both of us suddenly a lot more sober than we were, holding glasses of that ancient sloe gin – it's all that's left – and Dean tells me that he had his own special tea. The perfect meatballs followed by long, languorous sex with my aunt. Candles. Incense. Hot oil. The works. The full Scandinavian quiet night in. Then she wept. Then she dumped him.

'Said she felt a bit funny.'

'What about?'

'About you. About Oscar. About Suzanne.'

Felt a bit funny. I can see why he was hurt. As 'it's not you, it's me' break-up speeches go, it's a pretty lame one. Not much thought gone into it. I can see how it would make you feel small. Small enough to want to batter someone.

Dean's next move had been to go out and get wasted. To look for someone to smack. But the scent he was giving off was too strong, too obvious and too dangerous. The usual targets and victims had scurried away, sought out the shadows and hidden corners of the pubs and clubs. Trouble even hid from him in the Andromeda. So he'd come here to hammer home some truths with those big red Afghan-killing fists.

'I've been reasonable. Patient.'

'You got Alfie beaten up.' He looks confused.

'Who?'

'Alfie. My mate. Eye-liner. Gobby.'

Dean frowns. 'Him? I like him. He's got a bit about him. A bit of spunk. Why would I do him?'

'To get at me.'

Dean frowns harder, the line above his nose getting proper deep, turning him into a right old bum-face. He runs his hand over his bristly scalp.

'Christ, Billy, it really is all about you isn't it? If I wanted to get at you, you'd know all about it. I wouldn't need to involve a third party, you can trust me on that.'

And I know straight away it's the truth. I've been writing myself into someone else's soap opera. Someone else's *Life! Death! Prizes!* Whoever put Alfie in hospital it was because of him not me. Because of the way he is. Because of the way he smiles. Because of his pointy shoes. Because of the way he holds his cigs. Because of the way he seems to hear the sad echoes behind the banter of the nandos and the standard gavins. And then to pity them for it.

I can't think of anything to say.

'You OK, Billy?' Dean looms forward in his chair. He seems huge. Full-on wrestler huge. I try to speak. But I can't. He puts his great meaty hand on my shoulder. My face is melting. I shake his hand off and stand up. Slowly. Dean sits back. He just looks at me. It's down to me to say something. I take a breath.

'Come and see Oscar, Dean. Come and see him now.'

So we stand on chairs looking over Oscar's cabin bed, staring down in silence at his little puppy face as the dreams of guinea pigs and bear cubs flicker across it. Dean sniffs and blows his nose. I feel the blade in my pocket. Press my thumb against it till I feel that sudden pulse of blood.

I agree that Dean can come to the Christmas show. I'll square it with Toni. We help each other down off the wobbling chairs, giggling as we do it. Oscar doesn't wake, but he does talk in his sleep.

'Thank you,' he says, eyes dancing behind closed lids. 'Thanks Mum.'

As Dean leaves I ask him if he ever gave Mum a pair of Paisley pyjamas, and he thinks for a bit. 'Yeah,' he says in the end. 'Yeah, I think I did. Why?' I tell him no reason and then I ask how he got in anyway. And as I ask I already know the answer. 'Total Security Solutions,' he smiles. And I notice how red and swollen his gums are. He really has let himself go. 'I always get my guys to keep a copy of the key. You never know when it's going to come in handy.'

No. You never know when you're going to stagger into a place where terrible things are planned, and accidentally stop them with your ranting and your pain.

'You know what?' he says. 'I'll buy this place.'

I laugh. 'You – with a mortgage?'

Dean looks at me coolly. 'I won't need a mortgage, Billy.' There's a pause while I try and get my head around this strange new truth. Respectable Dean. Rich Dean.

He says, 'What is it going for? £250K? That's what I'll do. Buy it. Redecorate. Rent it out. Buy-to-let. Could be lovely. And it's a nice area. Near the park. That's what I'll do.'

I don't remember sleeping but I must do, and I wake to find Dean's gone and Oscar has got everything he needs. He's got his own clothes together, his backpack, inhalers, those sad-faced hippo wellies, everything. He's given himself a sensible breakfast – Oatibix – and when I stagger into the kitchen, he's listening to the *Today* programme on Radio Four like he was sixty-six instead of just a snapper. Maybe he really has got a syndrome.

I flick through a Christmas double-issue of *Life! Death! Prizes!* and discover this heart-warming nugget. Unable to afford to buy the comfy and festive Xmas slippers her Nan wanted, Delyth Morgan, 19, of St Davids, has made her some out of card, glitter, paint, Pritt Stick and, crucially, a couple of sanitary towels. Nan had declared them the best ever and the magazine has published a little photo of the slippers. A remarkable testament to the unrivalled inventiveness of the British people I think you'll agree. No wonder we've never been invaded.

The school show passes more or less peacefully, though the Christmas Pudding cries all the way through and even the baby Jesus can't stop that. He can cure the snowman of chronic grumpiness despite the Palestinian heat, but the Pudding's desperate sorrow seems beyond even his magic.

Later, as we tuck into fairy cakes and squash in the canteen, I see Mrs Bingley being cross-examined by a cold-eyed family court judge. Nick gives her some serious grief for casting his daughter, the Brit-art hopeful, as an archaic and fattening dessert. He thinks it's definitely emotional abuse. Mrs Bingley has sown the seeds of a future personality disorder. He could sue.

Most interesting is how Toni and Dean are with each other. They can't even look at each other properly. They circle around one another with such stiff politeness that I find myself thinking they're in love. Maybe they are actually in love. And then I think, maybe they should always have been together. Maybe Dean should have met Toni first, before Mum. Maybe it's like email and the phone, they arrived at the right place but in the wrong order.

Dean tells Toni he's going to buy our house – 'Market value. All above board' – and Toni tells Dean that she's moving to Brighton. 'In the summer, for when Billy starts uni.' He looks crushed.

'Come down weekends, Dean. Stay in a B&B or something.'

She's checked out schools and everything. Scoped out houses near the uni.

'And I'm giving up teaching,' she says.

I look at her. 'Why though? Why would you do that? You're happy here. You've got a life here. And you like teaching.'

She looks at me like I'm mad. 'I've never been happy here, Billy. I've never had a life here.' There's a pause. 'I've just stood in the shadow of other people's lives.' She shrugs and then she smiles down at Oscar who is managing to look anxious and overjoyed all at the same time. She says, 'And

242

I've never liked teaching. Truth is, Billy, I don't like kids very much. Children are horrid, nasty, smelly creatures.'

'Aunt Tonia!' squeaks Oscar, shocked.

'They don't even taste good,' says Dean. 'I don't know why people bother with children.'

And I could say, some people don't, Dean. Some people don't bother with their children for years at a time. But I don't.

Oscar says, 'I know you're joking. They're joking aren't they, Billy?'

I tell him that I think they probably are, and Toni looks me straight in the eye – she has Mum's eyes, I think, like Oscar has Dean's eyes. It's weird. It's suddenly like Mum is alive again and looking right at me.

Toni says, 'This way you can see Oscar whenever you want.'

And then I start to say something. I don't know what exactly, but I feel there's a big important something that needs to be said.

'Toni,' I begin, but she stops me.

'Just say thank you, Billy. Just say thank you.'

And I do and I realise that yes, that's all that needs saying right now. I was going to talk about the receipts – she'll have got them this morning – but I know now that we won't ever have to talk about them.

'Yay!' says Oscar, and then frowns. 'Can we take Butch and Sundance?'

'Who?' says Toni.

'Oh yeah,' I say. 'The flipping guinea pigs. I meant to tell you about them.'

'I love guinea pigs,' says Toni.

'So do I,' says Dean. 'Especially on toast.'

Oscar squeals. 'That's horrible!' He is plainly delighted

243

by Dean's transparent attempts to get down with the Year Twos. But I have a sudden lightness across my shoulders and I realise how tight they've been.

'What are you grinning at?' says Toni, but she's smiling too.

She pulls me into a hug. She's warm and her jumper smells biscuity. I feel a sudden damp heat behind my eyelids.

Families, huh?

As we drive home I see Lucy Avis hand in hand with a guy with impossible movie-star looks. Milan. He's like a ridiculous experiment that has fused the DNA of every brooding sad-eyed, slim-hipped idol you ever saw. He's Elvis. He's James Dean. He's Zadie Smith. He's something else. He doesn't walk, he glides. I almost laugh. What was I thinking of? How did I ever think I'd cut in on him?

But I did. I did. All right, I almost did.

I can still feel Lucy's perfumed warmth on my skin and I get this sudden ache for her. And I look at them again, Southwood's golden couple, with their alien sheen, a kind of crackling forcefield of shiny charisma that even seems to keep off the rain. Milan is talking and Lucy is nodding, serious.

I'll be happier than you, Lucy. I'm braver than you anyway. I won't be waiting in a small town with my baby, while my soulmate shags puppeteers across Europe. I'll be leading not following. And hey, Brighton's full of girls. Maybe one of them – beautiful in a vintage sixties dress, sad in the best kind of way, her hair held in place with a biro – is reading a history book in a bar right now, and wondering why no one ever asks her out. Why no one asks her to get down on her knees.

I look over at Oscar who is lolling on his booster seat,

almost asleep. I reach across the back seat and squeeze his arm. He sits up, gives me a questioning look.

'What's going to become of us, Oscar?' I say.

'We're going to live happily ever after,' he says promptly. 'You know that, don't you?'

Which is a pretty good answer.

Acknowledgements

Thanks to David Smith, my agent at Annette Green Agency, for his impeccable taste and extraordinary powers of persuasion. Thanks to my editor Helen Garnons-Williams for her reserves of patience, humour and calm good sense. Thanks should also go to Erica Jarnes, Jude Drake, Gabriella Nemeth and everyone at Bloomsbury for helping this book get on the shelves.

I'd also like to acknowledge the help of Adrian Barnes, Camilla Hornby, Sam Humphreys, Duncan May, Anthony Roberts, Gillian Stern, The Arvon Foundation, Jan Fortune-Wood and Carol and Charles Ockelford who all made contributions, directly and indirectly, to this book. Acknowledgement is also due to Pamela Stephenson, in whose fascinating book *Head Case* I first came across Avoidant Personality Disorder.

A NOTE ON THE TYPE

The text of this book is set in Linotype Sabon, named
after the type founder, Jacques Sabon. It was
designed by Jan Tschichold and jointly developed by
Linotype, Monotype and Stempel, in response to a
need for a typeface to be available in identical form
for mechanical hot metal composition and hand
composition using foundry type.

Tschichold based his design for Sabon roman on a
font engraved by Garamond, and Sabon italic on
a font by Granjon. It was first used in 1966 and has
proved an enduring modern classic.